JUST THIS ONCE

CHICAGO BILLIONAIRES SERIES

ALEXIS WINTER

I SWORE TO MYSELF THAT I'D NEVER CROSS THAT LINE WITH HER.

But when Savannah Monroe, my chief operations officer, shows up on my doorstep with a proposition that starts with her in my lap and a promise of *just this once...*The line disappears.

At fifteen years my junior and the smartest woman I've ever met, she's by far the greatest asset at Baxley Tech.
From the moment I hired her, we had a connection—as friends, as a mentor.
A lingering touch.
A stolen glance.
An unspoken attraction that lingers just beneath the surface, threatening to boil over.

So when she reveals a painful secret she's been hiding from me that involves my CFO, I don't hesitate...I take care of it immediately.
Or so I thought.
But the lies and corruption go much deeper than I ever realized and now we're in a tangled web of passion and secrecy.

After our one night together, everything changes.

The thought of her in the arms of another man turns me into someone I don't recognize—insatiable, hungry.
Indulging in every filthy thought I've had about her for three years is one thing, but losing my heart in the process wasn't part of the deal.

But here's the thing about forbidden fantasies...they usually come at a price.
And this one, just might be deadly.

When a blackmailer threatens to destroy her life and everything she's worked for, I take matters into my own hands.
Because when it comes to Savannah Monroe, there is no negotiation.
No backing down.
No Limits.
No Rules.
No losing her.

We promised each other it would only be *just this once*.
But now that I've had a taste...I want my fill.

A wonderful thank you to my amazing readers for continuing to support my dream of bringing sexy, naughty, delicious little morsels of fun in the form of romance novels.

A special thank you to my amazing editors Kimberly Stripling and Michele Davine without whom I would be COMPLETELY lost!

Thank you to my fantastic cover designer Sarah Kil who always brings my visions to life in the most outstanding ways.

And lastly, to my ARC team and beta readers, you are wonderful and I couldn't do this without you.

XoXo,
Alexis

PROLOGUE

SAVANNAH-THREE YEARS EARLIER...

"I got an interview!" I thrust my hands in the air in celebration as I stand up, my desk chair shooting out behind me.

I glance around nervously, trying to judge if anyone heard me. Probably not the best idea to be shouting about a new interview at my current job.

I sit back down and read the email again for a third time.

"Oh my God, I got an interview," I repeat in disbelief.

When I applied for the open Chief Operations Officer position at Baxley Technologies, I truly didn't expect a call back. Not to say I'm not qualified for the job; I feel I am, but most companies want to see at least fifteen years on your resume before they even consider you for the COO role.

I close my office door and grab my cell to call my best friend Callie.

"Hey, this is a lov—"

"I got an interview," I blurt out, cutting her off.

"An interview for—oh, for Baxley?"

"Yes!" I'm attempting to whisper but with my excitement it's coming out more in a whispered shout. "I'm in complete disbelief, like me? Seriously?"

"Of course you, why not *you*? First of all, you're very qualified. Your insane work experience in just six years speaks for itself, not to mention the MBA and undergrad from an Ivy League school, both of which you got into on merit and not because your family had money."

"I know. It's just that I don't want to get my hopes up if they're not serious about me."

"These are billionaires, sweetie. They wouldn't waste their precious time if they weren't serious about you. Now stop doubting yourself and get ready to go out and celebrate tonight. Think about where you wanna meet for drinks."

I smile into the receiver. If there's one person who will always have my back and gas me up, it's Callie. She's been my ride or die since the day we met freshman year at Northwestern. I didn't think she'd associate with me at all. She comes from a very wealthy family, old money, from the North Shore and I... well, I'm an only child, that I know of, raised by my grandma after my mom went to prison and my dad abandoned me.

I put my phone on my desk and turn back to my computer to finish up my workday. I feel too giddy to focus, but if this interview does actually turn into a new career opportunity, I don't want to leave this startup I've been at for the last three years high and dry. I need to finish up a few projects before I officially leave this place.

I knew from a young age I wanted a career, a big one. I busted my ass in high school, opting for any and every extracurricular and after-school program, even summer school. I graduated early with honors and was accepted into Northwestern University with a focus on business and finance.

Even through high school and college I worked any and every odd job I could find that would pay my bills and give me experience. I started in fast food, working my way up to a management position and then the corporate office that happened to be located in Chicago where I lived. Even through getting my MBA, I continued to move up the ladder until I was brought on as a project manager and financial advisor here at this software startup. In only three years we've grown from nothing to a multimillion-dollar company that's in the final stages of IPO.

I was determined to break the cycle of failure in my family if it was the last thing I did. Sometimes I still struggle with imposter syndrome when I look in the mirror. Like who is this girl who came from nothing and why does she deserve this opportunity?

I shake the thoughts from my head and power through the rest of my day before sending a text to Callie.

Me: *Leaving here in the next twenty. Mitzy's for martinis?*

Thirty minutes later I take the first celebratory sip of my dirty martini.

"Will Todd be surprised when you put in your notice?"

"*If* I ge—"

"When," Callie says emphatically with an arched brow.

"When," I start over, "I get the job, I think Todd will be sad to see me go for sure, but I think he knew from the get-go that I didn't plan to stay long term. I think when you jump in at the ground floor of a startup, it's a much quicker burnout period than other jobs, you know?"

She nods and takes a sip of her French martini, her eyes rolling back in her head for a brief second. "Yeah, for sure. You have literally put blood, sweat, and tears into that place. I hope he knows what he has with you."

"He does. He's always been extremely generous with pay, but as we all know, there's zero work-life balance when it comes to a startup. I'm only twenty-seven and I already feel like between school and all my jobs over the years, I've never had a chance to just breathe, enjoy life, and take some downtime."

I do feel a little guilty wanting to move on from Code Red Software, but I'm beyond excited that I even get the chance to interview at a tech giant like Baxley Technologies.

I SWALLOW down the fear in my throat as I stare up at the massive mirrored building on Franklin St.

I close my eyes for a brief second and take in a deep breath. "You've got this. You deserve this. You're going to nail it."

I square my shoulders back, lift my chin up, and march up to the massive revolving door emblazoned with the world-famous gold BT symbol.

"Please have a seat, Miss Monroe."

I take a seat in front of a large table where six other people are sitting across from me. "I'm Pierce Denton, Executive Vice President here at Baxley." The rest of the individuals follow suit with their name and title.

Round table style interviews are nothing new to me. I had to do them for my MBA program and when I came onboard with Code Red, but this one is intimidating. Not only is it filled with department heads, but the collective net worth in this room alone is more than I'll see in ten lifetimes.

"Mr. Baxley won't be here today for this interview. If we decide to move forward with second rounds, he'll be present for that one," Mr. Denton says.

I nod and try to consciously make eye contact with each person while not looking crazy at the same time.

"You have an impressive background, Miss Monroe. I'm sure it's not the first time someone has told you that."

I smile. "Thank you. Yes, I have heard that from previous employers."

We go through some general questions about my background, education, and then come the fun ones... the ones about how I'd be an asset to the company, why I should be considered, what value I'd bring to the company... a fight for my life or basically a modern-day version of a mock execution.

But this is where I come alive because I'm not just trying to blow smoke up these people's asses; I'm serious about my career and where I see myself, and I see myself at Baxley Tech.

I feel confident as I stand and shake each of their hands.

"Great job today, kid." Eric, the CFO who introduced himself earlier during the round table, gives me a wink and touches my elbow.

An instant *ick* feeling settles in my stomach but I don't let him see.

"Thank you. I feel very confident about the next steps." I maintain solid eye contact with him, refusing to let him make me feel out of place with his subtle comment about my age.

I'm more than aware that I'd be the youngest person in an executive position at this company, but that doesn't scare me one bit. It just stokes the fire of determination inside me.

"I have no doubt we'll be in touch shortly," Mr. Denton says after walking me to the elevator.

"Thank you and I look forward to it, sir." I step into the empty elevator and press the button for the ground floor. The moment the doors close, I toss my hands in the air again and do a happy dance.

* * *

IT'S BEEN four agonizing days since my interview and I am a nervous wreck. Every time I turn around, I'm either knocking something over or tripping over my own feet. My nerves feel like they've been juiced up with adrenaline and caffeine and all my breath work is for nothing.

I glance at the clock; it's 4:48 p.m. on a Friday. For most people, the workday is done already but for me, I'll probably be here till at least seven p.m. or later. I'm used to it at this point—that's not why I'm looking at the clock. I refresh my email for the fiftieth time, but there's nothing from Baxley.

"Hey, Savannah, doing anything fun this weekend?" Lynn, my coworker, pokes her head in my office.

I shrug. "Nothing on the books. Probably be here pretty late tonight. What about you?"

"Pete's uncle is taking his boat out on the lake so we'll probably join him. It's not exactly my cup of tea, fishing and drinking beer, but it'll be nice to get out in the sun."

"That does sound fun. And hey, maybe you can convince him to take you to that cute French bistro you saw the other week that you mentioned."

Her eyes light up, "You are so smart. I completely forgot about that."

I'm about to respond when my phone buzzes and I look at the screen.

Incoming call from Pierce Denton.

"Oh, I have to," I say, pointing to the phone, and she nods and waves, shutting my door behind her.

"Hello?"

"Hello, Miss Monroe. Apologies for the late callback. I know how annoying that is, but business gets in the way sometimes." He chuckles and I hold my breath. "Anyway, we would love to have you back for another round of interviews next week. That work for you?"

"Yes!" I attempt to readjust my volume as my excitement gets the better of me, "Yes, sorry."

"Great. I'll have Dorene from HR set it up with you. She'll send over an email with some proposed times."

"Will Mr. Baxley be there?"

"Yes, he will be—should be. You'll be interviewing with him and Eric Oliver, the CFO you met at the last interview."

"Oh, okay. Yes, I remember him." I try to sound positive, but I don't love the idea of having to speak to that man for several hours as these interviews can run long. At least Mr. Baxley will be there to hopefully correct him if he calls me *kid* again.

Per usual, I stay late tonight but with a little extra pep in my step. I double down and make sure I finish up as much as I can, knowing that there's a good chance I'll be gone from here in a few short weeks.

Normally, my Friday nights are a stressful battle between me trying to work late to finish things up so I'm not so stressed the next week and trying to appease my boyfriend via text with promises to spend every minute with him this weekend.

However, after several painful and teary conversations into the wee hours of the morning, Nick and I recently decided that after four years together, neither of us could offer what the other needed.

It wasn't easy but it was right, and we both agreed. The breakup was mutual and amicable, and I'm sure we'll stay friendly over the years. I promise myself that this time, I'll give myself at least a year off from relationships.

I grab my purse and head down to my car, already yawning. I received an email about an hour ago from Dorene with three times next week for my interview. I confirmed one for Monday morning so now I can actually relax over the weekend... at least until Saturday afternoon when I start panicking all over again.

* * *

I HOLD MY PURSE, plant, box of knickknacks for my office, and a bagel all in my hands as I walk through the revolving door of Baxley Tech, my new job where I, Savanna Grace Monroe, am COO. It still feels unreal.

Unfortunately and strangely, I have yet to meet Warren Baxley himself. He was called away on business before our interview so he was only able to attend via audio, sitting quietly on the call. I wouldn't have even known he was there if Mr. Oliver hadn't told me.

I purposely made eye contact with Mr. Oliver the entire interview because less than thirty seconds into it, his eyes dropped down to my breasts when I dared to look away for even a brief second.

"Hold it, please!" I say as my heels furiously click across the marble floor of the lobby. I dart through the closing doors of the elevator just as someone rushes up behind me to do the same.

I stumble as I feel two warm hands grab at my waist. I try to turn and see who it is when I hear his voice. "Whoa, kid. I'm sorry. Almost took a tumble on your first day." Eric Oliver flashes me a smarmy smile, acting like he isn't the one who caused me to stumble in the first place when his chest ran into my back.

I give him a slight smile and try to push my way to the back of the elevator.

"You need me to show you around? I can—"

"No, thank you. I know where I'm going. Much appreciated

though." I shut it down before he can offer anything else. "This is me," I say, exiting the elevator the second the doors open.

But it isn't me. I glance down to my right, then my left. I spot a bench and place my stuff down to pull up my email again to check the floor and suite number of my office.

"Shit, two floors up." I walk back over to the elevator and press the button. This time when the doors open, it's empty. I let out a sigh and step inside, but it stops after one floor and wouldn't you know it, he gets back on the elevator with me.

"You sure you don't need some help there, little lady?" He chuckles and pokes at my orchid that bobs over the top of my box.

"I'm sure."

"Well, listen, I mean it. If you ever want to get lunch and get a feel for the company or need a mentor, I'm here for you." It's like he has zero control of his eyes that once again look down at my breasts at least four times in that one sentence.

I spin around and exit on my correct floor this time, finally finding my office and placing my things down. I straighten out my button-down blouse and pencil skirt, second-guessing my very professional clothing choice... Maybe I should have opted for a damn potato sack.

I don't have many personal items to display in my office, not because I'm particularly private but because I have no family to have framed photos of or gifts or sentimental knickknacks. Besides my orchid, which I place on the corner of my desk, the only thing I have is a small five-inch-tall Eiffel Tower.

I click the button on the back of my iMac to turn it on, but nothing happens.

"The hell?" I mutter as I do it again and still nothing. I look under my desk and see that it's not plugged in. I reach under my desk and plug it in. I grab my chair to help pull myself back up, but it swivels, so I launch myself forward and land right on my belly on the floor.

"Glad to see you found your office. Everything okay?"

I hear a voice behind me as I right myself. I'm on my knees, read-justing my ponytail I just knocked askew. I am really not in the mood for this man's continued attempts at flirting or whatever the hell he's thinking. Time to let him know this won't fly with me.

"Sir, let me be very clear," I say with my back still toward the door. "I'm not your midlife crises, okay?" I stand up and brush down my skirt. "This is a professional setting."

"No, you're not, but I'm pretty sure I'm your new boss."

My spine stiffens and I feel my eyes bug out as I slowly turn around to face the man standing casually in my doorway.

Warren Freaking Baxley, in the flesh.

Shit.

1

WARREN

PRESENT DAY...

"He broke up with me."

Savannah flings her arms in the air before flopping down in the chair across from my desk, her silky chocolate hair pooling around her shoulders as she slumps down.

"Are you more upset that *he* broke up with you or that the relationship is over?"

I don't look up from the document in my hand. This isn't the first time Savannah has vented to me about her relationship woes and I'm sure it won't be the last.

We're an... unlikely friendship. She's outgoing and friendly, young and not afraid to voice her opinion. Whereas I'm fifteen years her senior and do everything I can to avoid human interaction outside of my business.

Yes, I'm her boss, but I'd say we're also good friends. Completely professional, of course, which is why I leave all the filthy thoughts that wander into my head about her, in my head.

"What do you mean?" The V between her brow deepens.

I put the paper down and remove my glasses, folding them in my hands.

"I mean, is it an insult that he's the one who dumped *you* or did you really think he was the one?" She chews her bottom lip as she considers my question.

"I'm not upset that he was the one who ended things because I can't handle being dumped. I'm hurt. We've been together almost a year and a half and this just came out of nowhere. I thought he was asking me to move in with him or maybe proposing at the—"

"Proposing?" That gets my attention. Sure, they've been dating that long, but I've never heard her speak about him like she's ready to marry the guy. I swallow down the panic that forms in my throat.

"Yeah, or moving in together. It's just—frustrating. Another failed relationship at thirty."

"Savannah, you have plenty of time to find *the one*. Stop putting that pressure on yourself and live your life. I'm sure Nick will regret his decision soon enough." I offer her a tight-lipped smile, but she just glares at me.

"Nick? Nick was my ex from three years ago. His name is Easton and you've met him twice."

"I have?"

I shrug nonchalantly, knowing full well that I met the smug prick twice. The first time he tried to offer me advice on my company's latest software launch by telling me that someone *my* age should be taking tech advice from someone in their twenties. And the second time, he was sloppy drunk at our office Christmas party and knocked over an entire table of champagne flutes.

"Maybe I'm not the best person for these kinds of talks."

She lets out a dramatic sigh. "No, you're probably right. I'll save it for overpriced martinis with the girls." She stands up and stretches her arms overhead, the bottom of her blouse lifting just enough to expose a sliver of her flat stomach. She pulls her long hair into a high ponytail, wrapping the tie from her wrist around it a few times.

"You doing anything this weekend?" she asks, coming around my desk to look at the paper I've been studying.

"The usual—work, maybe a round of golf or tennis at the club, and more work."

She leans in closer. The familiar scent of her floral perfume still lingers at the end of a ten-hour day. Her long, delicate fingers rest on her hip as she eyes the paper.

"This the Code Red proposal?"

"It is."

She picks it up and hikes one hip up to rest it on my desk. My eyes fall to where her hips flare out from her waist. It's a spot that I often fixate on with her. She has that classic hourglass figure that leaves me constantly desiring to run my hand over that dip in her body.

Sometimes I wonder if there's overt flirty undertones with her body language and actions, but I always settle on no because she knows how important discretion is to me. But also because I don't think for one second she sees me as anything more than a boss or mentor—fuck, maybe even a father figure in her life. It hasn't gone totally unnoticed by some of my male colleagues that not only is Savannah young and beautiful, but that I'm also rather protective of her.

"Good thing I didn't sell my stocks after they went public and I left the company. If this acquisition goes through, I'm poised to become a very wealthy woman. Might even knock you off the richest man in Chicago pedestal."

She winks at me and tosses it back on my desk. I lean back in my chair, attempting to put some distance between us.

"What about your weekend plans?"

I'm trying my hardest not to look down at her smooth, tan legs left exposed by her skirt riding up a little. Sometimes—okay, often—I wonder what her reaction would be if I simply reached my hand out and ran my fingertips up her silky skin.

In my fantasy, she parts her legs a little further for me, allowing me a peek at what she's wearing beneath her proper pencil skirts. In this particular fantasy, her on my desk at the end of a long day, she'd simply slip her panties off and hike her skirt up, offering me her sweet, wet pussy to devour.

"Oh, general wallowing I suppose now that I'm a single woman." Her response snaps me back to reality and I realize I've let my gaze settle on her thighs, but she doesn't seem to notice.

"I'm sure I'll let it all out with Callie and then rapidly go through the phases of grief, convincing myself I'm better off while I get it all out over a grueling spin class."

"That sounds miserable but I'll wish you all the best."

"You're welcome to join us for martinis at Mitzy's if you're bored." She smiles and while I know she knows I'll never take her up on the offer, I do appreciate that every weekend she offers to let me tag along on whatever crazy adventure she's up to.

"I'm afraid I'd be a bore. You don't want an old man, let alone your boss, to tag along with your friends." I wink at her and I swear I see a slight pink hue spread across her cheeks. For as much as we have kept things professional between us, once in a while it feels like these little tender moments are laced with flirty innuendo.

"Maybe I'll become a sugar mama. Find some twenty-one-year-old smoke show that needs beer money." She scoots back a little further on my desk so that she's now fully sitting on it and reaches down to pull off her heels. "You ever done that?"

"Been a sugar mama? Can't say that I have."

She slaps my arm playfully. "No, have you ever entertained someone considerably younger than you that you knew wouldn't be anything serious, just a fling?"

I debate on saying something to the effect of *no, but I'd be happy to if you're offering.* Instead, I answer truthfully. "No. I'm not really the kind of man who wants to be used for my money, but there's no shame in those who desire that kind of arrangement. It's just not for me."

"And what kind of arrangement does work for you? What is Warren Baxley looking for?" She crosses one leg over the other, briefly drawing my attention to her exposed flesh. I look up at her and she's leaning on one arm, palm flat on my desk as she waits for my answer.

"Who says I'm looking for anything?" She rolls her eyes. "I don't think I'm looking for an arrangement of anything. Just open, I suppose."

It's a vague answer, but the truth is I'm not sure what I actually want. I'm not exactly wanting to die alone, but what I want feels wrong. It feels selfish to want Savannah. She's young, has her entire life ahead of her, and I'm already in the second phase of my life. Besides, I've convinced myself that the things I'd want to do to her would scare her away.

"Look at us, both single with an amazing career, but no prospects." Suddenly her face drops and she lets out a groan. "Dammit! I completely forgot that Easton and I have our annual benefit dinner next month for the Northwestern University Alumni Association."

"I'm sure he'll behave accordingly if that's what you're worried about."

She shakes her head. "That's not what I'm worried about. I just hate having to make a public appearance at a place where everyone knows he and I were previously dating. It's like a public statement letting everyone know we failed. Like back when your friend would change their Facebook relationship status to it's complicated."

"I think you're being a touch dramatic, Savannah. And if it's really that uncomfortable, just don't go. Make him be the one who has to tell everyone there that he made the biggest mistake of his life and dumped the smartest, most accomplished, and beautiful woman he'll ever meet. He'll look fucking stupid."

Her frown morphs into a huge, genuine smile that reaches her eyes.

"Look at you, Mr. Sentimental." She pokes me with her bare foot, and I bat it away, but she does it again, this time trying to poke me in the ribs, but I reach my hand out and catch her foot. The warmth of her skin tingles against my palm. The moment we make contact, it's like something shifts between us. The air grows thick with unsaid desires and tension.

Her smile fades and I swear I see a sharp intake of breath between her open lips. I don't let go of her foot right away. Instead, I do something so stupid—I run my thumb up her insole and her eyelids flutter. Something is definitely happening between us, and it feels magnetic, like I couldn't stop it if I wanted to. But then it's gone when a soft knock brings us both back to reality.

"Hey, boss, got a min—oh, sorry, didn't mean to interrupt." Eric shoves his hands in his pockets as he looks between us.

"Not interrupting. Come on in."

Savannah jumps down from my desk and scoops up her heels.

"I'm heading home," she says to me as she slips on her heels. "Have a good weekend, gentlemen."

"What was that about?" Eric asks the moment she's gone. He walks over to the bar cart in the corner of my office and pours himself a generous amount of my liquor.

I shake my head like I have no idea what he's talking about. "Nothing. We were just talking about our weekend plans and Code Red."

"Last time I checked, my secretary doesn't sit on my desk when she's making small talk with me."

That irks me. I narrow my gaze at him and sharpen my voice.

"She's not my secretary, Eric. Those digs won't fly with me so cut that shit out."

I've always known Eric was a little more than jealous when I brought Savannah on as COO. He thought as the current CFO, he was a shoo-in for the position. He could have managed it—I have no doubt —but he's better with finances. He's not as good with the big-picture decision-making that Savannah does.

He raises his hand in a silent apology. "Speaking of Code Red, are things still moving forward?"

"As expected, yes. We'll make the announcement sometime in the next two weeks. How's Kane doing? Still no interest in coming aboard Baxley?"

I stand and walk over to the bar cart to pour myself a tumbler of whiskey. I'm not a big drinker, maybe a drink a week, typically on Friday night. It's a ritual; usually after everyone has left the building, I pour myself a glass and slowly sip it as I put on a record, kick back, and watch the city below.

"I'm working on it. Kid still thinks he wants to focus on building his own app. I told him I'm all for it, but it could really help him to get a few years under his belt working here. Really help him land some connections, and then he could develop the app with us or sell it to Baxley."

"Well, he's still young. I'm sure he'll come around eventually. It's good that he's so ambitious though. Just like you."

Eric and I have known each other for the better part of two decades. He was my mentor out of grad school at my first major job. He was a director, and I was just starting out. He saw something in me, took me under his wing, and helped me become the man I am today. So when I started Baxley Technologies fifteen years ago, he was the first employee I hired.

"More like you. I still remember you telling me six months after you started at DataTech, you said *Eric, I give myself five years before I start my own company and ten to make it a billion-dollar enterprise.* I thought you were crazy but here we are." He raises his glass to me and we both drink.

"Shit," he says, looking at his watch, "the Mrs. will be calling me any second if I don't get home. Maybe if I'm lucky I can sweet-talk her into giving me some of that action you and Savannah almost had." He winks at me and I just ignore the comment. "Have a good weekend, boss. See you Sunday at the club. Nine a.m. tee off; don't be late." He points to me as he walks out of my office.

Eric is on his fourth, possibly fifth marriage at this point. I can't keep track. His penchant for chasing after his next wife while still married to his current usually lands him in divorce court every few years.

His comment about Savannah and me lingers as I dim the lights and walk over to my records. I leaf through them briefly, finally deciding on "Something Else" by Cannonball Adderley. The smooth sound of jazz fills the office as I take a seat in my chair. I lean back and close my eyes, allowing the melody to carry me away.

2

SAVANNAH

"Wait, so you guys are broken up?" Callie gives me a sideways look and I nod as I take a sip of my mimosa.

I decided I couldn't wait till Saturday night at Mitzy's to spill the tea so we met for brunch at our favorite outdoor eatery in the city.

"Like not on a break but done?" Tessa, my old coworker, confirms.

"Yup. He said that we want different things and that he isn't ready to commit."

"I am so confused." Callie looks at me, then glances to Tessa who nods emphatically. "I thought you guys were in a committed relationship, so what is he afraid to commit to?"

I shrug. "I guess more of a relationship? I actually kind of thought when he took me out the other night that he was either going to ask me to move in with him or—propose?"

Callie's eyes bug out. "Would you have said yes?"

"Ye—no, I dunno. Doesn't really matter now anyway."

"What has me confused is how incredibly calm and nonchalant you seem about the whole thing." Tessa trains her eyes on me.

"Same," Callie agrees.

I am too. I've tried to spend the last week since the breakup rationalizing my thoughts... after my initial panic and breakdown in the shower that night. Is Easton *my person?* I don't think so, especially not now, but who knows.

"Well, I did have my initial cry, and then I had a very short denial phase followed by some solid wallowing and then hopeless panic and desperation. I signed up for a dating account that same night." The shock that flies across their faces with the audible gasps is a bit much. "Okay, calm down. I didn't murder someone. I promptly deleted it because I realized it was a manic state of thinking I'd die alone surrounded by cats."

"Do you still love him?"

"I think I do. I think the reality is he made a decision that was the right one; I just wasn't ready for it. I think he and I loved or still love each other, but we aren't in love. Ugh, I hate saying cliché-ass things like that, but I don't know how else to express it."

"But you're not over him."

I frown and shake my head. "I don't think so, no. I think part of it is the thought of starting ooooover. I'm thirty years old; the men that are out there are basically dragging their knuckles and pounding on their chest."

"What does this mean for you guys with the wedding? I know Jason, Patrick's brother, is one of Easton's best friends."

I feel dread well up as I remember that Tessa met her fiancé Patrick because his brother Jason was friends with Easton from college.

"Dammit." I flop back against my chair dramatically. "I completely forgot about that."

"Here's a thought," Callie says, quickly changing the subject. "Instead of looking for another relationship to jump into, look for a *situationship.* Just a fun, casual hookup buddy or buddies."

I open my mouth to protest because Callie knows I'm a relationship girl.

"I know, I know you're a relationship kind of girl, but hear me out. You had maybe three months between Nick and Ford and then another three to four months between Ford and Easton. You need to get out there and sow your wild oats."

"My oats aren't wild; they're in their thirties now and they're tired." I laugh.

"I agree with Callie. Make a dating profile, then go on some dates, and have some fun."

"The reason I ask is because I have that alumni association fundraiser soon and he's going to be there. I would love to show up with a date because—well, I'm afraid he will, and then I'll just look sad."

"Wait, is he seeing someone already?" Callie's eyes narrow.

"I dunno. I saw a picture on Instagram that some woman tagged him in at an outdoor concert."

"Lemme see," she says, holding out her hand. "And then you're blocking him."

I pull up his account and hand over my phone. Tessa leans in and she and Callie both study the photo with eagle eyes like they're trying to find Waldo.

"Well?"

"Looks a little sus, not gonna lie."

"Right? Like why is she laughing so hard and touching his arm like that?"

They sit back and Callie hands my phone back to me. "There, he's blocked. It's not your problem now, so it's time to just whoosah that shit and let it go so that you can open yourself up to better things."

I grab my mimosa and chug the rest of it. "Easy for you two to say. You're married and Tessa, you're engaged."

"Is this like a new leaf or something? I've never heard you be so obsessed with getting married. All you've ever talked about since freshman year was your career." Callie eyes me suspiciously.

"Yeah, and look where that's gotten me. I can't keep a man because I'm too focused on work. I spend most of my time with Warren."

Callie crooks an eyebrow at me, a devilish grin forming on her shiny lips.

"What? What's that look?"

"You still fantasize about Warren? Maybe he could be your hookup buddy."

"Ohhh, good idea," Tessa adds.

"Good idea? To sleep with my boss?" I wave them off. "You guys are both bad influences, you know that?"

"Just saying—that man is fine as hell and the way he looks at you."

"The way he looks at me?" I try to tamp down the giddiness in my voice, but my belly does a little flop when she mentions it. "When have you been around us?"

"Twice actually. When I came by your office to pick you up for lunch once, and then when I came to give you a new skirt because you ripped yours falling off the counter in your office trying to change that lightbulb."

"Yes, I remember the skirt-tearing incident; don't remind me."

I'd only been working at Baxley for six months when I noticed a lightbulb burnt out in the built-in bookshelves on the back wall. Shit like that bothers me so instead of waiting around for a maintenance ticket to finally be closed, I just grabbed a bulb from the maintenance closet and hopped up on the counter next to the bookshelf. Needless to say, when I lost my footing and shot my leg out to catch myself, it tore my skirt right up the back. And who would just happen to be coming to talk to me just then? Warren, of course.

He'd helped me up and grabbed a wet cloth from the restroom to dab on my now-bleeding, skinned-up knee. I remember beginning to sweat as his nimble fingers grazed my skin as I held on to the back of my skirt for dear life.

"Well, that man was clearly looking at you more than just as a simple coworker or boss type look. He likes"—she runs her fingers up and down as she points to me—"what you've got going on."

"Eww, don't be weird." I smack her hand as we all burst into a fit of giggles.

"But really, would you ever?"

I pretend to think about the question like I haven't a million times before. "Under different circumstances? Absolutely. But as my boss? No. We have an amazing dynamic; we're good friends, and there's a lot of trust there. I'd be scared to mess that up."

I'm seconds away from telling them about the intimate moment we had in his office the other night before dickbag Eric came in and ruined it. And the fact that I may or may not have spent a solid two hours that night trying to imagine how that scenario would have played out if he hadn't walked in. But I don't need to add gasoline to this already out-of-control fire.

"Really, you would? Even though he's like fifty?" Tessa looks surprised.

"He's almost forty-six; he's not fifty. And yeah, have you seen him? Six five with green eyes and that thick, silky hair?" I whistle. "Man looks like one of those sexy and vague Dior cologne commercials."

"Also because you have daddy issues," Callie says.

"And there's that," I agree. "Anyway, enough of that crazy talk. How long should I wait to do the online dating thing?"

"I don't think there's a rule about time. Do it when you feel ready."

"Don't tell her that, Tessa. She'll take three months, and by that point, she'll be back in another relationship."

"Hey!" I interject.

"It's true. Just make one this weekend. Better yet, let's go out and dance. You can practice your flirting skills."

"Ugh, the thought of some sweaty, drunk twenty-five-year-old bro grinding up on me and touching me? I can't. Those days are gone for me."

"Fine, how about we go to one of those fancy-ass business bars near your office. Where they play jazz and everyone drinks brown liquor in those crystal tumblers and talks about stocks and bonds or whatever."

"So my options are sweaty twenty-five-year-olds," I say, holding up one hand, "or most likely married sixty-year-old men looking for a sidepiece? No, thanks. Just let me think about things this weekend, and if I feel the urge, I'll set up the account. Now, if you ladies will excuse me, I need to go meet the delivery driver for a new dresser I ordered."

"Okay, fine, but try to have some fun on Sunday. Go down by the lake and join in a volleyball game or something," Callie says.

I know she only wants the best for me, and she'd made it clear that she didn't think it was Easton. He wasn't a bad guy, but she always said I could not only do better, but I deserved better. As she liked to say, *nobody deserves to raise someone else's thirty-year-old son.*

"I will be putting together my dresser and watching *Real Housewives.*"

We say our goodbyes and I head down the street to meet the delivery guys at my apartment.

* * *

I PACE MY APARTMENT FLOOR, a text response already typed out to Warren. I'd sent him one about twenty minutes ago asking if he was home to which he replied with a simple—

Warren: *Yes. You need something?*

I try to hype myself up to send the text. If I hadn't had the conversation earlier with my friends about the way he *looks at me*, I wouldn't be this nervous... Actually, scratch that. If we hadn't shared that weird yet intimate foot holding moment earlier, I wouldn't be this nervous.

"Send it, just send it. It's not weird; he's helped you out before."

So I hit send.

Me: *Hey, so... I have been trying to get this insane dresser I bought put together for two hours and I'm at my wit's end. Any chance you feel like being my knight in shining armor and helping me out? I really don't want to call Easton and grovel.*

I hold my breath as I see the three little dots bouncing.

Warren: *Of course. Be right over.*

I don't know why I'm so nervous. It's not like he knows the intimate thoughts I was having about him earlier. I'm going to make it weird when he gets here if I don't get it together.

I sprint to my bathroom and pull down my messy bun, running a brush frantically through my hair before reapplying deodorant and a spritz of my favorite perfume. I curl my lashes and slick on some sheer gloss.

I do a double take around my apartment, making sure there's

nothing crazy lying around before changing into a cuter pair of shorts and t-shirt.

My apartment is large and in an amazing neighborhood in the city, The Gold Coast. I really struggled to sign the lease with how expensive it was and the fact that it's more space than I need, but I reminded myself that this is what I busted my ass for, for so many years. I make good money—okay, great money—especially for my age. I'm a smart little saver so I figure a little splurge on my apartment is well earned.

I'm about to panic and drag my entire dresser out into the hallway when I realize that it's in my bedroom and any minute Warren Baxley is going to be standing in my freaking bedroom. A knock sounds on my front door and it's too late.

"Hey." I smile as I pull the door open. "Thank you. I feel like an idiot."

He returns the smile and steps into my apartment looking like six foot five of pure seduction wrapped in a black V-neck t-shirt and black jeans.

"Idiot is probably the last word anyone would ever use to describe you. You can't be perfect at everything." He removes his shoes and glances around my apartment. "Where's the untamable beast?"

I giggle and instantly feel embarrassed. *What the hell? I don't giggle at Warren Baxley.*

"Uh, in here." I point down the hall toward my bedroom. He follows behind me as I start walking.

"Okay," he says, crouching down on the floor and reading over the instructions. I stand back and take in the sight of Warren in socks on my bedroom floor like we're just a regular couple putting together some furniture.

"Seems manageable. Then again, if you couldn't figure it out, I might be in trouble." He looks up at me as he says it and it feels like my heart stops. His hair isn't perfectly styled like it is at work; it's flopped down over his forehead, and he's smiling so wide his eyes are framed with a few lines. It takes my breath away in this brief, seemingly inane moment. I realize I'm staring and I clear my throat.

24

"How about you tell me which parts you need and I'll hand them to you."

"Teamwork, just like in the office," he says and we get started on finishing the dresser.

Thirty seamless minutes later, the dresser is done, and Warren didn't struggle once.

"Now where do you want it?" he asks as he looks around my room.

"Oh, in my walk-in closet actually." I step around him and flip on the light. "Over here in this corner."

"Okay, you grab one end and I'll grab the other."

We walk it backward into the closet and toward the corner.

"Hang on. There's a bag here I don't want to smash." He reaches down and grabs for the bag. He misses one handle so when he picks it up, the contents spill out onto the closet floor.

My hands shoot up to cover my mouth as I watch in absolute horror when I realize it's the bag I shoved a bunch of items Easton had bought me that I planned to get rid of in some grand gesture of moving forward and forgetting the past. There lying on the floor with a bunch of random knickknacks, a t-shirt, perfume, and a photo album is a bright-pink vibrator.

"Oh my God." I lunge toward the pile and grab the vibrator first, shoving it back into the bag with the rest of the items. "Just some shit I'm throwing away," I say as my face feels like it's on fire.

He doesn't say anything as we finish placing the dresser into position and exit my bedroom.

"You want to stay for a glass of wine or anything?" I do everything but make eye contact with him while silently praying he says no.

"I would but I have some work I should get to this evening."

"Thanks again, so much." I reach around him for the door as he bends over to put his shoes on. "And I promise, I won't be bugging you for this kind of stuff now that I'm single."

He stands up and crosses his arms over his broad chest and it literally makes my mouth water. How the fuck is this man so fine and single? I want to just come out and ask him, but I think I've done enough embarrassing myself for one evening.

25

"Never a bother, Savannah. I always enjoy spending time with you."

"And sorry about the—" I can't bring myself to say the word so I just point my thumb over my shoulder toward the bedroom, hoping he gets what I'm saying.

He chuckles as I open the door. He steps out into the hallway and turns back to face me, but I'm staring at his shoes because I cannot look in this man's eyes right now. I see his hand slowly come up till it hits my chin softly, tipping it upward.

"Nothing to be ashamed of. We all have needs and sometimes men are shit at satisfying those needs the right way. No shame in improvising." He winks and walks down the hall toward the elevator.

I close the door, my legs feeling like jelly as I lean against it and let out a long, audible breath.

Did that seriously just happen?

3

WARREN

I should have kept my damn mouth shut.

I punch the button for the elevator and step inside when the doors open. I reach down and adjust my hardening cock, images of Savannah stuffing herself with that pink toy now flooding my brain.

"Fuck me," I mutter.

How the hell am I supposed to go back to my already almost unbearable work situation now that I have that image in my head?

I grip the railing in the elevator so tight it digs into the palms of my hands. Penance, I tell myself, knowing full well that when I get home tonight I'll be putting those images to good use.

I lied to Savannah. I don't technically have any work that I need to get done tonight. Yes, there's always something I can be working on, but I just knew I wouldn't be able to handle the temptation of being in her private space after seeing that toy.

I walk the six blocks back to my penthouse. The breeze coming off the lake is a welcome feeling against my too-warm skin.

"Evening, sir," Steven says as he opens the door to my building.

"Hey, Steve, looking sharp." I give him a friendly pat on the shoulder and wave at Thomas behind the front desk.

Instead of even attempting to sit behind my desk and distract myself with work, I pull off my shirt and go straight to my gym. I kick my shoes off and don't bother changing out of my jeans. I grab a set of heavy dumbbells and lie back on the bench.

After forty minutes of nonstop, grueling lifting, I'm sweating profusely. I stand up and walk to mirrored wall. My stomach contracts with every heavy breath as a few drops of sweat run down my chest. I place my hands on the mirror and lean forward, letting my head hang loosely as I catch my breath.

For some reason I have the unhinged urge to snap a picture of myself in the mirror. Shirtless, sweaty, hair a mess… and send it to Savannah. Would she respond? Maybe I undo my jeans and let them hang open a little lower.

"The fuck, man? You're almost forty-six years old; leave it to the younger men." I've never sent a photo of myself to a woman, not even a selfie.

I push off the wall and run up the stairs to my bathroom and turn on the shower before I completely go off the rails. I kick off my sweaty jeans and underwear, remove my socks, then step into the steam. I turn the water to cool after a minute, hoping it tamps down the burning desire inside me, but it's no use.

I close my eyes and lean forward, my forearm resting against the shower wall as the other grips the base of my cock. I'm already at full mast. I stroke myself gently at first, images of my hands on Savannah's full tits flooding my mind. I imagine what color her nipples are, how they'd stiffen when I swirl my tongue around them.

My slow pace quickens as does my breathing. I close my eyes as I imagine my lips trailing down her tits to her belly, down even further till I reach her sweet pussy. My jaw flexes, my teeth clenched so tight as my mouth pools with saliva at the thought of tasting her.

I feel my legs stiffen, my chest burning as my mouth falls open, and I let out an animalistic groan as I spill my orgasm on the floor.

I'm angry at myself. Every time it happens, I swear it'll be the last, but the reality is, I know it won't be.

Savannah Monroe has a hold on me so tight that if I don't allow myself this release, I might cross a line that neither of us can come back from.

* * *

"The announcement for the Code Red acquisition has been drafted and is with legal now. We have that meeting at four p.m. today with the guys from Merge Media for their upcoming app release, and here are the financials from Eric for last quarter."

Savannah sways back and forth like she always does when she's reading through a list. She drops the file on my desk and makes a note on her iPad. Her hair is swept up off her neck with a clip, half of it spilling over the top of it.

"How long till legal finalizes things?"

"They said end of the week, but you know legal; it could be two weeks." She rolls her eyes and takes a seat on the edge of the chair across from me. She moves from her iPad to her phone, tapping furiously before clicking the screen off and looking up at me.

"How was the rest of your Sunday night?" I ask and immediately regret it because I know by the rosy glow that appears on her cheeks, we're both thinking about that pink vibrator spilling out onto her closet floor.

"Oh, um, good." Her voice goes up several octaves. "I just chilled out, put my clothes in the new dresser. Thanks again by the way, total lifesaver. What about you?"

Images of jerking off in the shower to thoughts of her flood my brain.

"Work stuff, got in a workout." An awkward silence falls between us and I panic, wondering if something as simple as the sex toy sighting can unnerve us both.

"Oh," she says, suddenly closing her iPad and sitting up straight. "I did a thing."

"A thing?"

She bites her bottom lip coyly and nods her head. "I signed up for a dating app! It's actually one of our clients' apps."

It feels like a bucket of ice water was just poured down my back. My body tenses.

"A dating app? Already?" I try to keep the shock out of my voice, but I don't do a good job.

"Well, yeah, it's a little soon, but I'm not using it to find my husband or anything. Just to like, you know—get back out there."

"So for hookups?"

Her lips part and then snap shut again before she speaks. "No, I am a relationship kind of girl. I just—well"—her shoulders drop a little—"my friends think I should get back out there and just have fun. Stop trying to be in a serious relationship for a while."

I study her for a minute. "And is that what you want?"

She shrugs. "No, but maybe they have a point. The reason I actually decided to go through with making the profile was because I have that alumni association thing this weekend and I really don't want to go alone. I know it's pathetic, but I think Easton is already seeing someone else and he'll probably bring her and I'm just not that thick-skinned yet that I'll be okay with it."

"So you'll use it to find someone for the event, then"—I pick up a paper, attempting to seem only partially interested in what I'm saying—"after you find the guy for a date, you'll delete it?" I place the paper back on the desk, unable to distract myself.

She shrugs. "I guess. I don't think I'm ready for another relationship yet, and according to my therapist, I have intimacy issues which is why I struggle with casual sex." Her eyes flash to me as soon as she finishes her sentence. While Savannah and I are close and I feel a sense of protection for her, we don't speak freely about our sex lives to one another.

"Sorry." She squeezes her eyes shut and rubs her temples. "Total overshare."

"For what it's worth, I don't think you not wanting to have casual sex means intimacy issues. It's just not for everyone." Then an idea hits me, a stupid idea I should have kept to myself but instead, I blurt it out. "What if I take you?"

She cocks her head to the side. "Take me?"

The way she says it is almost breathy and my cock jumps to attention. I know she's merely asking what I mean, but hearing the words *take me* slip past Savannah's plump lips has me wanting to bend her over this desk and do exactly that. Take her deeply and thoroughly.

"Yeah, to this event," I say casually, as understanding settles over her face.

"But Easton knows you're my boss."

I nod. "And? You still wouldn't be there alone."

"Yeah, but—" She glances down at the iPad in her hands and fidgets with the cover nervously. "He knows we aren't dating." She looks back up at me nervously.

"How does he know we aren't?"

"Well," she starts. "I guess he doesn't actually."

"Exactly." I smile and torture myself even further for some sick reason. "Perhaps after your breakup, you and I realized there was something between us all along and the breakup drove you into my arms."

She looks at me intently as I say the words. I see her throat move as she swallows.

"And you'd be okay with that?"

"With taking you? I wouldn't have offered if I wasn't."

A smile tugs at the corner of her lips. "I mean, of people thinking we're together?"

I want to tell her that I don't give a fuck what people think. That if it means every man in the world will never look twice at her again I'll do it a hundred times. It's fucking selfish and I know it, but I'm also doing her a favor so it can't be *that* bad.

"That's the point of me going with you, isn't it, sweetheart?"

Her cheeks have that rosy glow back and she smiles. Every time I let a small term of endearment slip when speaking to her, she gives me the same reaction and I love it.

"Okay. So, I'll just send you over the information and we can meet there?"

"It's a date, Savannah. I'll pick you up at your place."

"A 'date,'" she says with air quotes.

31

I want to tell her if she does that again, I'll show her just how real a fake date can get and she won't be able to walk straight for a week. Instead, I narrow my gaze on her.

"We'll know it's pretend, but everyone else there will think we're so infatuated with each other we fucked in the limo on the way there."

That was the kind of thought I should have kept to myself. Her lips fall open and I see a tinge of red creeping up her neck. Then again, seeing her flustered at the mention of me fucking her has my blood pressure skyrocketing. I don't know what possesses me to keep going but I do.

"Maybe I should mess up your hair or wrinkle your dress—really sell it." I wink at her. She's on the very edge of the seat, her hands wrapped tightly around the iPad that she's gripping.

"Or better yet, maybe I'll just f—" I'm about to take things into territory she and I have never gone when Eric, like fucking bad luck, interrupts us again.

"Everyone's in the conference room." He motions toward his watch.

Savannah jerks her head around toward him, then back at me before shooting out of the chair.

"Oh my God. I lost track of time." She brushes past Eric and scurries out of my office.

"What was that?" he asks, jerking his thumb toward her.

"Nothing, just going over the Code Red briefing," I lie as I stand and adjust my tie before following him out of my office toward the conference room.

While Eric Oliver has been my mentor and close friend, he has a knack for trying to butt his way into all my business.

When I first mentioned extending an offer to Savannah for the COO position, Eric didn't take it well. He figured he would get the position when it became vacant, but he wasn't the best fit. Eric is a numbers guy through and through, a financial wizard, and that's exactly the expertise he brings to Baxley Tech.

I wouldn't say his annoyance or jealousy of Savannah getting the role has caused any obvious issues in the office, but there certainly seems to be a general coolness between the two of them.

* * *

I ADJUST my cuff links as I look myself over in the floor-length mirror of my closet. Savannah's event tonight isn't black tie so I forgo one altogether and go with just a simple black suit and white shirt.

I grab my keys by the front door and make my way downstairs. I considered having my driver take us, but it feels more genuine, more intimate to drive her myself. Besides, it's not too often I get to drive my favorite car—my Aston Martin DB11. Being a billionaire is a life of pure luxury, no way around it, but usually I don't have the time to enjoy the luxuries I can afford.

I pull up to Savannah's apartment fifteen minutes later and put the car in park, hesitating briefly. My nerves are doing something funny in my belly.

"It's not a real date," I remind myself as I exit the vehicle and enter her building. I know the doorman. "Evening, Carl." I wave as I walk to the elevator.

"Evening, Mr. Baxley. Looking sharp as always." He laughs.

Everything feels like it's in slow motion. It felt like the drive took twice as long. It feels like the elevator is climbing at a snail's pace and the doors are trying to open through quicksand. I finally make it to her door. I inhale sharply, then knock. A second later, she swings the door open, and my breath gets caught in my chest.

Her eyes light up when she sees me, a smile spreading from ear to ear. Her hair is set in beautiful waves, swept off her face on one side by a sparkly clip, the rest cascading over her shoulder. It looks darker against the blush-pink dress that falls over her delicate curves and rests just above her knees.

"Come in," she says, stepping to the side. "I'm putting on my jewelry. I'll just be a minute."

I follow her inside and close the door. She spins around to walk back toward her bedroom as she speaks to me, but I'm not listening. I can't focus when I see the back of her dress. Delicate straps crisscross over her bare skin and tie at the base of her dress that dips low.

I head straight to her refrigerator and grab a bottle of water, downing half of it before I catch my breath.

"Okay, I'm ready." She comes back out of the hallway and into the kitchen.

Now I can fully take her in. The dress swoops across her breasts, thin straps holding it up.

She's definitely not wearing a bra. Fuck! My eyes drop down to her breasts, then to her waist and back up.

"Water?" I ask, holding out the bottle.

She shakes her head. "Ready?"

I finish the bottle and toss it in the recycling as I silently follow her out of her apartment and toward the elevator. We step inside and it's just the two of us.

"You look nice," she says, looking over at me. "No tie, huh? You always wear a tie."

I reach down to my open collar. "I do, don't I?"

"And how do I look?"

I look over at her and feel like an asshole that I didn't say a single word about her appearance. I was literally speechless at how stunning she looks. I take the opportunity to drag my eyes slowly up her body. Her toned legs have a sheen to them; they look absolutely mouthwatering in the sky-high heels that adorn her feet. I swallow when I get to her breasts, the coolness of the elevator hardening her nipples just enough that I can see them poking against her dress.

I chuckle because there's only one way I can think to describe how she looks and I know I shouldn't but— "Mouthwatering."

She blushes and nervously adjusts one strap of her dress that rests against her exposed collarbone.

"You asked," I say as the doors open and I place my hand on her lower back. "Shall we?" I gesture toward the lobby, but she's frozen in place. "Savannah?"

She looks over her shoulder at me, making eye contact briefly before her eyes lower to my mouth.

"We're going to be late." My words come out in almost a whisper.

"Barbie and Ken?" Carl whistles and then laughs as he sees us, walking over just as the elevator doors begin to close again.

I know I have two options right now. I can reach around her and hit the button for her floor again. Tell her that we aren't going to an event tonight while I pull her against me and bury my tongue in her mouth or I can push the door open button and step outside.

She makes the decision for me as she blinks rapidly and turns to push the door open button. We step out into the lobby as Carl claps, causing her to smile.

"Oh, stop." She pretends to be coy as she does a little spin. Carl grabs her hand and spins her again, then pulls her in for a quick dance.

She's beautiful inside and out. The way she engages people so sincerely and shares herself with them is intoxicating. I'm envious of her openness. It's like she never worries about whether things will go wrong; she always chooses to see the positive side.

"You're a very lucky man, Mr. Baxley." Carl waves to us as we exit the building.

"You drove?" She spins around as I step toward her, reaching around to open the passenger side door. The movement causes her to practically be in my arms, her chest centimeters away from mine.

"I did, it's a date." I smile and open the door for her. She slides into the seat, and I walk around and climb in.

I try not to notice the way her dress has ridden up slightly to expose a few inches of her tempting thigh. I also try not to notice her sultry perfume that fills the car.

"So, you sure about this?" She holds her clutch in her lap as she looks over at me.

"What's not to be sure about?" I don't let her answer. I put the car in drive and take off through traffic.

When we arrive at the event, the valet opens Savannah's door and helps her out of the car. I hand him the keys and reach for her hand. Her fingers intertwine with mine and I realize that this is the first time she and I have ever held hands.

"Nervous?" I ask as we walk through the door.

"A little," she says, and I squeeze her hand.

I want to ask if she's nervous about being seen with me in public or if it's seeing her ex for the first time, but I also don't want to know the answer. I hate the fact that I'm here because of another man. I know it's my own doing and I'd still rather be here than not, but not as her fake date.

I want to be standing next to Savannah Monroe as her man.

4

SAVANNAH

I glance around the room, seeing a dozen familiar faces, but all I can focus on is the warmth of Warren's hand wrapped around my own, his description of me echoing through my head.

"Mouthwatering."

What would have happened if Carl hadn't been there? A tingle forms in my lower belly and settles between my thighs when I feel Warren's hand release mine, then slowly slide up to my lower back again.

"I'm going to run to the restroom briefly," I say as we enter the grand hall.

"I'll grab you a drink," he says as we part ways.

I turn the tap on cold in the restroom and run my hands through it as I take in a few deep breaths.

What the hell has gotten into me?

I grip the edge of the sink and close my eyes, letting my head loll forward as I imagine Warren closing the elevator door and grabbing me, thrusting his hands into my hair as he backs me against the elevator wall, his tongue demanding entrance to my mouth as his lips caress my own.

"Oh my God, is that Warren Baxley?"

I snap my head up, my eyes popping open as Brenda Deeter, head of the student alumni association, walks up to the sink next to me. "I had no idea he was coming. Is he a donor?"

"Oh yeah, he's a big supporter of the university."

"Didn't he go to Harvard?"

I nod. "He did but he's my boss and he knew I had this event tonight and he is a big supporter of education and likes to keep his finger on the pulse of things." I completely pull that out of my ass, but it sounds legit and she seems to buy it.

"The board will freak when they hear he came tonight," she says giddily before drying her hands. "Guess I should get out there and introduce myself to him." She fluffs her short hair and pinches her cheeks before rushing out the door.

I laugh. Good to know Warren has this effect on most women and it's not just me. I exit the restroom and stand at the edge of the grand room. I take a look around but don't spot Easton yet. Instead, my eyes fall to Warren who is leaning against the bar as Brenda talks his ear off.

He looks up and catches me staring. An instant smile breaking out on his face, he tosses me a wink. That feeling is back in my lower belly. It's just because I'm nervous about seeing Easton I tell myself, but I know better. The thought of seeing Easton right now is the furthest thing from my brain.

Warren excuses himself from Brenda and approaches me with a drink in each hand.

"Old-fashioned or dirty martini?" he asks, lifting them both up.

I reach for the martini, my favorite drink. "I only drink old-fashioneds when I'm trying to not remember the night."

"Good to know I haven't driven you to that point yet tonight."

I take a sip of the cocktail and then another, the numbness hitting my tongue.

"Sorry about Brenda by the way. You might need to open your checkbook tonight."

"I figured when I offered to bring you to a charity event. I already made a donation before we got here."

I look over at him. "You did?"

He nods and takes a sip of his drink. "In your honor. In the memo I wrote, *In honor of the brightest mind that ever walked these halls and the biggest heart that this institution will ever know.*"

"Is that really what you think of me?"

"Yes. And so much more but we'll save that for another time. Don't want your head getting too big." He reaches his hand out and brushes my hair back over my shoulder. "Have you seen him yet?"

The question breaks the trance he has me in. "Who? Oh, Easton. Not yet."

I glance around the room again, and then I see him. He's surrounded by several people who are laughing. That's Easton, always making people laugh and smile. He was always the center of attention, the life of the party. I smile when I see him, but he doesn't notice me. I feel a little tug at my heart. I haven't sorted through all my emotions surrounding the breakup yet, but this one doesn't feel like jealousy. Just loss. I lost a good friend and it does hurt.

"Hey," Warren whispers and places his finger beneath my chin, pulling my attention back to him. "How do you want to play this?"

I look down at my drink. "What do you mean?"

He takes it from my hand and places our drinks on the high-top table next to us. He grabs my hand and slowly leads me out to the dance floor where a few people are slowly swaying to the music. He pulls my hand, my body moving forward as his arm wraps around me, and he pulls me against him.

A soft breath escapes my lips as he presses himself softly against me. Any thought of Easton or anyone else floats away as I close my eyes and feel his warmth slowly encapsulate me.

"Do you want me to make him jealous? Is that the plan for the night?"

His breath is warm against my cheek. I don't answer right away; I just want to live in this moment. My eyes are closed as his hand slowly sinks lower down my back, his fingertips burning a trail on my exposed skin as his hand settles right above the curve of my ass.

I feel like my body is seconds away from bursting into flames. I slide my hand from where it rests on his chest, up around his neck.

"I think it's working," he murmurs and my eyes pop open.

"Hmm?"

"He's staring at us," he says as he presses his hand more firmly against me. "He's probably wondering at what point we realized there was something between us. Was it while you two were still together?"

He spins me around so that I'm facing away from him, his hands coming to rest firmly on my waist as my ass presses against the front of him. One hand slowly slides across my waist to rest against my belly as he continues to whisper against my neck.

"Maybe he's wondering if you were thinking of me when he was touching you, kissing you." He runs his nose up my neck and I let my eyes close, my head falling to one side. "When he was inside you."

The small strap of my dress falls off my shoulder as my breath begins to quicken. It feels like there's nobody else in the room but us.

His hand slides up my bare arm, his finger hooking the strap and slowly placing it back on my shoulder just before his lips come down and touch my skin for only a second. It sends a lightning bolt of pleasure shooting through my body.

Suddenly I'm very aware that goosebumps just broke out across my skin and I squeeze my thighs together as a small gasp escapes my lips. My eyes pop open in shock. I spin around to face Warren again, my hands resting against his chest. His eyes are dark; I've never seen them like this before, but I recognize the look.

Pure, unbridled lust.

His hands slide up my entire body unapologetically and into my hair. He tilts my head as he leans the other way. His eyes are on mine as he leans in, his lips so close I can almost taste them.

"Savannah." I hear my name and someone clears their throat behind me.

Warren's eyes go from dark and lustful to annoyed in an instant and he steps back from me.

I turn around. "Easton, hi." I smile and pull him in for a quick hug.

"You look beautiful, just like you always do."

"And Mr. Baxley, nice to see you here." Easton extends his hand toward Warren and I spin around.

"Yes, yes, this is my date, Warren." I link my arm through his and he forces a smile at Easton.

"Nice to meet you," Warren says, clearly letting Easton know that despite meeting him twice previously, he's inconsequential to him.

I feel bad. I don't want to hurt Easton, even though he hurt me. I smile at him as Warren pulls me tightly against him.

"Maybe we can catch up soon."

"Yeah." I smile and Easton nods and walks away.

Warren releases me. "I'm getting a drink," he says before walking toward the bar. Gone is the intensity that was between us just seconds ago.

"I'll take one too," I say, following after him.

"Two old-fashioneds," he says to the bartender. He won't look at me.

"What was that?" I ask. "You okay?"

"Yes," he says, tossing some cash in the tip jar. "You're still in love with him," he says, shoving his hands in his pockets.

"Easton?" I think for a moment. "No. No, I'm not."

His eyes lift and meet mine. "Seemed like it just now."

He's almost acting jealous and I want to remind him that this was his idea to come along, but I'm also extremely confused on why he would be jealous.

"It's not love like you think. It's—loss. I think he and I fell out of love with each other, but we still cared deeply for each other. He was one of my best friends and now he's just a guy I used to date."

I feel Warren's arm wrap around me again as he pulls me in for a hug. I settle against his chest.

"I'm sorry. I know it's not easy."

"Here you are, sir." The bartender places the drinks on the counter and we separate, both reaching for our glasses.

"To getting over exes," he says, lifting his drink to mine and we both take a sip.

"Who was your last ex? You over her?"

He squints and looks off in the distance. "Definitely over her."

"Who was it? Did I know this one?"

"This one?" He laughs.

"I feel like you're always so secretive about who you're dating."

"Or maybe none of them mattered enough that I felt the need to introduce them to you."

I eye him suspiciously. "That sounds like a cop-out answer."

"Ask whatever you want; I'm an open book." He gestures with wide-open arms.

"Okay." I keep my eyes on his, taking a sip of my drink. "So you care about my opinion of your significant other?"

His lips curl into a slight frown. "Yeah, I think so. I do. Is that strange?"

I toy with the stirrer in my glass, butterflies dancing in my belly at the thought that Warren Baxley cares about what I think.

"No, I do too. Which is why it bothered me that you pretended not to remember Easton's name or that you met him for the *third* time tonight." I raise an eyebrow at him, and he chuckles.

He places his glass down and reaches for my waist, pulling me so I step closer to him. It's weird how quickly this feels natural to us both. Apart from our one dance each year at his shareholders' event, Warren and I don't touch much.

"That's because I don't give a shit about that guy."

"Well, I did so you should." I point my finger in his chest playfully.

We're in a roomful of people, some powerful elected officials and other billionaires, and all either of us seem to notice is each other.

"You're right. I'm sorry. I promise I'll be better with the next guy."

My smile fades and I quickly take another drink, the old-fashioned burning through my chest as his words hit me. I somehow became so wrapped up in this little charade so quickly that I let myself actually believe I was going home with Warren tonight.

"You okay?" His eyes search mine as he slowly rubs his thumb across my hip bone. I step back, needing the space to clear my head and remind myself that this isn't real.

"Yeah, just drank this too fast." I smile, holding up my now empty tumbler. "Hey, what were you going to say in your office yesterday before Eric came in and interrupted us?"

His eyes dart nervously from mine to the floor. "Uh, I don't recall actually. You remember what we were talking about?"

I debate on opening that can of worms, but I just shrug it off. "Nah, nothing important." I place my glass down and grab his hand. "I think the best way to get over someone is to *pretend* to be over them, so let's get back on that dance floor."

Warren spins me around, then hooks his arm behind my back as he dips me, causing me to erupt into a fit of laughter.

If there's one word I would use to describe the Warren Baxley 99.9% of the world sees, it's stoic. He's not cruel or moody or bossy; he's just serious and keeps to himself more than anyone I've ever met. But tonight I get to see that side of Warren that he reserves for very few and it makes my heart flutter.

After a few turns about the dance floor, I take him around to meet a few other important people from my university. Back is the serious and reserved Warren.

"Thanks again for coming with me tonight. I never would have thought to ask you."

"No? Why not?" He shifts the car into gear and navigates through traffic.

"Well, for one, you're my boss, and two, we both know how much you hate these public events. I'm not so sure you'd ever leave your penthouse or your office if you could get away with it."

He smiles over at me briefly as he pulls the car into a spot in front of my building.

"I had good motivation tonight. A 'date'"—he uses the air quotes I used earlier—"with the prettiest woman in Chicago."

I laugh and unbuckle my seat belt. "Flattery will get you nowhere, mister." I turn to face him as he opens his door and steps out to come around and open mine. "Thanks again," I say, stepping out.

"Let me walk you up," he says as he ushers me toward the entrance.

Carl is just leaving for the night, and we say our goodbyes to him as we climb into the elevator.

"You're being awfully nice this evening."

He reaches around me, his one hand still on my waist. "Am I not usually nice?"

"Nice isn't the right word. More—sweet or flirty." I surprise myself a little at how easily the word just slipped out.

I see a devilish grin form at the corner of his lips as the doors open and we step into the hallway. He walks me to my door.

"Would you disagree?" I press further as I place my key in the lock.

He steps back a little, sliding his hands into his pockets. I look back at him over my shoulder.

"No, I wouldn't disagree with flirty, but sweet? Hmm." He casually removes his hand from his pocket, bringing it to his jaw. His eyes stare into mine. It feels like there's something on the tip of his tongue that he wants to say but he's fighting it.

I don't know what to do or say in this moment. It feels like there's something hanging between us and I don't know if he's waiting for me to invite him inside or pull him to me.

"Did you wan—" I point toward my door just as his pocket starts to ring.

He reaches in and pulls it out. "It's Eric. I have to take this. Have a good night, Savannah." His demeanor has changed in an instant and he waits for me to step inside and close the door before answering.

I close the door and hold my breath, waiting, hoping he knocks after he finishes his call with Eric, but a knock never comes. I walk to my bathroom and turn on the tub, deciding a nice soak with lavender Epsom salts will take away the tension in my feet from wearing these heels all night.

I kick off the shoes into the corner of my closet and reach behind me to undo the tie on my dress. My eyes catch the bag with the vibrator that I had every intention of throwing out but never did. I let the dress fall to my feet and step out of it, looking over my shoulder like someone could see before reaching into the bag for the toy.

I hold down the power button and shockingly it still has a charge. It buzzes in my hand and I drop down to my knees on the floor of my closet. I pull my panties down my thighs, then slowly drag the toy down my body till it settles against my clit.

I jump at the initial sensation but quickly my chest is rising and falling as a warmth takes over my body. I lie on my back, my thighs falling open as I imagine Warren's lips against my neck. The smell of his expensive cologne still burns in my nostrils as I remember the way his fingertips felt against my flesh.

I'm panting, my back arching as white stars burst beneath my eyes that are squeezed shut. I turn the toy off and let it fall from my hand as I slowly open my eyes and stare up at the ceiling, Warren's unfinished words from earlier taunting me... *"Or maybe I should f—"*

I want so badly to know what he was going to say. I know what I wanted to hear him say but I just can't imagine him saying those words to me. For a minute I think that maybe my friends are right. Maybe I should make the offer to him and see if we both need to just get it out of our systems once and for all.

* * *

I HOLD two coffees in my hand as I ride the elevator up to Warren's floor. It's already been a busy Monday morning and it's only going to be busier with the Code Red acquisition announcement happening this week.

Warren is also hosting his annual shareholders' event on his private yacht on Lake Michigan. It happens every year and every year I have to convince him that yes, he has to be there since it's his company, his party, and his yacht.

The elevator stops and the doors open a few floors from Warren's floor. Eric steps in and my back stiffens.

"Good morning," I say flatly. I'm always cordial to him but never friendly. I never want him to think for one second that there's anything but professionalism between us.

"Morning, doll face." He gives me a big smile, his mustache curling a little with the movement. "Bringing the boss his coffee? Isn't that Sophie's job?" he asks, referring to Warren's assistant.

"Not her job, no."

"Ah, so you're just making sure he's not sticking his dick in her too then, huh?"

I roll my eyes and try not to squeeze the coffee cups so tight I spill them. "This is a workplace, Eric. I think we should behave as such."

"Is that what you tell Warren when you're sitting on his desk playing footsy with him? Last time I checked, getting on your knees for the boss isn't keeping it professional."

My mouth falls open slightly and I can feel my heartbeat in my ears. The doors open and he steps out, instantly flirting with Sophie and making her laugh.

"Hey, Sophie, can you give this to him?" I say, handing her the coffee before turning around and marching back into the elevator to go back downstairs. I'm in no mood to pretend like things are okay with Eric standing next to me, and I'm not about to tattle on him to Warren.

I should have nipped this in the bud when I was hired on three years ago, but it's only continued to escalate. Today wasn't half-bad. Usually he asks me straight-up if I fucked the boss today because he's in a good mood. I know if I told Warren, he'd take care of it, but I also know that for as much as I hate Eric Owen, his financial genius is a huge asset to this company and he's been Warren's mentor for the better part of two decades.

As a woman working not only in corporate America but also tech, you can get labeled as a "bitch," "not a team player," or "disruptive" very easily if you start reporting stuff to Human Resources.

I shut myself in my office and turn on a brief meditation video to work through some breathing exercises and remind myself that if all I have to put up with is a few nasty remarks from a soon-to-be retired old man, I can power through if it means keeping my dream job.

5

WARREN

I fix my bow tie in the mirror for the third time.

I fucking hate parties, especially ones filled with other billionaires. It's just a bunch of ass-kissing and back-slapping. Isn't it enough I make them richer each quarter they collect a big fat dividend check?

I practice my smile in the mirror and head down to the main deck of my yacht where Eric is schmoozing already.

"Hey, buddy. Is Kane coming tonight? I'm curious about this app of his."

Eric turns around to face me. "No, he's out of the country at the moment. Doing some big deal in China and then meeting with some investors in Dubai."

"Well, tell him to give me a call. I'm happy to hear how things are going with it. Might be able to suggest a few investors to him."

I slap him on the arm and make my way to another group of individuals. I glance around, looking for Savannah, but I don't see her. She told me she'd be a little late tonight.

Since the alumni association event last week, she's seemed a little off. I haven't had the chance to speak with her privately about things, but I'm nervous I may have crossed a boundary or upset her. When I'd left her at her apartment, she seemed fine, more than fine. We'd shared a moment and I think she was about to invite me inside when I got a call from Eric.

Maybe that's the issue. Maybe she feels like I didn't make her a priority and blew her off for work.

"Warren, amazing party as always." I feel someone's hand on my shoulder and I turn to face Brian Snyder and Terrance Fuller. "Heard some great things are coming down the pipeline. Code Red?"

They both lean in, waiting for my response when I look up and see Savannah walking up the stairs to the main deck. She looks breathtaking. Silver silk flows over her body, accentuating the flare of her hips and the dip into her waist. She recognizes someone and smiles brightly, waving at them as she makes her way across the dance floor.

"Code Red, Warren?" Terrance repeats and I turn my attention back to them.

"Yes, yes, Code Red. Gentlemen, why don't you grab a drink and we'll talk about it over here."

We're deep in conversation, Terrance giving me his in-depth analysis of how our acquisition of Code Red will disrupt the software market and make us a contender as the leader in the market share.

I look up and see Savannah staring back at me from across the room. That cute little smile slowly forms as she rolls her eyes at me. This is a game we play every year at this party. It's called *let's see how long I last down here before retreating up to my private quarters to hide.*

I finish up my conversation with the men just as she slowly approaches with two glasses of champagne in her hand.

"Hey, gentlemen. Sorry to interrupt, but could I borrow Warren for a few?" She bats her eyelashes and throws them a flirty smile, something I'll tease her for later.

"Absolutely. We were just finishing up and if I can be so bold, Miss Monroe, you look exquisite this evening." Terrance leans in and places an air-kiss against her cheek.

"Yes, I was just about to say the same thing," Brian echoes.

"Oh, thank you, gentlemen. You know how to make a lady blush."

Both men smile and head over to the open bar.

"Well, damn, I'm not sure I can follow up those compliments." I wink and take the glass she extends toward me.

"Oh, please. You can do much better than that."

I take a sip of the alcohol. "I could but I'm afraid my compliments weren't going to be quite so nice."

She looks at me sideways. "Do your worst."

"I was just going to say that with the trail of broken necks and jaws on the ground you left walking over to me, it's safe to say that dress has every man in here imagining it on the floor."

Her cheeks redden with the comment. "Told you it wasn't a nice compliment."

She looks down at the bubbles in her glass, then back up at me. "That include you?"

Fuck, I didn't think that through.

I laugh. "I plead the fifth," I say, downing the rest of the champagne and placing it on the tray of a passing waiter.

It feels like something has recently shifted between us. Like our friendship has morphed from just friends and coworkers to little innuendos and flirty exchanges. I'm not sure how I feel about it. I know how I want to feel about it. I want to kick everyone off this fucking yacht, then drag her upstairs and strip her out of this dress so I can devour every square inch of her tempting little body.

"How much longer do I have to stay down here?" I ask.

She looks around the room. "Honestly, I'm impressed you're still down here. I'd say at least another hour. You know people don't tend to stay too late anyway. They'll probably be heading back to shore by then."

I look at my watch. "Okay, one hour. Then you better grab one of those bottles of champagne and come find me."

6

SAVANNAH

It's been sixty-three minutes since I told Warren he had an hour left at his party. Sure enough, he's nowhere to be found.

Like I told him, several people have already left or are boarding the ferry now to head back to shore. There are still about a dozen people on board, milling about, but I'm sure they'll all be on the next ferry that leaves.

I walk toward the bar and grab a bottle of chilled champagne and two glasses, then duck into the cabin and climb the stairs up to Warren's private quarters. I pause when I get to the top of the stairs and take him in. He's standing with his back toward me, one hand in his pocket and the other on the railing in front of him.

Everything about this man drives me wild. The way he stands, his legs a little farther apart than most, his shoulders square and back. He commands a room without saying a word. I want to walk up behind him and wrap my arms around him, but I can't figure out what's going on between us.

Warren has always been protective of me, treated me like more than a colleague, not in a creepy way, but more in a parental type of way. My friends always joke with me about my daddy issues, but when your dad was an addict that abandoned you after your mom

50

went to prison, it stands to reason you'll have issues. Warren never holds my hand like he doesn't think I can't handle something; instead, he's the voice in my ear telling me I have what it takes and to never feel like I'm not worthy of sitting at the table with everyone else.

That's the constant fear in my head when I think about pursuing these urges with him. While I know that my feelings run a lot deeper than just wanting to see what's under those bespoke suits and all the fantasies I've had of his large hands exploring and commanding my body—I don't want to lose what we have.

"Plotting your next hostile takeover?" I ask as I walk up behind him.

He turns and looks at me with that smile that always sends a little flutter through my body. "You know me too well."

He reaches for the bottle of champagne in my hand and pops the cork, pouring us each a generous glass before placing it on the ground next to us.

"To being a money hungry titan of industry, fueled by power and bloodlust that takes no prisoners and is always planning his next hostile takeover."

I laugh and we both raise our glasses and take a drink. The air has chilled a little, but it's a welcome coolness compared to how warm my body feels standing next to him. We stand in silence for a few moments, looking out over the glassy lake.

"How's the dating going?"

His question surprises me a little. We haven't spoken about it since I told him I created a profile and he offered to be my date to my alumni event.

"Oh, well, I haven't actually gone on any dates—er, any more dates since ours." I smile. "I will though. Just need to take the time and sort through my options."

"Sort through them, eh? How many guys have hit you up?"

I blush. "I didn't mean it like that."

"Don't be modest, Savannah. We both know you could have any man you want." He stares at me and my breath catches in my throat.

"I don't know about that. I have been dumped recently and not for the first time." I laugh nervously.

"Yeah, but would you say those are the kind of men you want or men you settled for?" He leans against the railing, his full attention on me, and I'm not sure where this conversation is going.

"Uh, I don't know. I think they were okay. I don't know if I'd say I was settling."

"Ah, yes, what every man dreams of hearing—*you're okay.*" He laughs and it makes me laugh too.

"What do men want to hear?"

He looks down into his glass as he responds. "Probably the same thing that anyone wants to hear. That you want him, that you can't stop fantasizing about him. That no matter what you're doing you constantly find yourself thinking about him. That you feel safe with him, protected like he'd never allow a single thing to hurt you. That even the most mundane things seem exciting and fun if he's with you." He looks up at me. "Is that how you felt about them?"

I slowly shake my head no, my mouth feeling far too dry to form words. I take a few sips of my drink.

"Have you ever felt that way about a man?"

I smile nervously as I open my mouth to reply, but then shut it again.

"I'll answer your question if you answer mine." He looks at me questioningly. "What were you going to say in your office before Eric interrupted us? What was the end of that sentence?"

His eyes drop from mine. "You know what the end of that sentence was." He finishes his champagne and reaches for the bottle to refill our glasses.

"I do?" I want him to say the words.

"Savannah," his voice drops an octave as he steps closer to me, "we both know what I was going to say and it's a good thing we were interrupted because it wasn't appropriate for me to say it."

That is not what I wanted to hear. My eyes shift away from his and I feel embarrassed. I thought this was moving in a different direction. He reaches out and pulls my chin so that my eyes are back on him.

"I still thought it and wanted to say it, but there's some lines we can't cross."

I nod my head and I stupidly feel a tear prick at my eyes. I can't tell if he notices it too, but he changes the subject.

"Go pick out the song you want to dance to." He motions with his head toward the stereo in the parlor area off his bedroom. I step inside and drag my finger over the small record collection next to the table.

This is our tradition. Every year we share one dance up here instead of down on the dance floor where everyone else is. He's asked me why I don't dance with him downstairs and I always brush it off, but the truth is, it's because of Eric. I don't need to add fuel to that fire if I can help it.

I don't know why I bother looking. I pull the same jazz record I always do, Miles Davis. I place the record on and step back out onto the deck.

"Same one three years running," he says as he reaches for my hand and gently pulls me toward him.

"What can I say? I'm a sucker for the classics."

We sway back and forth, the music carrying us away as it softly drifts off into the night. Warren's hand gently rests against the back of my neck for a few moments before he drags it slowly down my back, pressing it firmly against me.

"You know I'll dance with you downstairs, right?" I look up at him, and he tilts his head down. "In front of people."

"I know, you've told me and you did dance with me in public a few weeks back."

"Is it more than just not being surrounded by people?"

My eyes shift. "Just prefer the privacy, I guess."

He can see there's something more to it and I guess he's done letting it go. He stops dancing, his arms still wrapped around me though.

"What is it then?"

"Just don't want rumors and stuff said." I let out an exasperated sigh and step out of his arms.

"What are you referring to, Savannah? Did something happen I don't know about?"

I wish he'd just let it go. "Nothing," I say and rest my hands on the balcony.

"Savannah, look at me." His voice is deep and commanding.

"It's Eric, okay? I just don't want him having more ammo is all."

"Eric? What are you talking about?" His brows knit together and it's clear he truly has no idea how disrespectful Eric is toward me.

"He just has this weird thing that he won't let go and has continued to harass me about for years."

He steps forward, his head dipping down like he isn't sure if he heard me correctly. "Harassing you? Eric? Savannah, what the hell is going on?"

I'm frustrated now because there's no getting out of this, so I just blurt the words out.

"He thinks you're fucking me."

Warren shakes his head a little. "He said that? He said I'm fucking you?"

I nod. "In a variety of sometimes creative ways. He's made comments to me over the years about how I got the job, about us having long closed-door meetings that end with me on my knees." I shake my head and cover my face in embarrassment.

"Hey, hey, this isn't on you. I—I had no idea, Savannah. That motherfucker." He goes to step past me, but I stop him.

"Please don't go make a scene. He's going to know I told you and make my life hell." I'm practically begging him and he stops.

He pulls out his phone and scrolls through his contacts. "I'm going to step inside and make a call really quick. Don't you dare go back down there." I nod and he steps around the corner and out of sight.

I close my eyes and try to relax when I hear footsteps coming up the staircase to my right. I turn my head just as Eric's head comes into view.

"Well, well, well. How'd I know I'd find you up here, hot on Warren's ass. Where is he?" he asks, glancing from right to left.

"He had to step away and take a call." I turn back toward the water, in no mood to entertain this douchebag's advances.

"Thought for sure I'd find you trying to claw your way into his bed." He laughs and comes to a stop right next to me.

"What do you want, Eric? I'll tell him to come find you as soon as he's off the phone. Better yet," I say as I go to step around him, but he reaches out and grabs my arm. I stop and try to jerk it away, but he tightens his grip.

"Why are you his favorite little thing? Hmm? What the fuck did you do?"

I pull my arm away. "Nothing, you asshole. That's what makes you so mad, isn't it? You know I've earned my place in this company and I took a position you thought you'd get without even trying." I know I shouldn't, but I'm sick of letting this bastard walk all over me so I goad him. "What is it that bothers you more, Eric? That I'm half your age or that I'm a woman?"

His face goes from pale to tomato red in a second and I see his jaw clench tightly.

"You're a little cunt, you know that?" His eyes drop down to my breasts and then my belly. "You just eating more or can we expect a little announcement soon?" he says as he places his hand against my lower belly.

I recoil instantly and smack it away just as Warren steps around the corner.

"What the hell are you doing, Eric?" Warren's expression doesn't give anything away, but I can tell it's not his usual demeanor.

"Hey, boss." He flashes him a fake smile. "I was just coming to tell Savannah that the last ferry already left but your pilot Norm is landing the chopper now."

I go to step around Eric to walk downstairs when Warren's hand shoots out and grabs my arm. He pulls me back till I'm standing right next to him.

"She's staying on board tonight," he says firmly to Eric.

Eric's eyes dart from Warren to me, then back to Warren, defeat settling over his face. "All right then, have a good night." He turns to walk down the stairs.

"I'm not done speaking to you," Warren says firmly, and Eric stops in his tracks.

His arm releases mine and shifts to my waist. He holds me firmly, turning his face till it's a few inches from mine.

"You okay?" he asks softly and I just nod my head. He doesn't let go of me. Instead, he drags his hand slowly up my body from my waist to my neck, his touch burning a path up my body as his thumb grazes my breast.

His eyes are on mine, but then they fall to my lips and he leans in, pressing his mouth to mine so softly for just a brief second before gently pulling back. I think he's done but he leans in again, and this time his tongue delves into my mouth and he sucks gently on my bottom lip before releasing me.

"Go inside. I'll be in in a minute."

7

WARREN

I wait till Savannah is inside and motion for her to close the soundproof sliding glass door and she does.

"Look, Warren, I was just teasing her. She's being overly sensitive; it was all in good fun."

I stand there staring at the pathetic man before me as he nervously tries to excuse his vile behavior. One trick I've learned in business over the years, let the guilty party tell on themselves. If you have knowledge, it's power. It'll make a bully like Eric fall to pieces in a few minutes if you just let them dig their own grave.

"It's none of my business who's with who." He laughs and raises his hands. "I get it, man. She's young pussy. I'd do the same thing if I were you."

I ball my hands into fists. "Shut the fuck up," I say slowly, but he keeps speaking.

"But seriously," he lowers his voice, "what's she like? Hot thing like tha—"

I grab his tie and wrap it around my hand twice, pulling him toward me. He stumbles and tries to catch himself on the stair in front of him, but I lift the tie higher so he can't. His face is turning red as shock resonates through his eyes.

"Don't you ever fucking speak about her like that again. Don't even say her name, you pathetic old man." I release his tie and he gasps, coughing as he stands up.

"What the fuck!" he shouts as he loosens his tie, his fat face glowing.

"Clean out your desk when you get back to the office. You're fired," I say dismissively as I turn my back to go inside.

"Seriously? After everything I've done for you, you're going to throw away our friendship over a dumb bitch?"

My spine stiffens and I remind myself not to do something stupid, something I can't undo. I turn back around to face him.

"What have you done for me, Eric? Hmm? I raised the capital from investors to start this company. I was the one who built it from the ground up. In fact, I lost two of my original biggest investors *because* of you. When they found out I was bringing you on board as CFO, they ran for the hills and that should have been a sign for me but I gave you the benefit of the doubt."

"I've always been there to help you out when you needed advice and even when you didn't want to hear it. Like now, you need to stop thinking with your cock and get your head out of your ass about this woman."

I can't help but laugh at his pathetic attempt to try and convince me he's the good guy here. "It's always been about you, Eric. You always brag that you were my mentor, about what *you* did for me. You never congratulate me; you never tell anyone about my accomplishments unless your name is attached to them. You're not loyal and I won't have that in my organization or in my life."

I look up and see my security, Kevin, approaching but Eric doesn't. He lunges toward me just as Kevin reaches him, grabbing him from behind. Eric spits at my feet.

"Fuck you then!" he shouts as sweat drips down his brow.

I smile at him and then close the distance between us till we're nose to nose.

"You should be grateful you're an old man because otherwise, I'd have personally thrown you off this yacht and made you swim back to shore. If you ever talk to Savannah again or attempt to go behind my back, I will fucking destroy you."

I turn and walk back toward where Savannah is. "Make sure he gets on the helicopter, Kevin."

"Is everything okay?" Savannah walks toward me as I step inside and close the door behind me.

I nod. "Yes, I took care of things."

She pulls back and looks at me. "What does that mean?"

"It means I handled it and he won't be a problem again." I place my hands on her upper arms. "Look at me," I say and she tilts her eyes up toward mine. "I'm sorry I didn't know this was going on. I feel like I should have known. How long?"

Her eyes shift. "Since I first interviewed."

I close my eyes and pull her in to wrap my arms around her, resting my head on top of hers. "I'm so sorry. I feel like I failed to protect you."

She pushes back from me and shakes her head a little. "It's not your fault. I didn't tell you and he obviously didn't do it in front of you. But also, Warren—you don't need to protect me; it's not your job."

I stare at her for a moment, trying to read between the lines, trying to understand what she's not saying.

"What are you saying?"

"Just that. That I'm not yours to protect."

"Whose are you then? Who protects you?"

She laughs and shakes her head. "Nobody's. I'm not anyone's. I can take care of myself. I appreciate you standing up for me, I do. I just, I don't want you feeling like you have to."

I nod. "Well, at my company, you are mine to protect and so are the rest of my employees. I'm not singling you out, Savannah. I know you can take care of yourself." I step toward her again and brush her hair behind her ear. "I'd be lying, though, if I said I didn't think we had a special connection."

She stares at me and nods. "Yeah, we do."

The moment grows tense. Neither of have spoken about the kiss and I'm afraid to bring it up.

"Besides, who's going to protect our unborn baby?" I smile as I place my hand against her belly.

"Oh my God." She laughs and shakes her head. "Do I seriously look pregnant?"

"Not a chance." I place my hands on her waist and step back a little as we both look down at them. "If I squeeze you," I say as I tighten my hands on her, "I could almost touch my fingertips together; there's practically nothing to you."

I release her. "Did you ever tell him that you and I weren't together?"

She shakes her head no. "I don't think so. I just ignored him or told him to mind his business."

"So he still thinks?"

"That we're fucking?" she says. Hearing that word on her tongue instantly has my mind spinning on all sorts of ways I'd love to fuck her.

"Uh, that but also that you're pregnant?"

"I guess, if he's an idiot, he does. I had a glass of champagne in my hand when he said it. I'm sure he was just trying to get under my skin." She rolls her eyes. "Guess he'll just have to be surprised in nine months when no baby appears."

I don't know why I say it, but I do. "We could fix that."

She either doesn't hear me or chooses to ignore it. She reaches down and pulls off her heels.

"I'm exhausted. I would really love to just change into something comfortable and go to bed."

"Absolutely. You can choose any room downstairs; they're all made up."

"I, uh, didn't expect to be staying on board tonight. I don't have any pajamas."

"Let me grab you some." I walk through the doorway into my bedroom closet and grab her a t-shirt and pair of pajama pants. "Here."

"Thank you"—she takes them from me—"for everything tonight and sorry it got so weird."

"That's nothing for you to apologize for. Eric is the one who caused this."

She smiles, her eyes looking heavy and tired. "Good night, Warren." She turns and heads down the stairs.

I take a quick shower and change into pajamas myself, opting to sit on the balcony of my bedroom and take in the stars for a bit. I still feel too wound up from earlier to fall asleep. As much as I hate Eric in this moment, it's still an unexpected loss that I know will take time to fully understand.

I lean back in my chair, closing my eyes and picturing Savannah in bed right now. I've talked myself out of walking down to where she's sleeping a dozen times already. She's been through enough tonight; the last thing she needs is for her boss to make things more uncomfortable by infringing on her personal space.

"Can't sleep either?"

Her voice startles me and I sit up, turning around to see her standing in the doorway. Her legs are bare, the t-shirt I gave her coming down to her mid-thigh.

"Where's your pants?" I thought I only thought the words but clearly I just said them.

"They kept bunching up under the sheets." She tugs on the bottom of the shirt a little, like I've made her uneasy pointing it out.

"I can't sleep." She walks toward me. "It makes me so uneasy being out in the middle of the lake while trying to sleep."

"Well, for what it's worth, we won't encounter any tsunamis or hurricanes on the lake."

She flops down in the chair next to me. "Do you ever sleep?"

"A little. You're more than welcome to sleep in my bed. I'll sleep in one of the other rooms."

"I don't like sleeping alone on your yacht." She looks over at me and I stare straight ahead.

"I'll sleep on the sofa, that way you're not alone."

"Thanks." She stands up and heads back into my room. "Good night."

"Good night."

I don't follow her. I know that if I see her get into my bed, I won't be able to stop myself from following her. And I sure as hell won't be able to keep my hands off her. I can still feel her lips against mine, the warmth of her tongue as she kissed me back earlier. I wanted her to bring it up, but she didn't.

I feel my own eyes finally grow heavy and I walk back inside to see Savannah curled up in my bed. Her long, dark hair is splayed across the pillow. She looks so small in my king-sized bed. I take a seat on the edge of the bed and look down at her. Her eyes flutter a bit before she opens them.

"Hey," she says softly, reaching her hand from beneath the sheets.

"Go back to sleep," I say softly. I watch as her eyes shut again before standing up to walk to the sofa.

"Stay." Her hand darts out and grabs mine before I take a step. I look down at her and she rolls on her side and tugs at me gently.

I look at the sofa, then back to where her warm body is beckoning me to join her. I pick up the covers and slide my body into bed behind hers. She lets out a soft moan of contentment as she settles into my chest, and I slide my arm over her body to pull her in tighter. I bury my nose in her hair and ignore the alarm bells going off in my head that says we're entering dangerous territory.

I tell myself as I drift off to sleep that just this once I'll allow myself to fall asleep with Savannah in my arms, imagining what life could be like if she were mine.

8

SAVANNAH

The next morning I wake up alone.

By the time the sun is streaming through the glass panels of Warren's onboard bedroom, he's already dressed and in a meeting... on land.

"He had a meeting?"

"Yes, a breakfast meeting at the office."

I eye Kevin suspiciously. "It's a Saturday." He just nods and doesn't give anything else away. "So he's not here as in he's not on board the yacht?"

"That's correct, ma'am. He asked me to give you these and said you can stay as long as you need. Norm is on standby to chopper you back to shore."

I take the bag from Kevin. "Thanks. Can you give me like fifteen minutes to get ready, and then I'll meet you on the helipad?"

"Yes, ma'am. I'll let Norm know."

I take the bag and pull out a pretty floral sundress and a pair of sandals. A note written in Warren's handwriting flutters onto the bed.

Savannah, apologies for the sudden and early departure. I had a meeting that I couldn't miss. I know you didn't have anything to wear besides the

63

gown from last night so I hope the dress I picked up is your size. Have a good weekend.

It's a little cold for Warren, especially after the night we shared last night. I have some questions for him and I'd hoped we could talk this morning and enjoy breakfast together but that's clearly not happening. I can't help but worry he made up a meeting just to skip out on me and avoid talking about the kiss and sleeping together.

I pull out my phone and send a text to Callie.

Me: *Hey, sorry to spring this on you but could I stop by this morning? I'm in serious need of some advice... and need to vent.*

I toss the phone on the bed and head to the bathroom to shower and change. I open the cabinet in the bathroom to find a comb. It's filled with Warren's things. I grab the small bottle of cologne and open it, inhaling the scent as my eyes close.

"That was creepy," I mutter to myself as I put the cologne back and shut the door. My hair is wet but at least I find a comb to untangle it. My phone chirps and I walk over to pick it up and see a response from Callie.

Callie: *Yes! Brendan went to golf at like 6 this morning and I've just been trying to find an excuse to miss spin class so you gave me one! Come over whenever.*

I grab my dress, clutch, and shoes from last night and put them in the bag that Kevin handed me earlier with the new clothes and head up to the helipad.

Once I'm back on shore I pick up some coffees and take an Uber to my neighborhood. Callie only lives a block and a half over from me so I make a quick stop at my place and put on a pair of clean panties.

"Holy shit," she says in disbelief for the third time in a row. "So what happened to that guy then? Eric?"

I shrug and sip my coffee. "Dunno. Warren said he handled it."

She eyes me. "Did he throw him overboard?"

I laugh. "No! But that's what I was hoping to talk to him about today before he mysteriously bailed for his 'meeting.' I also wanted to ask him about..." I hesitate.

"About what?" Callie scoots to the edge of her seat.

"About why he kissed me." I say the words slowly as I raise my eyebrows and she gasps, her hand shooting up to cover her mouth dramatically.

"Lead with that next time!" She slaps at me playfully. "Okay." She situates herself in her chair and leans toward me. "Tell me everything in detail."

I laugh. "Honestly, there's not a lot of detail to tell." I launch into the story, trying to make sure I include absolutely everything. "But the thing is, we've had some other little *moments* lately." I tell her about what he was going to say in his office before Eric interrupted us and how he came with me as my date to the event for my alma mater.

"Okay, wow. Seriously, I feel like you've been holding out on me so much lately. What the hell?"

I knew she would feel this way and I do feel a little guilty, but I also needed to navigate things myself for a bit. Besides, if I had told her this stuff when it was happening, I'm sure I would have spilled the fact that I know I'm falling in love with him or possibly already fallen. And I know if I reveal that little bit of detail to her, she'll tell me not to act on any of this… and she'd be right. But that's not what I want to hear right now.

"So what's the plan? What are you thinking? Have you gone on any dates yet?"

I shake my head. "No, and I haven't even looked at the app in a week. I just—I feel like there's this insane tension between us, all this unsaid stuff that maybe we should just get out."

"You mean you guys should fuck?"

I blush a little and smile. "Yeah, maybe. Hear me out. What if I just lay it all out to him. Say, 'listen, we've got some serious sexual tension and we're both single so why not just have this one night of passion and then we move on from it?'"

She nods slowly but she doesn't look convinced.

"And then I'll start dating like crazy. I'll go on dates with all these matches from the app and it'll not only take my mind off things with Warren, but I'll have had a sexy little one-night stand so maybe I'll feel more liberated and confident." I'm completely talking out of my ass and I can't be certain but I think Callie knows I am full of shit too.

"Is that what you really want?"

I chew my bottom lip. "I don't know what I want, Callie."

"Open the app. Let's just see what kind of potential is out there."

I reach in my bag and pull out my phone, opening the app to see a flood of notifications.

"Damn!" Callie says, grabbing it from me and looking through several profiles. "Pass, pass, oh, he's cute. Eww, this guy's opening line was thong or G-string? Hard pass."

We laugh as we flip through dozens of profiles and roll our eyes at some of the opening lines the guys send me.

"Oh, this guy has a good one. It says *Heading to Whole Foods, need anything?* That's kind of cute and original."

"What's his profile say?"

She clicks on it. "Oh. Oh damn, this guy is a winner." I lean over her shoulder to get a glimpse of him and she's not wrong. His smile is bright and wide, accompanied by two perfect dimples.

"Barrett Westmore. He's six three, went to Yale. His job is listed as an entrepreneur slash business owner. Oh, and he has a puppy." She flips the phone around to show me a picture of him cuddling an adorable little chocolate lab.

"Barrett Westmore? Sounds made up."

"This guy is seriously a fantasy or maybe a catfish but either way, it can't hurt to respond to him."

She's typing on the phone and I lunge to grab it from her. "Hey, what are you typing?"

She turns her body away and the phone is out of reach. She laughs, then tosses it to me.

"I could use some really meaty sausage?" I read her response to him and grab a pillow to throw at her. "What the fuck, Callie!"

She's laughing hysterically and my phone chirps. We both grow quiet and look over at where it's lying on the table.

"Oh God, he wrote back!"

"What'd he say?" She jumps up and comes to sit next to me.

"He said, *LOL, not what I was expecting but I'll make sure I add it to my shopping list. When are we cooking the MEATY sausages?* Meaty in all caps."

"See, he thought it was funny. You're in!"

I scroll back to his profile and look at the rest of his photos. The guy really does look like a catfish. These photos are not only high quality but the angles are all perfect… or maybe he just doesn't have a bad angle. Maybe this is a sign for me to put myself out there after all.

I type out a response to him: *When works for you?*

"Are you going to see him?"

"He's responding back to me now. I asked him when works for him." His response appears and I read it aloud to Callie. "He says, *Currently out of the country for work but I should be home in a week. Could we plan for a date then?*"

"What do you think? Seem legit?" I ask Callie and she shrugs.

"Yeah, why not? I'd keep in contact with him till he's back in town though; maybe it'll give you time to figure out if you guys have stuff in common."

I send him a response. *Yes, works for me. What kind of business are you in?*

I close the app and turn my attention back to Callie.

"You still want to bone Warren?" she asks.

"Yeah."

"What do you think he's like in bed?"

I've thought about that question a million times it feels like, and oddly, I can't come up with an answer.

"I'm not sure. He's obviously extremely powerful and confident, but he's also so calm and not like a controlling asshole that I think he would be super gentle and attentive but quiet."

"Quiet?"

"Yeah. Like I can't see him doing dirty talk or like yelling or anything." I laugh.

"What makes you think that?"

"He's so focused on propriety. Like when he almost made a comment or joke about fucking me and wouldn't finish the sentence, he said that it was inappropriate for him to say it. I mean, it is because he's my boss but our relationship is different; we're good friends."

"That's not why he didn't say it, Savannah."

"What do you mean?"

"He obviously wants you. If he saw you as *just* a friend or *just* an employee, he wouldn't feel weird about making that joke for as close as you two are. I mean sure he might feel like it was inappropriate still, but I don't think he'd make such a big deal out of it. Plus, with all the things you've told me that he's said or done lately, that man is fighting everything inside him to avoid acting on his desires."

I check the time. "Let's go to a spin class."

"Ah, man, I thought I got out of it because you were coming over."

"Come on," I say, smacking her leg. "Let me borrow some workout clothes. I've got way too much drama rolling around up here. I need to work it out before I do something crazy."

Callie begrudgingly gets off the couch and I follow her to her room to borrow some clothes, knowing full well that I'm going to spend the rest of the day trying to talk myself out of going to Warren's penthouse tonight.

After our workout I go home and spend the rest of the afternoon trying to not think about him. I clean my apartment, take another shower, and even go back to flipping through my matches on the dating app.

I click open the messages and see a response from Barrett.

I work in tech. What about you? Also, I noticed on your profile you mentioned you loved to ski. Did I mention my family has a place in Aspen?

We send a few messages back and forth. I ask him if he's close to his parents and he says that his mother died when he was four but that he and his father are best friends. It makes me happy because coming from no parents, I've always heard it's a good sign when a man respects his parents.

I sigh and lie back on the couch, staring at the ceiling in silence. It's just after seven p.m. and the sun has started to set. I don't know why I keep checking my phone like I'm expecting a text or call from Warren.

Finally, I give in. I walk to my room and pull the sundress back on that he bought me. It doesn't require a bra so I don't bother. I run a brush through my hair and slick on some mascara and tinted moisturizer. I slide a sheer pink gloss over my lips and grab my purse and phone and head out the front door.

I tell myself that I don't know where I'm going, just out for a walk to clear my head, but my footsteps seem to know exactly where I'm going. Fifteen minutes later, I'm walking on Warren's block.

My stomach is in knots but there's no talking myself out of what I'm about to do. I duck into his building and stop to talk to the night doorman, Martin.

"Hey, Martin." I smile, and he shoots his hands up in the air, then clutches at his chest dramatically.

"It's Savannah! Long time no see, gorgeous. You look extra cheery in that dress." He whistles at me and I laugh and do a little twirl.

"Is Warren in?"

"I believe so, haven't seen him leave tonight. You want me to call him?"

"No, he knows I was stopping by. I just didn't give him a time." I smile through the lie and Martin waves me to the elevator as he follows behind me to give me access to the penthouse.

My legs feel like they're jelly. I tap nervously as the car rides to the top of the building, a single ding signaling I've made it. The doors open smoothly into Warren's foyer and I quietly step inside.

"Warren?" I say his name but I don't hear a response. I walk farther into the house and say his name again "Warren?"

I step around the corner just as he descends down the stairs.

"Savannah? I wasn't expecting you." A surprised look quickly morphs into a smile when he sees the dress. "Looks good on you."

"Thanks." I look down. "Sorry to just stop by unannounced. I, uh —" I don't know what to say. That I was in the neighborhood? I wasn't. That I called and couldn't get through? I didn't. So I decide to tell the truth. "I wanted to see you."

I can see my response intrigues him.

"Yeah? About anything in particular?" He motions for me to have a seat on the couch next to him where he takes a seat. "Did you want something to drink?" He starts to sit, but then stands up again.

"No, no, I'm fine. You can stay seated."

He looks nervous. "Okay."

He sits back on the couch and I fiddle with my purse before placing it on the coffee table and removing my sandals.

I walk over to where he's sitting on the couch and stand in front of him, between his knees. My heart feels like it's about to beat out of my chest but there's no backing out now.

"I have a proposition for you."

He looks up at me. "A proposition?"

His eyes are glued to mine as I reach down and slowly lift the hem of my dress up just enough to hike my leg and place my knee on the couch on one side of him, repeating the process with the other.

His hands instinctively reach out and rest on my hips as I slowly lower myself down onto his lap. Neither of us speak as I reach out and place the palms of my hands flat against his chest.

His firm pecs tense beneath my touch. I can feel heat radiating off his lap against my own warm center. The cool metal of his belt buckle presses against my panties.

"What are you doing, Savannah?" His voice is deep and thick with desire but he doesn't move to stop me or remove me from his lap.

"What if we have one night together?"

I say the words slowly as I lean in closer to him, my lips almost touching his. I can feel him growing firm against me and I move my hips the tiniest bit. His fingers tighten on me, pressing into me as an almost inaudible moan falls from his lips.

"Just one night. Just this once."

9

WARREN

"Just this once?"

I repeat her words back to her when I know I should be saying absolutely not.

She nods her head slowly, her lips parting as she closes the distance and presses them to mine. My hand shoots into her hair and I grip it hard, pulling her head back so I can look her in her eyes.

"Don't fucking tease me, Savannah. I'm not the kind of man you want to play with like this."

She grinds down harder against me, her fingers curling to grip my shirt.

"You don't know what you're asking." I say it as a warning, but it doesn't faze her.

"Are you saying you don't want me?" A cocky little grin forms on her lips as she asks the question that she clearly knows the answer to. She thinks she has me.

"No, I think we both know the answer to that." I grip her hair tighter and her head jerks back a little. "What I'm saying is you might think you can handle just one night with me but I'm not sure you can."

"Try me."

I grip her hips and lift her off me, half tossing her to the side as I stand up and put some distance between us. I walk to the all-glass wall that overlooks the city and press my hands against it. I have the woman of my dreams literally begging me to fuck her and I'm scared.

"Why now?" I ask as I turn around to look at her. She's tucked her legs beneath her on the couch. Her hair is mussed from where I shoved my hands in it and her eyes are big as she stares at me.

"You kissed me," she says softly.

I walk over to where she's sitting and look down at her. I crook my finger beneath her chin and run my thumb across her bottom lip.

"I did, didn't I?" I'm mesmerized by her.

"Why?"

"I tried convincing myself it was because I wanted to piss off Eric after witnessing that exchange, but the truth is… I just couldn't resist any longer. I've thought of little else since I tasted these lips."

She starts to move. "Don't," I say as I continue to look down her small body. I let my hand fall from her chin down to the strap of her dress. I push it gently off her shoulder and watch as it falls. I trail my fingertips over her bare skin and a shudder runs through my body.

"The thoughts I'm having right now—" I don't finish the statement. I close my eyes and grit my teeth.

"Tell me."

When I open my eyes again, I can't hold back. I reach down and hook my hands beneath her arms and pull her to her feet. I walk her backward till she hits the floor-to-ceiling window behind us, pinning her against it with my body as I grab her wrists and push them above her head to hold in place.

"Something about you drives me absolutely wild. I want to consume you." I drag my tongue up her neck, pausing when I reach her ear. "I want to fuck you in ways that you've never imagined." I kiss her neck, then bite down on it, and a moan escapes her lips. "I don't want just a taste; I want all of you tonight."

I slide my hand up the front of her neck, anchoring her in place.

"Are you mine tonight, Savannah? To do with whatever I want?"

"Yes." Her answer is a partial moan as my tongue swirls around her earlobe, sucking it into my mouth for a brief second.

"Good girl." I move my head back so I can look at her. "I'm going to use you any way I see fit tonight. I won't stop if you're tired or sore. I want you sore. Come Monday, every time you move in your chair or every step you take, I want you to feel where my cock has been inside you."

I release her hands and move mine to cup her face, pulling her mouth to mine. I tease her, kissing her softly, her lips parting as I snake my tongue inside her mouth. I press my rigid cock against her and deepen the kiss. It's erotic and wet, her mouth taking everything mine demands and more.

She protests when I finally break the kiss, both of us breathless. I look in her eyes for any doubt but all I see is pure unadulterated lust.

"I'm trying to decide," I lean in kiss her again, then whisper the words against her mouth, "how I want to fuck you first."

Her hands are back against my chest, gripping my shirt for dear life.

"How do you like to be fucked, sweetheart?"

Her eyes shift away from mine before darting back. "I—it's always just missionary, sometimes from behind."

I grab her hand and turn to walk us toward my bedroom. "I guess we should try them all and see which one you like best."

We barely make it through the door before I'm pulling her dress over her head and tossing it to the ground, leaving her standing in front of me in nothing but a lace thong.

"Fuck me." My hands reach out to cup her full tits. "They're so much better than I imagined." I lean down and suck each nipple into my mouth.

"Ahhh," she moans, her hands fumbling for my belt buckle.

I push her back onto the bed, her tits bouncing with the movement. I crouch down and place her feet flat on the mattress as she props herself up on her elbows.

"You can watch, but don't fucking move."

I drag my hand down her naked body, stopping when I get to her panties. I hook my finger beneath the edge and slowly pull it to the side, bringing her wet pussy into my view.

"So pretty," I mutter as my mouth begins to water. I run my finger slowly up her wet slit, then back down, parting her folds.

"Look at you quivering beneath my touch. That's just one finger, baby. You sure you can handle me? My cock is big and it's gonna hurt."

I don't let her answer. I shove my finger all the way inside her and she groans loudly. I repeat the process two more times before leaning in and replacing my finger with my tongue. Her thighs fall open as I tear her panties from her body, sinking my tongue inside her as I lap at her.

"Oh, yesssss." The word is a hiss as she grips my hair, pressing my face harder into her pussy as she comes.

"I could spend all night eating your little cunt, but if tonight is all I get, I need to fuck you now."

I unbutton my shirt, pulling it down my arms and tossing it to the floor before practically ripping my belt buckle off my pants as I reach inside and fist my cock, finally releasing myself.

"Holy shit." Savannah's eyes grow round as she watches me stroke myself. "How?"

I chuckle. "Told you it's gonna hurt. How's your gag reflex?"

She keeps her eyes on me as she maneuvers onto her hands and knees and then crawls to the edge of the bed. She looks up at me as she opens her mouth and wraps her lips around the head of my cock.

"Now this is a fantasy." I choke the words out as she starts to move her head, dragging her mouth up and down my length. "I'm never going to get this image out of my head. Oh yes, baby, suck my cock." I grip her head and thrust forward, causing her to gag a little.

"Too much?" She shakes her head no and I do it again. "You're a greedy little thing, aren't you?" She focuses her eyes on my cock as she reaches forward and wraps her hand around it, her fingers not even close to touching. She twists her hand up my shaft as her lips come down to meet it.

"Ohhhh, damn, where'd you learn to suck like that?" I'm losing grip. My hands are in her hair and my hips start to move in time with her movements. "Look at me, Savannah." She obeys. "Are you mine tonight?"

She continues to move her head, but I step back, my cock falling from her lips as she looks up at me.

"Answer me. Are you going to behave and do whatever I tell you?"

"Yes."

"Do you want to please me, sweetie?" I lean down and kiss her lips softly.

"Yes," she says again sweetly.

"I'm going to fill every part of you with my cum, you understand me? I want you to swallow me, but first, I want to see myself dripping out of your sweet little pussy."

I crawl over her body, kissing every part of her I can on the way up to her lips. I stop at her tits, swirling my tongue around her pert nipples as I position my cock at her entrance.

There's no more talking once I kiss her lips again. It's just panting and moaning as I stretch her tight little hole with my cock. I thrust in, her back arching as she struggles to accommodate me.

"Just relax, baby. Let me inside," I say through gritted teeth as I try to hold back from slamming inside her. I pull back and slide in a little more again and again till finally her wetness allows me to glide in and out.

"Fuck, you're tight." I grip her waist as I bury my face in her neck. I've never had a problem coming early, but damn, this is a struggle.

"Warren, yes. Oh, that feels so good." Her whimpers are driving me crazy. The way she says my name so erotically I don't think I'll ever be able to hear another woman say it again.

I can feel her getting close so I roll to my back and bring her on top of me.

"Ride me." I lick my thumb and place it against her clit as her hips begin to move. She gets maybe two full movements in before she's collapsing on top of me, her entire body shaking.

I grab a pillow and place it next to us, rolling her onto her back again as I pull myself up on my knees. With the pillow situated beneath her hips, I grab her legs and place one over each shoulder.

Her eyes roll back in her head as I enter her again. "Look at me," I shout and her eyes pop open. "I want to watch you come again," I say as I thrust into her harder.

Her breasts sway with each movement. I feel my balls tighten as my release builds. I grip her legs tighter, and just as I start to feel her walls tighten around me, I splay her thighs open and press down on her lower belly as I thrust even harder.

She screams in ecstasy as she explodes, her orgasm visible as she squirts all over my belly causing my own orgasm to release. I blink rapidly, the room spinning as I pump every last drop of my release into her. Her legs shake as I still grip her thighs in my hands.

"Did I just?" She looks down our bodies that are wet with the evidence of her ejaculation.

"Yes." I look down at where we're still connected and slowly pull my cock out of her. She whimpers and I see myself slowly begin to leak out of her, my cock jumping with excitement already.

I pull her up onto her knees, then press her back so her chest is down on the bed, her ass up in the air as I slide my cock back inside her.

"Already?"

"Don't resist," I say as I press into her further.

"Oh God," she moans as I don't give her time to adjust to me. I grip her hips, slamming into her over and over again till I'm shooting another load into her, leaving her a shaking, quivering mess beneath me.

I roll off her and onto my back, trying to catch my breath as she does the same.

"You okay?" I brush her hair away from her face, worried I may have pushed her too hard too soon, but the satisfied look on her face tells me she's fine.

"Mm-hmm." She smiles lazily at me, then pushes herself up on her hands and crawls on top of me. "Kiss me."

She doesn't have to ask twice. Kissing Savannah alone gets my dick's attention. She must feel it because she breaks the kiss with a laugh.

"Seriously? You're hard again?"

"You have that effect on me, what can I say."

She rolls her eyes. "Let me guess, you say that line to all women."

I reach down and pinch her ass and she yelps.

"Ow, what the hell was that for?"

"Don't compare yourself to other women. There is no comparison." She stares at me for a moment and I'm tempted to say more, but I also don't want to confuse us on what tonight she is. She was clear with her proposition—one night, no strings attached.

"So was it as good as you imagined?" She grabs my hands and pins them over my head with that cocky little smirk.

"Oh, you think I've imagined this? That I've fantasized about fucking you seven ways from Sunday while you stand next to my desk and read over my shoulder? Like I haven't imagined stuffing my cock into every part of you while I beat off in the shower?" Her eyes get a little wider. "Oh, sweetheart, that's just the PG version."

I slide my hands free from her grip and flip her to her back, pinning hers above her head. "You blushed when I mentioned that every man on my yacht had imagined what was under your dress, but I can guarantee you none of them even came close to the filthy thoughts I have about you every day."

She swallows. "Like what?"

"You really want to know?" She nods her head slowly. "You really want to know that when you're sitting in a chair across from me in a room full of people all I can think about is your red lips wrapped around my cock while I release a full load down your throat?"

"Speaking of, I think it's time you finished sucking my cock." I stand up and walk to the chair that's in the corner of my room, sitting back and holding myself in my hand as I crook my finger and call her to me.

"After you finish me off, we'll take a shower because when we are done with that, I want you to sit on my face so I can enjoy your taste again."

She drops to her knees and wraps her lips around me again as my head falls back against the back of the chair.

"You're not getting any sleep tonight, baby."

10

SAVANNAH

I don't want tonight to end.

Warren's hands drag the soapy loofah over my body as the water cascades around us. I close my eyes and savor the remaining moments I have with him. Knowing that every time I glance at the clock, I'm praying time stands still.

"What's going through that pretty of head of yours?" His voice interrupts my thoughts as he snakes his arm around my waist.

"Hmm?" I smile and lean against him. "Oh, nothing. Just enjoying this amazing shower. I've never been in one this nice before," I partially lie. It's true, the shower is impressive with all the different water spouts and steam options, but I don't want to tell him that I'm dreading the morning.

"Does it make it more impressive that you're the only woman that's ever been in it?"

My eyes pop open and I turn around to face him. "Really?"

"Really."

"Why's that?"

He shrugs and reaches around me to put the loofah on a hook. "I'm not big on sharing my personal space. I think you know that. I value my privacy."

He places both arms around me now and maneuvers us so we're not directly under the water. He kisses me softly mid-conversation as my arms drape loosely over his shoulders. It feels so natural, like we're two lovers on a casual weekend morning just going through our routine. It feels good, normal, but at the same time terrifying because this isn't reality.

"So why'd I get a free pass?"

"Well, that answer is twofold. You just showed up at my home without an invitation"—he smiles—"and I selfishly want to spend the next hour with my face buried in your pussy." His hands start to wander.

I smile and close my eyes, turning my face to rest against his shoulder so he doesn't see the disappointment on my face. Instead, I allow myself to get lost in what his fingers are doing to me rather than the sadness of knowing that I'm not someone special, but merely a convenience that forced her way into his home this evening, and I have nobody to blame but myself.

* * *

"Shit." I grab my tumbler of coffee as it sloshes over the edge onto my kitchen counter. I take in a few deep breaths, trying to calm my over-active nerves.

All morning I've been on edge. I took way too long to pick out an outfit; my hair didn't want to cooperate, and I'm positive I'm getting a stress pimple on my chin.

I thought one flaming-hot night with Warren would give me clarity. Allow me to get all this nervous energy out with a few rounds of hot sex, but instead it's done the exact opposite.

After leaving his penthouse on Sunday morning, after another few rounds, I've been nothing but a wound tight ball of nerves.

Leaving was a bit awkward. We both weren't sure what to say about seeing each other on Monday morning but here we are—Monday morning and I'm still a mess.

All I can focus on is how the hell I'm supposed to act like I didn't just have the hottest, most satisfying sex of my life last night with my boss that I spend close to ten hours a day with. I roll my eyes at myself and grab my coffee to head into the office.

"Time to get it over with."

I'm feeling pretty good as I approach the building when suddenly I realize that I not only have to face Warren after he saw me naked in every imaginable angle, but I also have to deal with the aftermath of whatever went down between him and Eric after the yacht party.

I step into the elevator and pretend to be buried in my phone so I don't have to make small talk with anyone. I glance up briefly when the doors open, praying Eric isn't getting on, but instead it's Warren.

I do a double take as his eyes meet mine and that devilish grin slides into place. I smile back, then look back to my phone as my face starts to burn. It suddenly feels like there's a hundred people in the elevator car and they all know exactly what we did this weekend.

As the car stops on different floors and people exit, it's just him and me left as it makes its way to my floor.

"You have a nice weekend?" he asks with a smirk on his face.

I shrug. "Yeah, ya know, same old, same old."

His head jerks to look at me and I burst out laughing. He turns his body toward mine, stepping closer to me. He raises his hands and places them on the walls so I'm backed into the corner, looking up at him. My laughter dissipates when I see the burning look in his eyes.

"No man has ever fucked you like I have, sweetheart." He dips his head lower and I think he's about to kiss me when the doors ding and start to slide open. He drops his hands and steps back, the lust disappearing from his eyes instantly.

"Your floor, Miss Monroe?" He gestures toward the door as I struggle to put one shaky foot in front of the other.

I step out of the elevator, then remember Eric. "Oh, what can I expect today with the Eric thing?" I look to my right and left and lower my voice so nobody can hear what I'm saying.

He furrows his brows for a moment, giving me a look like *how do you not know?*

"I fired him, Savannah."

My mouth falls open just as the doors start to close and I shoot my hand out to keep them open. "You fired him?"

"Come to my office," he says, pulling me back into the elevator.

I wait till we're in his office and he closes the door behind us.

"I'm so confused. I thought—well, I don't know what I thought, but fired? Warren, he was a financial genius; you said it yourself, and we have the acquisition announcement today."

He shrugs like none of that even matters. "I told you I handled it. I wasn't about to keep you working in a hostile environment like that. He's an adult; he made his bed."

I slowly sink down in the chair across from him as he casually leans against his desk.

"I just feel so bad; he was your mentor and your best friend."

"Exactly and yet he chose to do the things he did to you of all people." He shakes his head when he says it and I want to ask what he means. "Savannah." He pushes off the desk and comes to stand next to me. "If I had to choose between losing him or you, it's him every time."

I nod slowly. I want to ask him if he'd fire him for anyone else or if it was specifically because he was harassing me, but I don't.

He reaches his hand down to where the strap of my purse is pulling my blouse away from my neck and runs his finger over my bare skin. It startles me.

"Is that a bruise?" He slides my purse strap from my arm and grabs my elbow to pull me upright. I'm standing in front of him as he moves my blouse further away from my neck.

"I dunno, maybe." I try to see the spot he's referring to. "I think you bi—" I stop myself, not sure if I should even make reference to the things we did this weekend, but he finishes the sentence for me.

"I bit you. I'm sorry, I lost control." He studies the mark intently as he traces it with his fingers before slowly leaning in and planting a featherlight kiss against it.

My eyes flutter closed and I inhale a sharp breath as I clutch my coffee tumbler for dear life.

"Does it hurt to sit down?" His voice is low in my ear, his warm breath against my cheek as I clench my thighs together.

"Yes."

He guides his hand up from my neck to my chin, and he holds my face in place as he stares at my mouth. I close my eyes. I can feel myself leaning in the smallest amount, but he never closes the distance. Suddenly he steps back. I rock forward an inch and right myself as he steps around his desk and takes a seat.

"So with Eric gone, it will put us under a little more stress, but Diego knows the ins and outs of the acquisition and I've been eyeing him as Eric's replacement for the last year anyway. Eric recommended him as well when he first mentioned possible retirement in the next few years."

And just like that, Warren's stoic facade is back in place and the moment has dissipated like a cloud of smoke.

"Okay, yeah, Diego is great. I usually always work with him anyway. I'll reach out to him this morning and make sure our ducks are in a row with legal and go from there." I turn on my heel, feeling a little weird about how to end the conversation. I start to head toward the door when he says my name.

"Savannah?"

"Huh?" I turn back around.

"You go on any dates yet?"

"Pardon?" I'm not sure if this is another joke about us this weekend, but his expression says otherwise.

"The app."

"Oh, uh, no. I was kind of preoccupied this weekend." I try to sound flirty, but Warren's blank expression says he's completely past whatever exchange happened between us just a few moments ago.

"Okay. I'll be in meetings till later." He looks back down at his desk, essentially dismissing me.

Confused and disheartened, I make my way back down to my office and let out the massive sigh I've been holding in. I'm not sure what I expected when I came in to work this morning, but the whiplash of him touching me, kissing my exposed neck, only to dismiss me so coldly wasn't it.

His comment about the app reminds me of Barrett and I pull my phone out to see if there are any messages from him.

Hey, thinking about you. Hope you have a nice weekend. Can't wait till we can actually meet. Soon! Have a great Monday and kick some ass.

I smile at the sweet message from the still-a-stranger. I don't have a clue who this man is other than what he's curated on his profile, but I feel a little flicker of hope that maybe I'll be able to actually enjoy hanging out with him and get over this crush I've developed on Warren.

I send a quick text to Callie to see if she wants to grab lunch today which she confirms she does. We try to make a habit of getting lunch together a few times a month since her graphic design firm is only a few blocks away. We agree to meet at one of our favorite salad places before I put my phone down and dig in to work.

* * *

"No, no, you didn't. I don't believe you." Callie shakes her head furiously as she shoves a forkful of spinach into her mouth.

"Whatever you say." I shrug.

"How are you so calm then? Like how did you spend a night with your boss having mind-blowing, porno-style sex and you just casually mention it to me over a fifteen-dollar salad?" She's leaning halfway across the table right now, her eyes about to bug out of her head.

"I needed time to let things sink in and"—I wince as I adjust myself in my seat—"I'm telling you now."

"Did you just wince? Did he leave you sore? You have to tell me everything. I can't eat." She pushes her salad away and leans back in her chair, crossing her arms over her chest.

I drop my fork. "I don't think a public place is the best for details, but yes, it was amazing and no, it won't happen again. But I just—" I can't help but hide my disappointment and she clearly sees it.

"Oh, sweetie," she says, reaching across the table to grab my hand.

"It's not that I'm in love with him or anything. I just… Barrett, that guy from the app, is the kind of guy I should be going for, ya know?

Someone my age, he's in my industry, and he's driven and outgoing and wants to have fun."

"Is that what you *want* or is it like you said what you feel like you should want?"

"Both, I guess? How'd you know that Brendan was the one?"

I've known both of them since college although they didn't really get serious about their relationship till after we graduated. They'd hooked up a few times and gone to some parties, but they'd both dated others along the way.

"I think I always knew he was the one. I know that sounds weird since we didn't get together until years after we met, but I think I knew it was like a right person, wrong time situation early on so I was confident we'd find our way back to each other."

"Ugh, I'm jealous. I wish I was as carefree and confident about love as you are."

She shakes her head. "I wasn't for a long time. I can say it like that now because we're happily married and through all that shit, but it was hard. There were a lot of doubts and fights and tears shed. I knew we were meant to be together, but the waiting on the timing thing was killer. He wasn't ready to settle down and get married, and as much as I wanted him to be ready, I wasn't either. We both had to grow up, and luckily we both were willing to wait for each other."

I smile genuinely at her because I truly am so happy that she found her forever and that he's an amazing guy.

"Speaking of, has Tessa been freaking out lately? I know she was stressed that Patrick wasn't doing enough for the wedding and only focused on his bachelor party, but I feel like all women feel that way at some point in the wedding planning process."

"She's better now. She's so ecstatic for the bachelorette weekend in Vegas. Hey, maybe that's what you need. Maybe this trip will help get you out of your own head."

"Yes!" I say, lifting my hands up dramatically. "With everything going on with work, I had actually forgotten about that trip."

"Any word back from Barrett?"

I nod and swallow down a bite. "Yeah, he's still out of town but he sent me a sweet message over the weekend. I think," I say, having a moment of clarity, "I'm going to go on a date or two this week. There are a couple guys that reached out that seem promising."

"Oh, yay! I can't wait to hear how they go. And you know, if you ever want me to be in disguise in the back of the restaurant, I got you." She points her fingers at her eyes, then mine and we both laugh.

* * *

I STARE at myself in the mirror, turning to double-check that my skirt is a reasonable length and isn't tucked into my underwear. I've never actually had that happen, but for some reason it's an irrational fear of mine.

I smooth the edges of my white crop top and hike my skirt up just a tad higher so only a few inches of my stomach are showing. It's a cute outfit, one that makes me feel confident and flirty, the energy I need to be putting out into the dating world.

"Okay, you've got this. You've dated before. Don't talk about work the entire time and don't talk about your exes." I point to myself in the mirror and plaster on a huge grin. "I look insane."

I grab my purse and lock my door as I make my way down to the Uber that's waiting to take me on my first official date since being dumped by Easton. His face flashes through my mind from the last time I saw him at the alumni event. He'd sent me a sweet text a few days later saying it was nice to see me, but I didn't bother responding. That night wasn't as awkward as I thought it would be between us actually. Any nervousness I felt was channeled into Warren and the way his eyes lingered on me, the way his fingertips touched me so delicately yet so seductively.

I shake the thoughts of Warren from my head and get into my Uber. The last thing I need is to be thinking about him when I'm trying to forget about all the delicious ways he satisfied me this weekend.

"Peter?" I ask as I approach the nervous-looking man who's eyeing everyone in the bar like his head is on a swivel.

"Wow, Savannah? Wow," he says again as he looks me up and down.

"Hi, yes, it's me." I give a silly little curtsy and hold out my hand to him.

"Nice to meet you. I'm sorry, but holy shit, you're really fine."

I blush and we take a seat at the bar.

"Thanks, and thanks for the date. I hope you weren't waiting long." I order a drink from the bartender, and he orders his second or possibly third; I can't tell from the empty glasses near him.

"Nah, I just downed a few drinks to calm my nerves and set the mood." He gives me a wink and I laugh nervously. I haven't been on a date in a long time and maybe he hasn't either.

We make small talk about our jobs, but he quickly changes the subject back to how I look and while I don't mind the compliments, he's laying it on a little thick.

"So what made you pick this bar? It's really nice, I like it. You come here often?"

I look around the place and it's definitely swankier than most bars I'd expect someone to recommend for a first date. It's near Warren's place actually, and it's the kind of bar you'd expect to see old white-haired guys sipping brandy and having cigars.

"I've always seen it and wanted to check it out. Plus, it looks hella fancy, so ya know, brownie points." He wriggles his eyebrows at me. "Plus, I'm trying to break into the tech world so I know this is a good place to possibly meet investors. When I saw you mentioned that you worked in tech on your profile, I was like niiiiiice."

I'm not sure if I should laugh or be offended that he's just admitted to possibly using me for connections and certainly using our date as a secondary pickup spot for investors.

"Yeah, feels like everyone works in tech these days." I finish my drink and wave down the bartender for some water.

"Do you think you could introduce me to anyone here?" he asks, and at first I think he's joking, but his expression is serious.

"Oh, oh, you're serious. Um, well, I don't think I know anyone here," I say as I casually start to look around the dimly lit bar. "I don't think it would be appropriate though, even if I did, to just approach someone and introduce you because I don't really know you. I'm so—"

"Holy shit, is that Warren Baxley?" Peter's eyebrows shoot upward as he stares past me.

I almost fly off the barstool as I turn around to see where he's pointing.

"I don't see who you're talking abou—" My words catch in my throat as I turn to the final corner of the bar and do a double take at the dark figure sitting at a table with another man.

The last person I figured I'd ever run into at a bar when I'm on a date, let alone on a weeknight, is Warren Baxley, but there he is, staring right back at me.

11

WARREN

I was wondering how long it would take for her to notice me.

I can see shock resonate on her face that quickly morphs into disbelief, probably mostly over the fact that I'm sitting in a bar.

She spins back around in her seat, but her date continues to look at me as he speaks to her. I see her shake her head before grabbing her purse and sliding off her seat to head to the back of the bar.

"I'll be right back, Art." My lawyer waves at me dismissively, preoccupied by the evidence on his iPad we've been discussing.

I take extra-long strides across the bar, catching up to Savannah just as she's pushing into the women's restroom.

"Hey, what the hell?" She looks over her shoulder at me as I grab her arm and lead her to a small alcove next to the emergency exit. "What are you doing here?"

"I feel like I should be asking you that. You're in my neighborhood."

"Your neighborhood? We don't live that far apart, Warren. Besides, since when do you go to bars?" She smiles, but I don't return the sentiment.

"So you didn't purposely bring him to my neighborhood at the bar that my lawyer frequents?" I look down her body at the delectable little outfit she's wearing. "Dressed like that?"

"What's with the weird attitude? I didn't pick the place, my date did." She rubs her arm where I grabbed her.

"Did I hurt you?" I reach out to touch her, but she jerks her arm away. Her reaction angers me. "Your *date*, huh?" I don't mean to spit the word out, but I hate the way it feels in my mouth.

She gives me an annoyed look. "Yes, my date. Is there a problem with that, Warren?"

I can't help but laugh, but it's not a genuine, ha-ha, this is funny kind of laugh... it's a *are you fucking kidding me? You're already on a date after we fucked like animals less than forty-eight hours ago* kind of laugh.

"What's going on? Things were perfectly fine at work today and now you stalk me to the bathroom and give me the third degree for being on a date. Might I remind you..." She cocks her hip and places her fist firmly on it. "That you were the one who asked me today if I'd gone on any dates from the app." She points her finger at my chest, and it pisses me off.

How the fuck can she seem so perfectly unfazed after how we spent Saturday night?

"Might I remind you," I say as I lower my voice and step forward, "who's cock was buried deep inside you all Saturday night?" She recoils a little further into the alcove as I tower over her, anger flashing through her eyes.

"Are you—fuck this," she says as she goes to step around me, but I don't let her pass. "Seriously, Warren? What?" she says in exasperation, flailing her arms. "What is it that you need to say? Because you've been hot and cold all day and now—"

I grab her firmly by the back of the neck and smash my lips against hers. My lips cover hers as I move them against her, sweeping my tongue inside her mouth. She pushes against my chest, her breath coming out in jagged puffs as she stares at me before grabbing my tie and pulling me back to her.

I don't know what I'm doing, but I know it's wrong. I didn't even know what I was going to say to her when I followed her back here.

She paws at me, like she can't get close enough, like we can't get enough of each other. My cock throbs as her tongue swirls around mine. I drag my hand up her bare thigh, rubbing my thumb against her panties before sliding them to the side.

"You're soaked already." I want to lift her skirt to see her glistening, but I can't wait.

She moans, her fingernails digging into my skin through my shirt as I plunge two thick fingers deep inside her.

"Ohhh." Her head falls forward, resting against my chest as I tease her. I slide my fingers in and out of her, circling her clit with my thumb. My other hand rests against the back of her neck as I hook my fingers and reach her G-spot.

Little moans and pants fall from her lips as I feel her legs begin to shake.

"You have no idea how fucking wild it drives me to hear you moan like this. To watch you completely come undone with just two of my fingers. Come for me, sweetheart. I need to taste your release."

She obeys, falling forward so that I'm holding her up against me as she rides out the waves of pleasure that roll through her body. Her eyes are glassy, her lips puffy. I pull my fingers from her warm center and bring them to my lips, savoring every last drop as I lick my fingers clean.

My cock is rigid, digging into her hip so hard it's painful. I reach down to adjust myself and her eyes follow as her tongue darts out to lick her lips.

"Come home with me," I offer without thinking and her eyes go from cloudy with lust to focusing back on where we are and what just happened.

"I—I can't. I'm on a date." She situates her skirt, pulling it down as she works to put space between us. "I thought we said just one time."

"We did. I guess I didn't realize the rules were so rigid. You really think that kid out there knows how to make you come like that?"

Her eyes flash to mine. "I didn't say I was going home with him either; it's just a first date." She steps around me and reaches for the door of the restroom.

"Right, go sew those wild oats. Hopefully I gave you enough to fantasize about when he's trying to find your G-spot later." I smack her ass and instantly regret it. Not because her hand in return lands square across my jaw, but because it was a shitty thing to say and completely out of character for me.

"I deserved that," I say as I rub my jaw.

"What the fuck, Warren? We sleep together and you suddenly turn into an asshole? I thought I got rid of that when you fired Eric." Her eyes are filled with tears.

"I'm sorry, Savannah, really. That was disgusting and out of line. I'm sorry."

I turn and head back down the hallway to pay my tab and head home. I tell Art that we'll finish our discussion later this week, then I walk the few blocks back to my place. I feel like shit, lower than shit. I've never once behaved that way, let alone with Savannah.

I sink down in my chair in my home office, music blaring through the speakers to drown out my thoughts, but it doesn't help. For three years I've pined for her. I always told myself that it was nothing more than lust, but now that I've had her, it's more than that. I've never connected sexually with a woman like I have with her. I've never spent days thinking of nothing but spending time with someone like I have with her.

No, this isn't just lust. This isn't just an unmanageable desire to satisfy her in every way possible.

This is passion and jealousy and need. A need to protect her, to make her happy.

I feel my chest tighten at the thought that all I might ever have with Savannah is that one single night.

12

SAVANNAH

To say the date was a complete fail is an understatement.

By the time I walked back to my seat, Pete was in deep with two older men, pitching them some idea and talking about the metaverse. After three failed attempts to get his attention, I paid my tab and left, sulking the entire way home.

I flop back on my couch, second-guessing on whether I should have taken Warren up on his offer of going home with him.

"What the fuuuuck?" I grab a pillow and bury my face in it and scream. Why the hell did I blow him off for some dude who clearly had zero interest in me. I lean over the edge of the couch and grab my purse where I tossed it on the floor. I check the time, debating on if it's too late to text Warren and tell him I messed up.

After some serious back and forth, I end up settling on not reaching out to him. Instead, I open up the dating app and see another message from Barrett.

So, I was thinking. Since I won't be back for a bit but still want to get to know you, let's send each other some fun questions. I'll go first. You get my answers after I see yours.

1. *Favorite movie (yeah, I know this is basically impossible).*

2. *Favorite food (last meal on death row favorite).*
3. *Last thing that made you cry (yikes).*

I smile at the message and sit up to type out my responses. I'm impressed by his question about crying, good to know this guy seems to have some emotional depth. I think through my answers.

1. *Okay, don't judge me because it's... Actually go ahead and judge, I'm not ashamed! You've Got Mail. I know, I know it's cheesy and cliché but come on, a modern-day love story based on the beginnings of the internet at the forefront of the Information Age? Classic.*
2. *Hands down, baked ziti. Has to have a ton of that almost burnt but still gooey mozzarella on top though.*
3. *Oh boy... I think it was this social media post about this dog that had been left for dead and someone ended up rescuing him. He made a full recovery and found his forever home but damn, his journey was heartbreaking.*

I put my phone into airplane mode, deciding that a nice night of some yoga and sushi is in order after the insanity of today. I scroll through a few streaming apps, settling on rewatching a Kevin Hart stand-up special that always make me laugh, but tonight I can't seem to focus.

I take my phone out of airplane mode, anxious that I may have missed a text or call from Warren, but there's nothing. The crazy thing about all this is, I was this way before we ever slept together. I've always had a *thing* for Warren. A crush, whatever you want to call it. The reality is, I've been hung up on him for the better part of three years and it hasn't gotten any better. Maybe it's time I finally let this go. I close my eyes and tell myself that this obsession with him ends now. Starting tomorrow, I'm going back to pretending like nothing ever happened between us. We're coworkers, friends, and nothing more. I won't read into his comments. I won't try to read through the subtext for hidden meanings and innuendos.

Tomorrow is like it's three years ago all over again.

* * *

"Good morning," I say, maybe a touch too chipper as I place Warren's coffee I pick up for him a few times a week on his desk.

"Morning to you too." He eyes me suspiciously, but I ignore it.

"Okay, Todd is coming in today from Code Red to finalize a few things. He and I are actually going to lunch to just catch up so I might be out of the office a little longer today." I scroll through my calendar, seeing if there's anything else I need to discuss with Warren.

"Oh, Diego said he has the final financials done for the acquisition and he's ready to present to the board so I told him we'd make that happen."

I glance up and Warren is just staring at me. I look back down at the screen and double down on my focus.

"Savannah." His voice is even, with a tone that says *I need to say something*, but I really don't want to hear it.

"And in case you forgot—"

"Savannah." This time his tone is clipped and I look up at him. "We need to talk."

I sigh and turn off the screen on the iPad. "Sure, what's up?"

"I appreciate you pretending like nothing happened here, but I owe you a formal and serious apology."

My shoulders drop. "No, you don't. You already apologized."

"Well, I want to do it again. I had no right to say what I said, and it really was out of character for me. I hope you know that. I respect you, even though my actions said the exact opposite this weekend."

"Thank you, I appreciate that. No hard feelings."

"Good." I can tell he has something else he wants to say so I sit patiently. "So will there be a second date?"

I laugh. "No, there won't. I think he was more interested in you and every other rich guy there than me."

"Well, I'm sure you have an endless line of prospects begging to take you out."

I shrug. "There's a few."

"Anyone in particular catch your eye?"

I debate on saying anything about Barrett but figure this might actually be the time to get some normalcy back between us. Before, I never thought twice about complaining about my dating life to him so why stop now?

"There might be a guy."

"Oh?"

"Yeah, he's pretty spot-on with what I'm looking for. Great career, went to Yale, good family relationship. Doesn't seem to be looking to use me for connections. Ticking all the boxes."

"Sounds like a dreamboat." He laughs.

"Yeah, we'll see. Going on our first date soon so I'll keep you posted."

He smiles and I stand up to head back to my office.

I'm almost to the door when I stop and turn back to face him. "Were you apologizing for the weekend or last night? Because last night wasn't the weekend; it was Monday."

He smiles a lazy grin before leaning back in his chair. "Last night. You're right; that wasn't the weekend."

"So, you're not sorry about this weekend?" We both know what I'm asking and while I promised myself I wouldn't pull at these threads anymore, I have to know if he's sorry about sleeping with me.

"No, Savannah," he says in that deep register that sends electricity straight to my groin. "I'll never apologize for what I did to you this weekend."

I barely make it to the elevator before I'm pulling at my blouse, trying to get some airflow to my body as images of what exactly he did to me this weekend flood my brain.

"Just three more days," I tell myself. "Three more days and you're off to Vegas."

* * *

IT's Thursday afternoon and much to my surprise I've been able to stick to my plan with Warren this week.

Even when I caught him trailing his eyes slowly up the back of my legs as I bent over to retrieve a file from my drawer.

Even when I stood pressed up against him in the cramped elevator yesterday.

Even right now, watching in agony as he slowly rolls his shirt-sleeves up his toned, tan forearms.

Why the fuck is that such a sexy move on a man?

"Vegas, huh? When was the last time you were there?"

I tap my pen against my chin, knowing full well it was for a work event with Warren right after I started here. I'd spent the entire trip trying to think of ways to spend more time with him, but he spent it either in his room on the phone doing business or in a conference room doing business. The only action I got was accidentally ending up in his lap in a tangle of embarrassment.

"I think back when I first started here?"

"Oh, right, I remember that trip. You accidentally sat on my lap when Eric stepped on your foot and you fell."

I laugh. "You remember that?"

His eyes light up. "Of course I remember that."

Something flashes between us, a moment of tension like we used to have before I screwed things up by sleeping with him. I swallow down a lump in my throat. I want to run into his arms and ask him if we're still friends. If we'll still share those little moments like on his yacht or at the annual Christmas party when he hides away in a random corner waiting for me to find him.

"You ladies have any fun plans?"

"The usual bachelorette stuff. Dancing, flirting, cocktails, maybe one of those Magic Mike type shows."

"Flirting?" He cocks an eyebrow.

"Yeah, just innocent stuff. Oh, and we have reservations at the pool. Really excited about that."

"Flirting? The pool? Sounds like you ladies have a fun time

planned. Don't forget your sunscreen. But most importantly, have fun. You deserve it."

"Thanks. If you don't need anything else, I'm heading home."

"I think we're good."

"Great." It's a little awkward between us so I make it worse by shooting finger guns before heading toward the door.

"Savannah?"

"Hmm?"

"I, uh, if it's not too much trouble could you just text me when you land? So I know you're safe?"

"Yeah, of course. See you next week."

I close the door behind me and the little butterflies are back. Relief washes over me as I realize that he still cares and I haven't completely ruined things between us.

* * *

"OH MY GOD, you're about to be a married woman." I fawn over Tessa as we get ready to head to the pool. Our flight got in a little bit ago and we came straight to our hotel to change and hit up the pool for our reservation.

"Please don't start getting emotional already, Savannah. You're only on your second cocktail and we have bottle service at the pool. Pace yourself."

I roll my eyes at Callie and grab my swimsuit from my bag, along with the cover-up. I step into the restroom and slide on the hot-pink triangle bikini. I tug nervously at the top that covers what it needs to cover but still leaves little to the imagination. I turn around and look at my ass in the mirror.

"Oh God." It's way more cheeky than anything I've ever worn before. I open the door and peek my head out. "Hey, guys. Uh, either of you pack a second swimsuit?"

"Why? What's wrong with that new pink one you just bought?" Callie wrinkles her nose.

"It's, uh... a little too small for my comfort level."

She walks over and rips the door open.

"Hey!" I grab my cover-up, but she pulls me out into the room.

"Drop it, come on. Let's see it."

I close my eyes and drop the cover-up, standing there in my half-naked glory.

"Holy fucking shit!" Tess says as she grabs my arm and spins me around. I try to reach my hands back to cover my ass, but she holds them away from my body. "Are you kidding me right now? You have this body and you're scared to show it off?"

"I've tried telling her for years. Savannah, if you don't wear that, I will, and we both know I've got twice as much going on so I will be hanging out and flaunting that shit all over Vegas."

I laugh at Callie as my face grows red. "I need another cocktail then."

We have been at the pool for just over an hour. I'm sun-kissed and feeling buzzed but not enough that I forget to reapply my sunscreen. I put the can back in my bag when I suddenly realize I never let Warren know we landed.

"Shit." I rummage for my phone and pull it out to see one single text from him. It's the bright-orange emoji with the curse worse across the mouth. It makes me laugh because I know the exact face he'd be making if he were standing here right now.

Me: *So, I forgot to text but I did make it. Currently at the pool.*

I place the phone on my chair, but he responds immediately.

Warren: *I was about to send out a search party. Wearing your sunscreen, I hope?*

Me: *SPF 35, just reapplied.*

I flip over to my stomach and grab the sunscreen from my bag, holding it up to smile and send him a selfie for proof.

Warren: *You've been drinking?*

Me: *Yeah, a little. It's vacation. Why?*

Warren: *Look at the photo again.*

"Huh?" I remove my sunglasses and click the photo I just sent him. "Oh God." I stare as I realize that my entire ass in my thong bikini is in full view in the background of the photo. I'm about to apologize and explain that it was an accident when the liquor takes over my brain.

Me: *If that offended you, you won't like the rest of the suit.*

Warren: *Send me a picture of it.*

Me: *It's really offensive, you wouldn't like it.*

Warren: *Picture NOW.*

"Hey, Callie, I need a favor." She lifts her sunglasses and looks over at me. "I need to take a sexy photo in my swimsuit."

"Oh, new dating app picture?" She sits and grabs my phone.

"Mm-hmm," I say and stand up to head over to the edge of the pool. I lie on my back, one leg bent with my foot on the ground, the other out long as I arch my back a little and stretch my arms overhead.

"Oh my God, yes." Callie squats down, snapping several pictures from different angles. "Okay, now stand up and do that sexy Insta-gram girl pose where you kind of hike the waist of your bikini up and look off and down to one side."

I do as she says and she stands behind me to take the photos. When she hands the phone back to me I'm shocked as I look at the photos. I can't believe that the woman in them is me and even more, I can't believe that I'm sending these to Warren.

I don't think twice. I select the two best ones and hit send. I stare at my phone, expecting a response right away, but I don't get one. I see the three dots dancing, then they disappear, only to reappear for a moment, but still with no response. Ten minutes later my phone dings.

Warren: *Needed a moment.*

Me: *So not offended then?*

Warren: *Offended? No. Satisfied? Twice.*

My mouth falls open and I shove the phone into my bag, glancing around like anyone knows what's being exchanged between us.

"You ladies ready to go take a nap before we go out tonight?" Tessa yawns and stretches, and Callie and I second her suggestion.

I don't respond to Warren. I figure it's best to let that situation marinate for a bit and maybe for my brain to sober up before I take us right back down the sexting rabbit hole. Though I'd be lying if I said I wasn't curious about what kind of sexter Warren would be or if he ever has sexted.

Taking a nap does nothing to squash my curiosity about earlier. I take my time getting ready, attempting to casually check my phone now and then to see if he's messaged back but he hasn't.

I pull out the dress I was also too scared to wear but packed for this trip anyway and try it on. It's basically a giant piece of material held together by a string that is draped haphazardly over my body.

The glow from the pool time earlier makes the red satin pop against my skin. I opt for a pair of nude stilettos that make my legs look a mile long and rub on a bit of shimmery oil over my body.

"Damn, you are killing it this trip." Callie whistles as I fluff my hair in the mirror.

"As the resident single woman of this group, I'm taking it upon myself to act up a little." I wink and they both giggle at the courage the alcohol has given me.

"Oh, I got us something!" I say as I scurry to my bag and pull out three large penis straws. "And," I say as I shake them, "they glow in the dark!"

"Oh God, not the penis stuff," Tessa groans as Callie snatches hers from my hand.

"More like hell yes, penis stuff!" she says, stuffing it in her purse. "Now let's go get some drinks and enjoy this sexy male review show."

We make our way down to the show and a waiter brings around our cocktails. We place our straws in them and cheers to Tessa.

"Okay, selfie. I have to send this to Brendan." We all lean in and take a silly photo of the ridiculous penis straws in our mouth.

The show is about to start, but I pull out my phone and turn on the front facing camera. I look down to make sure my boobs look good, then place the penis straw at my lips. I make my best sexy, flirty face with the tip of my tongue on the straw and send it to Warren with a casual message.

Me: *Cheers. Hope you're having a nice night.*

The music comes on and the lights dim as the announcer begins to speak. I check my phone quickly and see a response from him so I slide it open.

It's a mouthwatering selfie of him in a fitted black suit with a black shirt and no tie. His top two buttons are undone and his hair is styled a little differently this time. Instead of perfectly combed, it's a little bit mussed and instead of a perfectly shaven face, he has a strong five-o'clock shadow.

He's never sent me a picture of himself before and I'm about to throw all caution to the wind and tell him he looks so goddamn fuck-able I just came in my panties when I see the text that accompanied the photo and my heart sinks. It feels like a giant knot just took over my stomach and I grab my drink to wash it away.

Warren: *Is this acceptable for a date?*

Now I get why he lashed out when he saw me on a date. Is this him getting back at me?

I don't respond. I turn my phone completely off and shove it in my purse, turning my attention to the eight hot men who are grinding on stage.

13

WARREN

I wait patiently.

It's nearing eleven p.m. when I see a group of three women tumble out of an Uber, laughing and falling over each other as they walk into the hotel.

Although I'm ready to throttle her for teasing me earlier, I can't help but smile at how happy Savannah looks. That being said, the scrap of material she's wearing for a dress has my cock ready to tear through my suit pants. I've never been a controlling or jealous asshole, but knowing every man got the pleasure of seeing her in that dress all night has my stomach in knots.

The three women are walking right toward me, but she hasn't noticed me. Why would she? I'm pretty sure the last thing she expected was for me to hop on my private jet and fly to Vegas to teach her a lesson.

"No, the blond one!" she says to her friends while fanning herself. "He could get it." She bursts into laughter, then turns her gaze directly at me. I can see it doesn't register that it's me at first. She looks at me, then back to her girlfriends, then stops dead in her tracks as her head snaps back to me.

"What the hell?" her friend says as they plow into the back of her.

I walk slowly over to her till I'm standing in front of her. "Savannah."

"Oh, *oh!*" her one friend says as they realize who I am.

"What are you doing here?"

"I came here to see you."

"Why?" Her shock is now replaced with curiosity or maybe it's snark.

I look at her friends as I shove my hands into my pockets. "We need to have a talk."

"Okay." She crosses her arms over her chest, her breasts almost spilling out of the top of her dress, and I have to stop myself from reaching down to pull it up. "So talk."

It's definitely snark.

"Ladies." I look at them again. "I promise I won't interfere with your trip, but I'm going to take Savannah up to my room for a little talk."

"Your room? You're staying here?" She points her finger toward the floor.

"I promise I'll have her back in the morning." I reach out and take her hand as I start walking toward the elevator.

"In the morning? I thought we were talking?"

I chuckle as I scan my card for the penthouse and the doors to the elevator close, leaving us alone. "We are and then"—I turn to look directly into her eyes—"I'm going to spend the rest of the night taking out my frustration on you."

I run my thumb over her lip, and she swallows, hard.

"Frustration? You're frustrated with *me*?"

I step behind her, placing my hands on her waist as I turn her to look at her reflection in the mirrored wall of the elevator. I let my hands glide down her hips a little where they rest. These tempting hips that taunt me every time she walks into my office.

"You know exactly what I mean, don't you? I'm going to use this tight little body of yours exactly how it was meant to be used, for pleasure." I run my hand up the back of her thigh and slip it between them, not touching her panties, just softly resting it an inch away as I lower my mouth to her ear. "Even though you've been a very naughty girl."

Her eyes give her away. They flutter and roll back in her head slightly just as the doors open with a ding.

"After you." She steps into the penthouse, and I walk over to the kitchen as she sits down on the love seat. "Would you like some water?" She shakes her head no, but I pour her a glass anyway and hand it to her. "Drink it."

"I said I didn't want any."

"Are you drunk?"

She rolls her eyes. "No. I had like four drinks over a twelve-hour period."

"So you were sober when you chose to wear that napkin as a dress?" I motion to her body, and she looks down. When her eyes find mine again, she's angry.

"Is that why you came all the way out here? To scold me?"

"I told you why I came here."

"Yeah, to yell at me." She stands up. "This is ridiculous. Go home to your date."

"Savannah, sit down."

"You're not my dad, you know that, right?" She's ready to storm out of the room and I'm ready to bend her over my knee.

"Sit down!" I raise my voice and it startles her because she drops right back down in the chair and her mouth snaps shut.

"No, I'm not your father. I have no interest in being your father, but I do think you need to be punished." I close the distance between us and lift her face up to look at me. "You know what I mean when I say I want to punish you?"

She nods. "Yes."

"What?"

"Spank me?" It comes out as a question.

"Good girl, you're learning. That's part of it, yes, but I want to remind you how good it can feel when you obey me. When you don't follow through on your word to text me when you land and then taunt me with those seductive little pictures, that tells me that you're not worried about how I'll react, but you should be, Savannah. I told you I'm not the type of man to be played with."

"Is that the only reason you came?"

I shake my head no. "I haven't had my fill of you yet, sweetie. I need more." I pull her upright till she's standing, then kiss her deeply, my tongue dancing with hers before I pull back and kiss her lips again.

I want to tease her.

I want her trembling with desire, gasping, begging me to take her.

"The night you came to me, I was caught off guard. I didn't get to explore all the things I wanted to with you." I drag my hand up her arm to settle against her neck, my thumb pressing slightly against her throat. "Will you let me explore you, baby?"

Her eyes search mine as she nods. I love the way her words fail her when she's nervous under my touch. Gone is the snarky attitude she threw at me only moments ago, replaced with need.

"Even if I'm rough with you? Demanding things of your little body you haven't experienced before?"

"Like what?" Her question is almost breathless but it's thick with anticipation.

"Have you ever been choked?"

Her eyes grow wide. "Choked?"

"Gently," I whisper as I squeeze her throat a little harder. This time I lean in and tease her mouth with my tongue as I let my other hand find her panties. I slide my hand up her body, pulling her dress up so I can dip my fingers beneath her waistband. I drag my finger between her folds, slick with desire already.

"Mmm." I bring my finger to my mouth and lick it, savoring the tang of her juices and fighting every urge to rip her panties off and bury my face in her. "Something tells me you enjoyed it."

I step back, breaking all contact while I reach for my watch and undo it. I take a seat and reach down to untie my shoes, kicking them off along with my socks. I lean back on the love seat as she stands there dazed, looking at me.

"What are you doing?" Her words are heavy with need.

"Thinking," I say as I drag my eyes lazily over her body.

"About?"

"About what I want to do to you."

I pat the cushion next to me and she sits down. Reaching for her foot, I pull it onto my lap to remove her shoe, repeating the process on the other foot. I motion for her to stand and I situate her in front of me. I reach beneath her dress, hooking my thumbs in her thong and dragging it down her thighs. Next, I pull her dress off in one smooth motion, tossing it onto the couch.

"Your body is a fucking playland." I drag my hands up her body as I stand, cupping her breasts. "Look at me. It's not going to be gentle, not the first few times at least. I need to fuck you hard and deep."

I wrap my hands around her ass, planting them firmly one on each ass cheek as I press my lips against her pubic bone. Her hands shoot down to my shoulders, but I don't move. I want to savor this moment of just having her in my arms. Her hands find their way into my hair as I tilt my head upward to look at her.

"What are you doing?"

I don't respond, afraid that if I do, I'll confess my true feelings to her. Instead, I sit back and guide her to straddle me as my hands leisurely glide over her thighs and hips to settle against her waist.

"You make me feel like I'm losing control." I'm gripping her tightly as I lean in to plant delicate kisses against her breasts. "You have no idea what you do to me. I could spend hours just staring at you." I know I'm betraying my facade of just wanting to fuck some sense into her, but I can't seem to keep it inside. I let my head fall back against the back of the couch as I grip her hips tighter, pulling her down against my hard-on and lifting my hips to grind against her.

"Mmm," her moan comes out as a purr and I do it again. I want her frantic with desire like I am right now. Her eyes open and she looks down our bodies. "Your pants."

"What about them?"

"I'm—they're going to be we—" The words come out broken as I roll my hips against her and she falls forward.

"Fuck the pants, baby."

She grabs at my belt, pulling it through the buckle as she fumbles with the zipper. "Off," is the only word she utters.

I grab her hands and still her movements. "Patience," I say as I press against her hips, angling her back a little so I can look at her. Her hands shoot back to rest against my knees, giving me a better view. "I want to see you."

She watches me intently as I bring my thumb to my mouth, popping it inside to get wet and then gently swirling it over her tight bud.

"Oh." Her eyes flutter as her fingers dig into my thighs. I slowly repeat the movement again, and her mouth falls open.

"Mmm, look at you glistening, sweetheart." I watch as her pussy pulses with my movements. I can feel my hands begin to shake as I hold myself back. "So mouthwatering."

"Please," she begs finally.

"Please what, Savannah?"

"Please make me come." Her pleading does something to my ego.

"Look at me," I command and her eyes pop open and find mine. "Do you want me to continue using my hands or do you want to get fucked?"

She searches my eyes, looking for guidance.

"Tell me and I'll make you come."

"Fucked." She barely gets the word out before I'm standing up with her still in my arms and planting her on her feet.

I guide her to the bedroom where I've already laid out a few items. Her eyes move from one to the other, then to me. "What's all this?"

I lean forward and pick up the silk tie. "I figure this is more gentle than handcuffs." I spin her and cross her wrists one over the other as I gently bind her.

I pick up a second item, a bright-pink vibrator. "I think we both know what this is. I've had endless images of stuffing you with this since I saw one similar in your closet."

"And that one?" She points to a much smaller item.

"This," I say, picking it up, "I'm going to stick in your tight little ass while I fuck you from behind."

"What—my ass?"

I snake my hand around her neck and kiss her softly. "Mm-hmm. It's going to feel good, sweetheart. Don't worry."

"Why do you want to do that?"

"It's control, Savannah." I brush her hair out of her eye. "It's just a kink I have. I want to see it inside you. You have such a delicious little ass. I'd love to fuck it if I'm honest, but I know it'll take time to get there. I want to mark every inch of your body, Savannah, with my cock and my tongue."

"Your tongue? Even my ass?"

"Yes. You've never had a man eat your ass?" Her eyes grow a little wide and she shakes her head no. That makes me even more turned on, knowing I have access to parts of her no man ever has. "Oh, Savannah, the things I'm going to do to you."

Her eyes search mine and I can see an emotion on her face that I don't recognize.

"Are you okay? What are you thinking?"

She lets out a small laugh. "Honestly, I don't know. I just didn't expect you to be so—to talk like this with me. You're always so serious."

Her response makes me chuckle. "Well, I never found the right time in all our years at work to bring up the fact that I want to impale my cock in your ass. Does it turn you on?" I reach down and toy with her again, finding her soaking wet.

"Yesss." Her head falls back as she answers me, her words a half moan.

"Savannah, I could write a book with all the filthy things I want to do to you and it still wouldn't satiate my desires." I reach down and free my aching cock while I talk. I bend her over the bed, guiding her to turn her face so that her chest falls against it while her knees push her ass up in the air.

"What really turns me on, is that everyone who sees you has no idea of the filthy little slut you want to be for me."

I crouch down and grip her cheeks, spreading them wide as I drag my tongue lazily up her slit to her asshole. She groans loudly as she presses back against me. I repeat the process, hungrily devouring her before I stand back up, my nerves on the verge of tearing her apart.

"If I could fuck you for hours every day, it wouldn't be enough." I grit the words out as I position myself at her entrance and push in an inch.

"Ahh." She attempts to shift forward, but I grab her hips and pull her back, causing me to drive into her further.

"I warned you." I can feel sweat beading on my forehead as I try to hold back from completely breaking her in half, but it's no use. I lose any control once I feel her slick heat encase me.

I rear back and slam into her harder. I repeat it a few more times till we're both moaning in ecstasy. I grab the butt plug from the bed, holding it while I spread her cheeks and spit.

"Relax, baby. I'm going to stick this in your ass." I don't give her much time to protest and before she can, it's in place. "Oh, fuck yes, that looks so fucking hot."

I don't even know what I'm saying; I've lost all control. I grip her so tight I'm sure there will be bruises in the morning, but I don't care. My chest burns as I pull myself out fully, then slam back into her deep and hard. I repeat the process over and over. My hips piston hard and fast till I'm shouting and coming inside her. I fall onto her back, untying her hands while I try to even my breathing.

I know she didn't finish so I flip her to her back, leaving the toy inside her as I crawl up her body. I spend time sucking on each nipple before moving my lips to her mouth. I'm still rock hard so I slide myself back inside her, her back arching as her mouth falls open.

"Do you trust me?" I lazily slide in and out of her. She nods her head, unable to form words as I continue to fuck her.

I place my hand at her throat, squeezing gently as I quicken my strokes just a touch, making sure I'm going deep to her G-spot. I can feel her begin to quiver, her legs shake, and I tighten my grip on her throat as her release builds.

I pull myself up on my knees, my hand still tightly wrapped around her throat as her eyes plead with me to let her finish. I drop my other hand to her clit and apply pressure just as she squeezes her eyes shut and an orgasm takes over her body.

I release my hand from her throat and watch as she inhales deeply, her orgasm taking her to new heights as I pull the toy from her ass.

I lay back against the headboard, my upper body slightly propped up as Savannah is stretched out over me, the sheet halfway covering our still-naked bodies after hours of lovemaking.

Lovemaking? I feel panic rise in my chest, but the movement of her lifting her head up to look at me keeps it at bay. She looks satisfied and so damn beautiful it makes my chest clench again.

I've known for years that the feelings I have for Savannah aren't platonic. I've tried a variety of reasons in my head: I'm a father figure to her, a mentor; she's ambitious and reminds me of me... but I know the real reason is I'm in love with her.

It would be so easy in this moment to say it. To just open my heart up to her and tell her that for the better part of three years I haven't wanted to wake up to anyone else. She's the only woman who excites me, who makes me want a future—but I'm terrified. Because if she doesn't feel the same way, I know there's no going back to how we used to be. Hell, I'm not sure there is now but at least I haven't scared her away yet.

"How are you feeling?"

She smiles lazily, then yawns. "Utterly abused."

"Good."

She kicks the sheet off and maneuvers herself till she's straddling me, her bare breasts right at my mouth level. I lean forward and swirl my tongue around one nipple.

"Can't you control yourself?" She giggles, crossing her arms over her breasts.

"Not when your naked tits are right in my face; are you kidding?"

"Pretend we're in your office then, going over some business."

"You think that would stop me? If you had these out in my office, I'd bend you over my desk and not give a fuck who walked in that door."

"No, I mean—fine." She grabs the sheet and pulls it over her body. "There, now it's like we're in the office. Fully clothed."

"You think I don't imagine what your tits look like when you're fully clothed, standing in my office?" Her smile fades and I slowly pull the sheet back down.

"Sweetheart, I've imagined every vile thing I can when you're sitting next to me on my desk. I'm sorry if that scares you, but I'm no different than any other man who watched you walk across my yacht in that dress. The only difference between me and them is, my fantasies were probably the most graphic."

I lean forward and run my nose up her chest to her neck. "I know how you smell. I know how it feels to hold your waist as you stand next to me. I know how it feels to have your full tits pressed against me… and that was all before I ever even had you."

I can hear her breathing grow rapid as her hand finds its way into my hair and her hips begin to move slowly against me.

I tighten my grip on her back as I slowly roll her over till I'm on top of her. Our eyes meet as she lifts herself up to kiss me. This time as I bury myself inside her I go slow, her eyes on mine as I lose myself in her.

Keeping my ultimate fantasy of calling her mine to myself.

14

SAVANNAH

I search Warren's face as he lazily pumps in and out of me. Gone is the controlling, sex-crazed look in his eyes, replaced with something softer, something I've been wanting to see for years.

"Please," I beg over and over, but I don't know what I'm begging for.

"Does this feel good, baby? You need more?"

"No, just like this. Don't stop." My pleasure is building like a slow burn that will soon turn into a full-blown explosion. My nails claw at the slick skin of his back as he slides into me again. "Never want this to stop." The words come out in a lust-fueled haze.

He stills for a second, looking down at me, and panic rises in my chest. He kisses me, his eyes still trained on mine as he slowly begins to move again. He reaches around to grab my hands, hoisting them above my head as he pins them to the pillow. He buries his face in my neck as he begins to pant.

"You have no idea what you do to me, Savannah."

"Tell me," I beg as he drags his tongue up my neck, making my toes curl.

"Someday," he murmurs, "when I'm not consumed with lust."

* * *

I BLINK, stretching my arms overhead.

My entire body feels like I put it through a grueling workout. I turn to my right to see a still-passed-out Warren, his arm extended out over my body, his leg pressed against me. His dirty blonde hair lays across his forehead and I reach over to brush it away.

He looks so peaceful and relaxed, a state I'm not sure I've seen him in. I don't want to wake him. I want to savor this moment after our exchange last night.

"Why are you staring at me?" He snakes his arm around my waist and yanks me toward him, cupping my breast and thrusting his erection against my backside.

"Good morning to you too." My laugh turns into a moan as he massages my breast, his lips leaving warm, wet kisses over my bare shoulder.

"It is a good morning waking up to you." He bites down on the nape of my neck, sending a shot of electricity straight through me. "So fucking good." He pushes his cock against me from behind as he bites down on me even harder. Another little Warren kink I've discovered.

"I'm going to be covered in bite marks and bruises."

"Mmm, that's the point." His hand is playing with me now, my arousal making me wetter by the second.

"Marking me?" I'm breathless as I arch my back and press myself against him. I turn my head over my shoulder and capture his lips with mine. His tongue lazily swirls against mine as he sloppily kisses me. I feel the tip of his erection press against me, then slide inside.

"Yes. I want the next man to know that I've had you. That I've used you in every way imaginable."

My eyes pop open and I want to stop him, but my body betrays me. I want to tell him that the only man I want to ever touch me again is him. Instead, I antagonize him.

"Except my ass."

He grabs a handful of my hair and thrusts his cock into me hard till I'm completely filled with him. I yell out and grip the pillow next to me.

"Shut the fuck up, Savannah," he grunts as he continues to thrust into me with hard, punishing strokes.

I can't form the words anyway so I close my eyes and allow myself to just enjoy the pleasure that tears through my body.

* * *

I TAKE a bite of French toast, tucking my legs under me as I watch Warren get dressed.

I lost count how many times this man made me come last night and this morning, but I know I'll be feeling it for a week.

"You look cute in that robe." He smiles at me and it makes my heart flutter.

"Thanks. You don't look too bad yourself." He winks as he slides his shirt up his arms. "So what happened to your date last night?" I ask, not really wanting to know the answer, but it's been on my mind since he sent me the text.

"My date?"

"Yeah, you asked me last night if the outfit you were wearing was okay for a date."

He pauses buttoning his shirt and looks at me with a smirk. "*You* were the date."

I pause, my cup of coffee halfway to my mouth, and smile. "Oh."

"You really didn't get that?"

I shrug. "No, I thought you were trying to get me back for the date thing the other day."

He doesn't respond, just turns back to the mirror in front of him. I stand and walk over to the vanity, taking a seat on it as I push his hands away to finish buttoning his shirt myself.

"You really have to leave already?"

He tips my chin upward. "Yes, I have a meeting in LA this afternoon."

"It's the weekend." I try to hide my pouty tone, but I don't do a good job.

"No rest for the wicked." He bends down and kisses me, pausing to pull back and look at me before kissing me again. "You'll see me Monday at work. Besides, I promised your friends I wouldn't interfere with your trip."

"Hey, I wanted to ask you about something." I fiddle with my bathrobe belt. "Tessa's wedding is in a few weeks and I was wondering if you'd want to go as my plus one?"

He loops his tie around his neck and looks at me. "As your date?"

I panic. "I mean more like just a fun plus one type arrangement." I say it like it's not a big deal, hoping he doesn't freak out at the mention of going somewhere as a couple.

He nods and tosses one end of his tie over the other. "An arrangement, huh? Let me guess, Easton will be there?"

"Oh, uh, I don't actually know." I tell myself it's not a complete lie, I don't know for sure if he's going to be there and he very well might not be since he's more friends with the groom's brother than the groom. Bottom line, that's *not* the reason I asked him this time.

"What about Mr. Dreamboat?"

"Huh?"

"Barrett from the app, the one who you said is ticking all the boxes. Why not ask him?"

"Oh." I feel my throat go dry and I don't know why but it feels like tears well up almost instantly. "Uh, we haven't gone on an actual date yet. He's traveling for work so I didn't want to spring a wedding with all my friends on him as our first date."

"Ah, so I'm the backup."

I stare at him, trying to decipher if he's joking but I don't think he is.

"No, I didn't ask him. I wanted to ask you and I did." He doesn't respond, just continues on with his tie. "Look, I don't want the pressure of having to entertain a guy I just met at a wedding with all my friends. I trust you and I want—I want you there."

"I'll think about it." His tone is clipped. I hop down from the vanity and walk back over to where my breakfast has gone cold and pick up my coffee.

"What's wrong?"

He doesn't look at me as he gathers up the rest of his items and places them in his suitcase. "Nothing, just running late and you need to get back to your friends."

"Right," I say, standing up and grabbing my wrinkled dress off the floor to head into the bathroom. I go to slam the door behind me, but his arm jumps out and catches it.

"Don't do this, Savannah."

"Do what, Warren? You're the one who went all Jekyll and Hyde on me because I asked you to go to my friend's wedding with me. Now, can I have a little privacy, please?"

"This is why I knew this would be a bad idea."

It feels like he just punched me in the stomach. "That what would be a bad idea?"

He looks down at his feet and shakes his head. "This"—he motions between us—"crossing this boundary. Now it's weird."

"Now it's weird? Ha." I toss my hands in the air. "Funny because that didn't stop you from fucking me. In fact, I didn't hear the word no come out of your mouth once."

"It should have." I recoil at his answer and his eyes soften a little at my response. "I'm sorry." He reaches for me. "I care about you, Savannah, and yes, I knew it could get complicated as friends and as your boss if we slept together, but you're right." He steps closer to me and places his hand against my face. "I didn't let it stop me before, but it will now."

"Meaning?" I can't hold back one big fat tear that tumbles down my cheek. He lifts his thumb to brush it away.

"Meaning I don't think we should do this again."

I push his hand away and storm out of the bathroom in search of my panties.

"Savannah." He says my name, but I ignore him.

"Fuck the panties," I mutter as I march toward the elevator.

"Savannah, stop it!" he shouts as he grabs my arm and spins me around to face him.

"Let me go, Warren. Go back home or to LA or wherever the fuck you need to be that's so important."

"I thought this is what you wanted? You came to me, Savannah. You propositioned me for one night, and I've given you two. Tell me what you want."

"I told you, I wanted you to go Tessa's wedding with me, but you acted like I was asking you to be make some grand commitment to me. It's just a damn wedding; it doesn't mean anything!"

He pinches the bridge of his nose and lets out an exasperated sigh. "That's not why I hesitated. It's because I—"

"Oh, I'm aware it's because you thought it would make things weird for us. You're right, Warren, but it didn't make it weird; it just made me realize where I stand with you." I punch the button to call the elevator and the doors open. I step inside, clutching my dress in one hand as I pull the robe tighter around my body. "Good to know you'll fly halfway across the country at the drop of a hat to fuck me, but you won't go to a wedding with me."

The doors close slowly as I watch sadness wash over his face. I don't care in this moment that he's hurting. All I can focus on is the giant hole that just ripped through my heart as I crumple to the floor in a pile of tears.

15

WARREN

I can't wrap my brain around what just happened right now, but I'm going to be late to my plane if I don't get out of this suite.

The words were on the tip of my tongue before she cut me off. I was going to tell her that the reason I was upset is because I wanted to go as her date. I didn't want to be a last resort or a mere chair filler because she didn't want to go to yet another social event alone.

"Fuck!" I slam my suitcase shut and pace the floor. It feels like rushing water is in my ears as I try to calm myself down. I knew allowing myself to touch her, to kiss her and hold her would bite me in the ass, not because I didn't want anything more with her but because I'm in love with her.

I want it all with her, but she's made it clear that I'm nothing more than an arrangement or proposition. I'm a human fucking dildo for her while she has fun before finally finding Mr. Perfect and settling down with him.

I grab my bag and head down to the car that's waiting to take me to the airport. Once on board, I settle in my chair and tell my flight attendant not to disturb me for the short flight. I open my iPad, pushing all thoughts of Savannah from my brain and dive in to the mounting evidence in front of me that Eric Oliver and his son Kane are not only defrauding investors but have a slew of other accusations to their name. Something else that I completely missed right under my nose.

* * *

I STARE at the ceiling in my bedroom, dreading the fact that today is Sunday which means tomorrow I'll have to see Savannah.

In three plus years of working together, I've never once dreaded seeing her. Usually, I spend my Sundays checking my watch at least a dozen different times, counting down the hours till I see her smiling face on Monday morning.

It typically consists of a cheery good morning accompanied by my favorite coffee, something I've tried to do for her, but she always insists it's her treat for me, a quick debrief of our day to come, and then a funny or dramatic story from her weekend outings.

I smile as I think about the ridiculous expressions she uses. *"So we were lost, I'm talking out where Jesus lost his sandals lost."* It feels like there's an elephant sitting on my chest as I realize that our last exchange may very well have ruined any chance of ever hearing those stories again.

I sit up and toss the covers off, checking the clock.

It's already 9:03 a.m. Damn, I never sleep this late.

Normally, I'm teeing off by now with Eric, but he hasn't been seen since I fired him and you couldn't pay me to associate with that fool again. Even if Savannah hates me and I never see her again, I'll never forgive Eric for the things he said to her, for the hell he put her through these last several years. Somehow in the span of a few weeks, I've lost both of my closest friends.

After a two-hour workout, a shower, and feeling sorry for myself, I decide lunch at the club and maybe some driving practice are in order.

"Warren Baxley, you devil, where have you been?"

I turn around to the booming voice of Teddy Marren.

"Hey, Teddy, long time no see to you too. Ester." I kiss her gently on the cheek as Teddy thrusts his hand into mine.

"What's been going on? I heard about the Code Red acquisition. Congrats. That's going to be huge for the portfolio."

"Thank you. I really have my COO Savannah Monroe to thank; she's the one that got the whole ball moving on that project."

"Oh, Savannah, she's so lovely," Ester says. "How is she doing? I haven't seen her since your yacht party last year. Sorry we missed this year by the way; we were in England for our youngest son's graduation from Oxford."

"You didn't miss much. I'd gladly be in England to miss those parties if I could too." I debate ignoring the Savannah remark, but they're both staring at me. "Savannah is great, kicking ass as always." I smile.

"Why don't you sit with us at lunch. We were just heading to our table."

I nod and follow them to their corner table.

"So when are you going to finally settle down, Warren? You're not a young man anymore." Ester nudges me playfully and Teddy glares at her.

"Jesus woman, give the man a chance to order a drink before you hit him with that stuff. Ignore her. She just loves to meddle and now that all of our children are married or engaged, she needs to channel it elsewhere."

I laugh and Ester just rolls her eyes, keeping her attention on me with a questioning brow.

"I, uh, well, I will eventually I suppose or maybe I won't. Haven't given it too much thought."

"Smart man." Teddy laughs and Ester just ignores him.

"What about Savannah? We always say how you'd make such a lovely couple and you have such a great rapport with each other. She always speaks so highly of you."

"I don—she does?" My curiosity gets the best of me.

"Mm-hmm. In fact, I think she has a little crush."

I swallow down the lump that's inching its way up my throat. This feels like a very strange conversation to be having about an employee, especially right after what just happened between us.

"Well, I am her boss and almost old enough to be her father. That doesn't really seem appropriate."

"Oh, please." Ester waves away my concern. "I was Teddy's secretary and he's twenty years my senior and we've never been happier."

"Well, Savannah is a wonderful young woman whom I respect very much, but I'm pretty sure she's seeing someone else."

I don't know why I said it, maybe to get them off my back about her or maybe if I say it out loud, it will be more real to me that she's not an option. She's found someone online that has piqued her interest and she's made it clear that it's not me.

Teddy can see my unease and quickly changes the subject. "Are you attending that Black Ties and White Lies bullshit? This one says I have to go, but if you're not going, I'm not going."

"I planned to yes. Certainly isn't something I'm jumping to attend, but I'm being presented some award this year unfortunately."

"Oh, that's wonderful! See?" She smacks Teddy's arm. "You have to go and support Warren." She turns back to me. "Who is your date?"

The waiter approaches and takes our order which I pray is my saving grace, but Ester's eyes turn right back to me once he walks away.

"I'm not sure I have one." I take a long drink of my water. "I don't have one actually."

"Well, that won't do. You can't go stag as the night's honoree." Someone catches her eye and she waves over my shoulder. "I'll be right back."

Teddy waves down the waiter again and orders us both a scotch on the rocks. "She's driving me batty lately. Always trying to fix someone up. I'm second-guessing retirement."

I laugh because as much he complains about Ester, she's his entire world. After forty some years in the tech world, Teddy retired last year. Retirement for Teddy is only going in to the office five days a week instead of seven. The man only knows one thing: work. For as much as I love my work and the company I've built, I'm going to end up in the same boat as him if I'm not careful, only I won't have an Ester by my side.

"So, what's this I hear about you firing Eric Oliver?"

I pick up the tumbler and take a sip of the liquor, savoring the burn. I knew it was only a matter of time before that can of worms spilled out in our circles.

"I did. Had to be done." I roll the glass between my palms. "I'm in love with her, Ted."

"Oh shit," he murmurs. "What happened?"

I don't have to tell him who *her* is. He knows all too well.

"Found out that Eric had been harassing her. Making disgusting comments about she and I that *weren't* true… at the time."

His head shoots up and he looks at me. I just hang my head.

"We tried and it turns out we don't want the same things."

"Ah fuck, man, I'm sorry. Ester didn't know; she didn't mean any harm with what she said."

I wave away his concern. "No worries. I know she didn't. But I ended up witnessing Eric's behavior and when I questioned Savannah, she confirmed it has been going on since she first interviewed."

"What the hell?"

"Yeah, made me feel like shit I missed it the entire time. I know he had a bit of an issue with me hiring her in the first place. I think her age was a big factor but mostly, he wanted to be COO, but that's not where his expertise lies."

Teddy agrees. "Eric Oliver is a financial genius, but he has no business sticking his nose outside that realm."

"And no business staying in it," I add on.

His tumbler slowly falls from his lips. "What are you saying, Warren?"

I lean back in my chair and look around, making sure the ears nearby aren't leaning our way.

"After I fired him, I knew that he could come back at me with some bullshit about wrongful termination, especially since he's never been reprimanded by Human Resources previously. I also knew that after seeing that side of him, I didn't trust him. So I started doing a little digging."

"And?" Teddy's on the edge of his seat, leaning all the way forward on his elbows.

"And I found some shit. I kind of had some suspicions about his son Kane. I'd offered over the years to bring Kane on board at Baxley, even offered to be an investor and introduce him to other investors when he started pursuing this app of his. Turns out the SEC already has a case opened against not only Kane, but also Eric."

"Well, I'll be damned." He rubs his hand over his bald head, his mouth hanging open in shock.

"Yeah, turns out that there were some complaints raised by a few investors, one of them being Riz Malik in LA."

"He tried to pull one over on Riz Malik? The man who owns half of LA?" He whistles. "That boy either has balls the size of bowling balls or he's a fucking idiot."

"Right? That's what I said. Arrogant little shit. Anyway, my lawyer and I have been gathering intel and going over things and I actually met with Riz yesterday in LA, and I can tell you, he's not rolling over on this one. He's serious and he won't back down."

"So he's pursuing legal action? Fraud charges?"

"Mm-hmm." I nod and Teddy leans back in his chair, stunned. "It sucks, Ted. I never wanted to find shit on Eric, and honestly I didn't think I would except for maybe some stupid tax bullshit but this, this is huge and I have to get ahead of it so that my name isn't dragged into this."

"Look who I found!" Ester walks back over to our table, a tall, thin raven-haired woman at her side with a megawatt smile.

"Maria Syler, how are you, sugar?" Teddy stands and walks over to her with open arms.

"I was just telling Ester that I've been meaning to call you guys. I've been so busy I just let time get away from me."

I stand and extend my hand to Maria. "Maria, good to see you. I trust you're doing well?"

I haven't seen Maria in over a year. I was a business acquaintance of her late husband Titus Syler. We weren't close, but we were friendly and carried a mutual respect for each other.

"Please sit down." Ester pulls a chair over to our table and insists on Maria sitting between us.

Maria is stunning, by anyone's standards. Her dark hair and dark eyes contrast perfectly against her alabaster skin. She's refined and sweet, gentle, and very classy. I don't think I've ever not seen her completely put together with designer items, and that smile on her face. She was raised with money, one of the few socialites left in the city and fit perfectly into our world of money and power when she married Titus twenty years ago.

"How's business?"

"Teddy, it's the weekend. Let the woman relax."

"It's okay." She gently touches Ester's arm. "Business is—stressful. It's good. We just closed out one of our most profitable quarters, but it comes at a cost." She smiles sweetly but you can see the tiredness in her eyes.

"You still acting CEO?" Teddy asks and she nods.

"I am but I'm hopeful not for long." She turns to me. "I'm actually so glad I ran into you here. I've been meaning to set up a meeting with you to talk about a possible acquisition."

"Acquisition? You want to sell Syler Systems?" My ears perk up with that comment. If she's serious about my company acquiring hers, that would make Baxley Tech the largest market shareholder in the industry by far.

She sighs, her fingers knotting together in her lap. "I think so. I hate that I'd be selling Titus' legacy, but I can't think of a better company to take over."

"I'm flattered truly. I will absolutely reach out to you and set up a meeting." I reach for my phone. "Do I have your number?"

"I know this is sudden, but is there any chance you're free tonight for dinner to talk about Syler Systems? I have to be out of town next week and I'd feel a lot better if we could talk through some things before I leave."

"Yeah, I can make that happen."

"Thank you. I feel so much better now that I've been able to get that on the books. Now I just need to find a date for this masquerade Black Ties and White Lies event." She laughs.

I glance up and Ester's eyes bug out. *Ah, shit, here we go.*

"Well, what a coincidence. Warren was just saying that he didn't have a date either."

I see Teddy looking at me with an apologetic look.

"Oh, would you want to go together?" Maria asks me.

"Absolutely." I down the rest of my scotch and plaster on the fakest smile I can muster as my heart plummets to my stomach when I remember that Savannah will also be attending the masquerade event.

16

SAVANNAH

"Okay, I'm only going to ask you once because something clearly happened with Warren last night but you're acting like it didn't so, as your best friend, what the fuck happened?"

Callie and Tessa both stare at me on our flight back to Chicago. Lucky me that I ended up in the middle seat so there's no getting away from them.

After I left Warren's suite this morning, I had a moment of hysterical crying in the elevator for about ten seconds before I realized I didn't have a key to get back in my room. So, I knocked on our door and when Callie opened it still half-asleep, I darted into the bathroom and shut the door behind me, telling her I had to pee really bad. Then I ducked into the shower where I had my full emotional meltdown in private.

"He stuck something in my ass."

Tessa spits her coffee out all over her tray table as Callie and I grab our napkins to help her clean it up.

"Dude." She looks around, but I made sure I said it quiet enough that no one heard me.

"Uh, okay, need to hear that story, but that doesn't explain why you're sulking. Or does it? He can't possibly be bad in bed."

"No, no, he's not. Trust me. Actually," I say, pulling my oversized hoodie away from my neck and shoulders to show them the bite marks and slight bruise he left. "I'm glad I packed this for the plane at the last minute."

"Hot damn, he's an animal."

"Yeah, so the physical stuff isn't the problem. The man can go for hours like back-to-back-to-back; it's insane."

"Okay, no need to rub our faces in it," Callie teases. "But why'd he come out here? Did you guys plan that?"

I shake my head no. "That was a surprise. You know those poolside pictures you took for me? Yeah, those were for him, and then I sent him a selfie when we were at the Magic Mike show with the penis straw in my mouth."

"Okay, so you antagonized the man." Callie laughs. "If I did that to Brendan, he'd rip me in half when he saw me. No wonder he did all that to you." She points to my neck.

"So you sent him some sexy pics and he came out and you guys had mind-blowing sex, so where did it go wrong? I'm so confused," Tessa asks.

"It's so stupid. I asked him to be my plus one to your wedding. Well, first, the morning sex was amazing; it felt like—making love." I cringe when I say it because I don't like sounding sappy. "It was super intense and passionate, and then when I asked him, he seemed dismissive about it. He made some comment about why I didn't ask Barrett instead. I told him I didn't want to take a dude on a first date to a wedding, that I'd rather take him because we're friends and I wouldn't have to entertain him all night. It just annoyed me."

"Wait, so he knows about Barrett?"

"Yeah, kind of. I told him that there was this guy who'd reached out to me and we seemed to have a lot in common, like the kind of guy that I'd date but that we—"

"Savannah." Callie gives me a look like *seriously*? "You told Warren about this guy who is 'your type,' meanwhile you're flirting with Warren and hooking up with him, then you invite him to Tessa's wedding as a *friend*?"

When she says it like that, I guess I can see why he got upset. "I didn't mean it as a backhanded compliment or anything to him. I just didn't want to put pressure on him about it. I want Warren to go with me because I like him and want to spend time with him."

Tessa crooks a knowing eyebrow at me. "Because you're in love with him?"

"What? No! No. He's fun and I like spending time with him, and yes, our sexual chemistry is off the charts, but he doesn't want anything with me. Trust me, he made that clear when he said he knew that things would get weird with us if we slept together. Meanwhile he never said no!"

I can feel my emotions start to take over. I lower my voice and shake out my hands in nervous frustration.

"Sweetie, I think there's more between you two than you realize or that you want to admit."

"What do you mean?"

"You basically told Warren after sleeping with him that you only see friendship potential with him, that this other guy has what you want in a man but that he'll do as a fill-in until you finally make things happen with Barrett. I know you didn't mean it like that, or maybe you did, but I can see why Warren got pissy. I'd be mad too if I flew across the country to see a guy and after a hot-ass night of sex he told me that I wasn't good enough to go to something as my date but that I could go as his friend."

I hear it and it hits me like a ton of bricks. "Oh my God." My hand clutches my chest as I realize not only how fucking stupid I am, but how cruel I must have sounded. "But I don't think he wants anything with me like that. He did say that we shouldn't have slept together in the first place and we certainly won't again."

Tessa grabs my hand. "Maybe he was too scared to tell you that he does want something more because you made it seem like to him that you didn't."

"Ugh, this is all so confusing, and I'm stuck on this stupid plane so I can't just walk over to his place and clarify everything."

"We'll be home in an hour, then you can scurry right over there and tell him how you feel," Callie tries to reassure me. "How do you feel about him?"

I stare at the plastic cup in my hand, the ice cold against my fingertips through the thin material as the words I've been too scared to ever admit to myself let alone out loud fall from my own lips.

"I'm in love with him."

* * *

BY THE TIME our plane lands, my nerves are at all-time high. Anxious energy courses through me as I fumble to get my luggage in and out of my Uber and up to my apartment.

"I should shower and look nice." I run to the bathroom and flip on the shower. "But what do I wear?"

I flip through my clothes while the water warms up, talking to myself the entire time about why this is a bad idea while simultaneously talking myself out of not doing it because it's worth the risk and I deserve to be happy.

I spend the next twenty minutes shaving every inch of my body, followed by a thick layer of lotion like this man hasn't already seen the most intimate parts of my body... and liked them.

I settle on the sundress he bought me a few weeks back after our night together on his yacht. I run my hands over the material. A smile plays across my lips as I remember the last time I showed up to his house in this dress.

I take the long way to his penthouse, going over in my head what I want to say to him. I feel the nerves start to build again with every step closer to his building. I round the corner, practicing my opening line to him. "I'm sorry for making you feel like you weren't enough for me, like I didn't want you by my side at Tessa's wedding because you're more than just my friend, you're the lo—" I look up as I take the final steps just as I see Warren exiting the building with a tall, dark-haired woman by his side.

My feet are glued to the sidewalk as my mouth hangs open. Maybe they're just walking out together; it's just a coincidence. But his hand comes out to press against her lower back as he leans forward to open the car door and usher her inside.

My entire world feels like it's tilting on its axis. Of all the reasons I'd come up with in my head that Warren reacted the way he did toward me in Vegas, not one involved him being with someone else.

Maybe that's why he came to Vegas, to tell me that it can't happen again after one last night together.

Then it hits me, I'm too late.

I'd made it so clear to him that he wasn't even on my horizon for a potential partner that even if he ever did feel something more than friendship toward me, he clearly doesn't anymore.

17

WARREN

I spin my cuff link mindlessly on the drive back to my building.

Dinner with Maria was successful. We spoke about the next steps and what it would look like for her if Baxley Tech acquired Syler Systems.

As someone who didn't sign up to run a Fortune 500 company, I can completely understand Maria's eagerness to off-load the company. I know it might seem as simple as hiring the right CEO to run it, but there's more to it than that. She's ready to retire and move to Paris to be near her only daughter.

"Evening, Martin." I give him a half-hearted wave as I keep my head down and trudge toward the elevator.

As huge as this new deal might be with Syler Systems, I can't get the pit in my stomach to go away after my night in Vegas with Savannah. I have no idea where we stand right now, but I'm dreading going to the office tomorrow morning, a feeling I've never experienced.

"Oh, Mr. Baxley, sir, someone left this for you."

I look over to the front desk where Steve is holding up a brown envelope for me.

"Thank you, sir." I take the envelope and tuck it under my arm as I enter the elevator and wave at the men again who both look at me with a perplexed look on their faces.

I feel lost, for the first time in probably my entire life. I don't have an answer. In business, I'm always a step or two ahead; I know what my goals and plans are; I know what I need to execute to get there, and I do it. But with this—this thing with Savannah, I'm in uncharted waters and I'm sinking fast.

I toss the envelope onto my kitchen island and walk to the fridge to grab a bottle of water. I debate on if I should put myself through a second grueling workout of the day to get my mind right, but I settle on bringing the envelope with me to slump down on the couch to catch up on some baseball.

I flick through the sports channels, settling on one to catch the highlights of what I missed this week.

"Cubs lost? Shocking," I mutter as I grab the envelope.

I flip it over and look for an address, but it's unlabeled. The small metal prongs on the top are the only thing keeping it closed; there's no actual seal on it. I flick the prongs open and slide my hand inside, pulling out the contents.

I blink rapidly, staring at the 8x11 black-and-white photographs in my hand. They don't make sense. I rub my eyes and look closer. I shoot upright, bringing the photos closer to my face as I flick on the light on the end table, realizing they're photos of Savannah and me.

"What the fu—"

I FLIP THROUGH THEM, each one more explicit than the other. The first ones are at the bar I saw her in a few weeks back when she was on a date. How the hell did someone even get these? I think back, trying to recall if I remember seeing someone in the shadows or even walking by the alcove we were in, but I was too focused on what I was doing to Savannah to notice. I remember there was a glass emergency exit door to the right, but I didn't pay attention to it since it opened to an alley.

The second set are detailed photos of Savannah and me in the throes of passion. I stare at them, my stomach rolling at the thought that somehow, someone managed to take explicit photos of something that happened inside my home.

A cold flush spreads over my body as I flip to the last two photos. They're photos of Maria and me leaving my building just a few hours previously.

I gather the photos and shove them back into the folder, rushing to the elevator. When the doors open in the lobby, I motion for Martin to come over to the front desk where Steve is looking at me, confused.

"Who dropped this off?" I hold up the envelope.

"I don't know, sir."

"How do you not know? You sit here all night."

"I had gone to the restroom for two minutes and Martin—"

"Some couple got into a huge fight and caused a commotion right out in front of the building," Martin interrupts. "So I was trying to usher them down the sidewalk. I don't know if someone stepped in and placed it on the counter while I was distracted because by the time Steve got back to the desk, it was just sitting there."

"Neither one of us saw the person come in."

"Did either of you open this?" I ask sternly, hoping they don't take offense, but I have to ask, considering the sensitive material.

"No way, sir," they both say while shaking their heads.

"Okay, thanks. No worries about not seeing the person. Steve, call your supervisor and see if we can get the footage pulled from the CCTV. Tell him to call me."

I slap the counter and head back upstairs to call my lawyer.

"Art, sorry to bother you so late at home, but we've got a problem." I explain in detail about the photos and what I know about how they ended up at the front desk of my building.

"There's no note attached to them? Nothing written on the back of any of them or inside the envelope?"

"Nothing," I say, tossing them down onto the coffee table as I begin to pace.

"This doesn't feel right. If someone is going to go to this kind of length to not only follow you but take intimate photos of you in your own home, they clearly want something."

"Yeah, that's what I was thinking too. My guess, it's step one in some elaborate mindfuck of a game they plan to play with me."

Art chuckles. "They picked the wrong man to do something like that to."

"No fucking kidding," I mutter. I'm stressed and pissed and feel like I'm completely out of control in this situation, a feeling I hate.

I can handle endless hours of negotiations, of depositions, of tedious and often monotonous ass-kissing to close a business deal but this—this I'm completely out of my depth.

"What do we do, Art? How do we get ahead of this?"

"You said they're going to pull the camera footage, correct? Let's get our hands on that first. Maybe the idiot was dumb enough to show his face right on the camera."

"And if he didn't?"

"I've got my private investigator on speed dial, Warren. We'll get it sorted. Don't worry. This guy was the one who nailed that state senator last month for insider trading. He's the best in the biz, can find out everything from just a single crumb."

I rub my forehead, a splitting headache starting to make its way from my temples to the base of my neck.

"He better. I can promise you the moment I find out who it is, he's a dead man."

I hang up the phone and slump down in my office chair, an audible exhale coming out in a rush as my back hits the chair. I stare at the photos, my mind racing with not only *who* would do this, but how and why? I live in the penthouse of a high-rise so either they were in a nearby building with a long lens camera or a drone.

The most fucked-up part about this is someone is following Savannah and me, and I have no idea why.

* * *

ALL I CAN THINK about while I get dressed for work and head into the office is the fact that someone out there has naked photos of Savannah, and I have no idea what they're planning on doing with them.

I pace my office floor as I glance at the clock for the fifth time in a minute. I know that she will be getting to the office any minute. I haven't thought of how I'll break this information to her or if I even will. In my mind, the best idea is to not tell her, just let my lawyer handle things with the private investigator and make sure that the photos never see the light of day again. But there's a nagging feeling in the pit of my stomach I can't seem to ignore—one that tells me if I hide this from her and she were to ever find out, it would absolutely ruin everything and I might not get the chance to ever make things right.

I start to strategize a plan on how I can keep an eye on her without giving away the information I have about a possible psycho trying to blackmail me. Part of me wants to tell her that I was wrong in Vegas, that I want to be in a relationship with her, but I know that's not the right thing to do.

It is what I want, more than anything, so it wouldn't be a lie, but me not being able to keep my dick out of her got us into this mess in the first place.

"Good morning." Her voice startles me and I snap my head up to look at her in the doorway.

Her beauty is striking. Her dark hair is down, loose waves cascading over her bare shoulders. She's wearing a cream dress that hits just above her knee, elongating her legs adorned with nude heels. Something shiny catches the sunlight and I notice a delicate gold chain on one ankle, something I've never noticed her wear before.

"Good morning." I smile, diverting my eyes away from the anklet, deciding that it would be inappropriate to ask about it, considering the circumstances.

"I wanted to go over a few things with you before our executive meeting this morning." She offers me a timid smile and it makes me want to grab her and pull her into my arms so I can feel her against me again. I want to tell her that I'll protect her, that I'll find whoever took those photos and destroy them.

"Yeah, absolutely." I motion to one of the chairs and she takes a seat, tucking her hair behind her ear.

"You okay?" she asks and I realize that I'm just staring at her.

"Yes. Yes, sorry." I force a smile. "So what did you want to discuss?"

It's like now that I've put the final nail in our coffin of a relationship, I'm noticing just how much I crave her.

How much I *need* her.

We talk through a few items and she stands to leave.

"Savannah, you have a few minutes?"

She glances at her watch, then slowly sits back down.

"Thank you. I know this is awkward and obviously the office isn't the best place to have a discussion about our—personal life, but I hope it's okay?"

She nods and I continue.

"I wanted to apologize, *again*, for my behavior in Vegas. I reacted poorly and emotionally and I'm sorry."

Her eyes soften as she drops her gaze to her hands before looking back up at me.

"It's okay. I'm sorry too. I—I want you to know I'm not angry with you. I don't hate you." She lets out a nervous laugh. "I actually miss you. I miss just how we were."

Relief washes over me.

"And I don't regret it. I want you to know that, even if it doesn't mean the same to you as it does to me, I don't regret any of it."

"I don't either. I meant what I said last time I apologized." I narrow my gaze on her and it feels like once again the energy between us shifts. "I'll never be sorry for any time spent with you or any physical touch you allowed me."

She blushes and it makes me smile.

"Can I ask what you want?" she says, motioning between us. "Between us, I mean."

I steeple my fingers beneath my chin, letting it rest there momentarily as I think. Do I tell her that what I want is to be with her or do I tell her I want it to go back to how it was before?

On one hand I'd be lying because I don't want it like it was before. I want to hold her in my arms at night. I want to look at her every morning and tell her I love her, but I don't feel I have that right. Not when there's something so heavy hanging over us that she doesn't even know about and I can't figure out how to fix it.

"What I want isn't the important question here; it's what you want," I say, hoping that it can bide me enough time on my end to sort this issue. "So what is it *you* want, Savannah?"

She chews her bottom lip for a second. "Can I think about that and get back to you? For now, let's just say we'll work on being friends." She nods. "And on that note, I'm going to go get some coffee and use the restroom before our executive meeting. You want some coffee?"

"I'm good. Thanks again for hearing me out."

She gives me a wink and walks toward my door, pausing briefly. "By the way, did you have a nice weekend?"

"I did," I say, my eyes averting her gaze because I know I'm full of shit.

"Do anything fun?" Her intonation goes up a little higher than normal and she eyes me suspiciously.

Am I reading into this too much or does she know something? Or hell, maybe it's because I am guilty because I'm fucking lying.

I shake my head, a frown forming on my lips. "Not really. Went to the club, same old."

Her smile stays in place as this time she turns and exits my office.

18

SAVANNAH

I close the door to his office softly and make my way toward the elevator.

Clearly, he's not ready to tell me that he's dating someone and that's okay. I get it. I didn't tell him that tonight I'm going out with Barrett for our first date.

A nervous butterfly flits through my stomach at the thought of my date. I'm honestly not sure if it's excitement, nervousness, or anxiety about the fact that I'm going on a date with a complete stranger.

"Excitement," I say, punching the button to head to the cafeteria for some coffee.

Barrett and I have continued to exchange messages on the dating app. He asked for my number, but I said I didn't feel comfortable till our first date which he totally understood.

After my small—okay, more like colossal—emotional breakdown when I got home from seeing Warren leaving his building with another woman, I'd reached out to Barrett and he'd cheered me up almost instantly.

The small talk over chat felt so welcome and not heavy with the possibility that at any second he'd tell me it was a bad idea.

I can feel myself wanting to move on from Warren, *needing* to move on from him, but my head and heart still can't get on the same page. I made a promise to myself last night when Barrett and I confirmed our date that I would not only be open-minded to him, but I'd allow myself the chance to truly be happy.

If after this date I still feel drawn to tell Warren that I'm in love with him and want the chance to pursue something real with him, then I will. I'll swallow my pride and put myself out there because I'd rather live with heartbreak and disappointment that he doesn't feel the same way, than live with regret of never being honest with him and myself.

* * *

I SNAP a photo of myself in my floor-length mirror and send it to Callie.

Me: *How do I look? First date appropriate?*

I don't know why but I'm suddenly second-guessing my choice of the flowery, off-the-shoulder top and high-waisted mint-green pants.

Callie: *Adorable! Says you're flirty and fun and approachable but that you also have class and a little sexy side. Where are you going? Send me the pin.*

I laugh at her response.

Me: *The Pour House Wine Bar. I'll send you the pin when I get there.*

I spritz myself with perfume and grab my clutch, double-checking our message log to make sure he isn't flaking on me, but he's not. In fact, there's a cute little note from him with the winky smiley face.

Can't wait to finally meet you! See you soon.

I hold my breath for what feels like the entire Uber ride to the bar. I walk inside and glance around the room, spotting a tall, handsome blond guy with a crooked smile and a subtle wave.

A smile burst across my lips as I make my way over to a small corner booth.

"Barrett?"

"It's me." He smiles as he extracts himself from his seat and stands to give me an awkward half hug and handshake. "Sorry, I never want to overstep boundaries."

"No apology necessary. That's super nice of you to care about that."

We take a seat and I can feel him nervously staring at me.

"I'm sorry again, but you are *way* more stunning than I thought possible. Seriously, not to be weird, but you were gorgeous in your photos so in real life it's just like—" He makes a fake explosion sound and demonstrates with his hands. "Wow."

"Thank you." I feel my cheeks warm. "Anyone ever tell you that you look like Chris Evans?"

He chuckles, his head bobbing up and down. "A time or two."

And just like that we flow into conversation like we've know each other for months. We order a bottle of wine for the table and a few appetizers to get started.

"So what's your take on online dating?"

I shrug. "Honestly, you're only my second online date and the first one didn't really last as a full date."

"Second ever?"

"Ever," I repeat.

"Damn, I feel honored." He touches his hand softly to his chest. "How'd you get lucky enough to avoid it this long?"

"Well, I've been fortunate enough to meet people organically. I'm a relationship kind of girl, always have been. Sorry if that scares you, but I'm not saying I'm looking for commitment tomorrow or anything just—yeah." I can feel nervous energy start to build. "Anyway, I had a long-term relationship through college and then two after. No major drama about how they ended, just not the right fit, I guess. What about you?"

He takes a sip of his wine, his eyebrows shooting up at the first taste. "Wow, this is great. I had a few long-term relationships as well that didn't work out so about a year ago, I decided the millennial thing to do was get on the apps."

His face tells me it hasn't been a fun ride. "That bad, huh?"

He just shakes his head before taking another drink of wine. "It's just—nobody is who they say they are it feels like. And don't take this as a personal attack; I just mean in my experience so far. It's like you meet someone, things seem to go well, and then bam, they show their crazy a few weeks in and you feel like the rug was ripped out from under you. I dunno, maybe the same thing would happen if I met someone organically, but it just feels like online is a lawless free-for-all at times."

"Makes you wonder what our parents would have said if we'd told them when they were our age that this is what dating would be like in the future."

"Right? I'd love to be able to talk to my mom about things now. I just—" He gets a far-off look in his eye for a moment. "I just wish I could meet someone the way my parents met, ya know?"

I try to sympathize, but the reality is I don't have that same desire or understanding. My parents met in a trap house so they weren't exactly America's sweethearts.

"How'd your parents meet?" I ask.

"At a bookstore actually. Mom was working the counter and my dad came in to get a book he needed for college. He says it was love at first sight, but Mom always said, 'I made him work for it.' Dad was twenty at the time and Mom was nineteen. They only dated for maybe six months before they got married."

"Sounds like it was meant to be, a true love story."

"Yeah, that's what Dad always said. He was devastated when she passed away. I thought he'd never come out of it, honestly."

Sadness fills his eyes as he reaches for the bottle to top off his glass.

"More?" He gestures with it toward me, but I shake my head.

"So did your dad remarry?"

He nods. "He did. His wife actually just left him."

"Oh," I gasp. "That is awful, your poor dad." I reach my hand across the table for his. He looks up at me as he wraps his fingers around my hand. I watch the gesture; it's small but sweet. I want to feel something, excitement, electricity, but there's only the warmth of his skin against mine.

"Yeah, he, uh…" He clears his throat and looks away from me. "He unfortunately just lost his job and it caused a pretty major issue for his wife and she couldn't handle it all so she bailed. Just like that."

He lets out a bitter laugh and something flashes across his face that leaves me feeling uneasy, but I tell myself not to fixate on it. His family has been through so much; I can imagine he has every right to feel angry at the universe.

"I'm sorry. Dammit, listen to me over here being a complete downer on our first date." He grabs my hand again and gives it a squeeze. "Tell me more about *you*."

"Nothing too exciting, I'm afraid. I love my job and I've worked really hard to get where I'm at. Sacrificed some things like marriage and kids and all that I suppose, but I don't regret it. I'm good at what I do, and I've wanted this career since as long as I can remember."

"Good for you. Where do you work?"

I hesitate, wondering if I should divulge personal information so soon, but I can't stay guarded forever if I'm hoping to meet someone.

"Baxley Technologies. It's over on—"

"Baxley, huh? Oh, I know where that's located; everyone knows that building." He offers a genuine smile. "I'm impressed. I hear that place is like a vault, hard to break into and like zero turnover."

I'm intrigued by his response. "Did you apply there or work there before?"

"Me? Nah." He shakes his head. "Just heard about it, ya know, being in the industry and all. Think a buddy of mine interviewed there right out of college a few years back. You like it?"

"I do, a lot."

"You work with the old man ever?"

"Old man?" I'm confused.

"Yeah, Baxley."

"Oh." I laugh. Warren would *love* to hear he's being referred to as an old man. "Yes, I do work very closely with him. He'd get a kick out of you calling him an old man."

I imagine what his response would be. Depends what mood I catch him in, but I can imagine it would either be a low chuckle followed by him agreeing that he's an old man or he'd make some innuendo about if I thought he was an old man and that maybe he should prove me wrong.

I feel a flush run over my body and creep up my neck slowly at the mere thought of Warren. I wonder what it would feel like to sit across from him on a date. Making small talk as we sip wine and flirt. Knowing that when I leave, I'm going home with him. With the anticipation of what he plans to do to me hanging heavy in the air.

"Where'd you go?"

I snap my head up, Barrett's voice sounding almost distant as I realize I completely zoned out.

"Sorry, just got thinking about a work thing." I wave my hand in the air as if to say it's nothing important.

"Must be *some* work thing to get that look on your face." He eyes me and I let out a nervous laugh before changing the subject.

"So we both admit to being workaholics, it seems. What do you like to do for fun?"

"Fun? What's that?" He laughs. "I feel like I'm always on the move with work, flying here, meeting with people there. When I do get the chance to unwind, I'm kind of a big homebody. I really like my condo and I'm a huge fan of just staying in with a good book or a TV show I'm binging and hiding away from the world."

"Now that sounds like music to my ears. That's always been a bit of a stressor in my past relationships. Because I do work so much, I don't tend to have much of a social life and I actually like it that way. I like to see my friends and I'm always down for a brunch on the weekend or a Cubbies game, but going out three times during the workweek? I can't."

"Going out during the workweek? That's insanity." He laughs mockingly since here we are out on a Monday night together.

"I didn't mean this, sorry." He brushes it off. "Just going out to clubs and bars several times a week isn't my scene. Sometimes I feel like the oldest thirty-year-old alive. I'm not into social media," I begin ticking off things. "I enjoy it, watching stuff and whatnot, but I don't post anything. I never know which celebrity is the hot new person. I feel like I'm five years behind on TV shows."

"Here's to us being in our early thirties, going on fifty." He raises his glass and I join him.

We spend the next hour talking about anything and everything. It feels nice, easy.

Exactly like it did with Easton... and Nick... and Ford.

"So, do I get to ask for your number now?" Barrett leans against the railing outside the wine bar as I wait for my ride.

"You mean I didn't bore you away from wanting a second date?"

He steps closer to me, his hand coming up to cup my cheek as he leans in. "You couldn't get rid of me if you tried."

I smile and grab his phone, entering my number and sending myself a text so I have his.

"Text me when you get home safe, Savannah." He holds my hand as slide into the back seat of the Uber, tugging on it so I look back up at him. "And thanks for tonight. I had a great time."

He shuts the door and I turn around to see him disappear as we drive away.

A small pit forms in my stomach and I realize that I have a pattern. I go for the guy who's nice and sweet, the one I know is *safe*, but who, in reality, I have no dynamic attraction to—no insatiable desire—like I do for Warren.

I hate this. I feel lost and guilty. I feel like a liar—lying to myself about what I want from Warren, lying to Barrett about being interested in him even though I want to be more than anything. I want to want him; that has to count for something, right?

Isn't this what I'm *supposed* to want? An age-appropriate man who has his shit together? Instead, I'm left daydreaming about an emotionally unavailable, potential daddy issue manifestation that has most likely ruined my ability to ever come with another man again.

After returning home, I send a text to Barrett to let him know I made it home and thank him for a lovely date.

I barely have the energy to strip out of my clothes, shower, and crawl into bed where I pray that a solid night's sleep will have me waking up tomorrow refreshed with clarity on what I should do.

* * *

IT'S 6:38 P.M. I know because I've been checking the time every minute, on the minute for thirty-eight minutes.

I open my office door and peek my head into the hallway. The almost silent hum of the air-conditioning is the only sound.

I check my messenger and see that Warren is still listed as available. I quickly shut down my computer and turn off the lights to my office before grabbing my things and taking the elevator up to his office.

"Hey, got a minute?"

His eyes immediately lift from the paper in his hand to mine.

"For you? Always." It's such a simple answer but accompanied by his adorable smirk and the way his eyes light up when he sees me, it feels like everything.

This. This is the feeling.

That toe-curling, nervous anticipation as you approach the person. The feeling of desire that courses through your veins, hoping, praying that there's even a hint of something in return from them. That secret desire for any reason to touch them.

"How was your day?" I ask as I perch on the edge of the seat across from him, my spine stiff as a board.

He pulls his glasses from his face and slowly folds them. "What's on your mind, Savannah?"

God, the way this man reads me. It's something so—insane yet it sets my entire body ablaze. I love the way he knows me. The way he can be in my presence for mere seconds and already sense my need.

"You asked me yesterday what I wanted or what I hoped would come out of this, between us?" I frame it as a question, but he doesn't say anything, just waits for me to continue. "I know what I want."

"Which is?"

146

"You," I say it confidently, keeping my eyes trained on him, but I can't read his expression.

He stands up slowly, walking over to the window that overlooks the city.

"For how long?" he finally says and it throws me off.

"What do you mean?"

He turns back around and comes to half sit, half lean on his desk, his arms crossing over his chest.

"How long will you want me? Till you and Mr. Dreamboat decide you want to be exclusive? Till you don't need me by your side at some event? Till you get your fill and then what?"

"I—" I'm shocked. He seems cold and callous. "Why can't we keep doing what we were doing? I have feelings for y—"

"You don't," he says curtly.

"Excuse me?"

"Did you have feelings for me before we slept together?"

I stare at him, blinking rapidly, unsure how to answer that. I did, absolutely, but for some reason I'm not so keen on answering truthfully right now, but I do anyway.

"Yes."

"Savannah." He sighs and I know I'm not going to like what he's about to say. "I think you're just confused. I think me indulging in sleeping with you just made everything worse."

"*Confused?*" I want to slap him. How dare he fucking question my feelings for him, especially after everything.

"Yes. Tell me, what role would I play in your life? A continual proposition? A chair filler at your next social event?"

"You motherfucker." I shake my head. "*You* were the one who offered to be my date to the alumni event." I point my finger at him. "I didn't ask you to do that."

"You're right, but then when you told me we could have just one night together which then turned into you immediately dating other people and then offering to bring me as friend to that wedding, you made it pretty clear how you viewed me. I'm the guy you sew your wild oats with, Savannah, the one you fuck till you find forever."

Silence falls between us and I'm seething with anger. I ball my hands into fists and close my eyes to try and regain some composure.

"Is it her?"

His eyes snap to mine, his eyebrows shooting up in surprise. "Her?"

"Don't play dumb, Warren," I say as I fly out of the chair. "Her, the dark-haired woman you were leaving your apartment with on Sunday."

"How?"

I realize I've made a mistake; I look insane.

"I—I was," I stumble. "I was coming over to your place to talk to you, but I got there right as you two were leaving."

"To talk to me or to seduce me again?" I glare at him. Why the hell is he being so cruel?

"What did you need to speak to me about?"

"Nothing, doesn't matter now."

"What you saw was a business dinner. Maria Syler is looking to sell Syler Systems to Baxley Tech. She wanted to talk candidly about things before we move it to the boardroom. I knew her husband for twenty years. It was business, Savannah. Nothing more."

I sink back down in the chair and bury my face in my hands as tears sting my eyes. I hate this. I hate that I feel like I'm a jealous, crazy person.

"Why are you belittling my feelings for you?"

"I'm not trying to honestly, but you're young and you have so much ahead of you that I feel guilty that I've put you in this position to believe that you're—that you have feelings for me because I took advantage of your trust."

"Don't do that," I say, shaking my head. "Don't try to make this seem like it's dirty and wrong because you don't want me anymore. If you don't feel the same way about me, then that's fine, but I don't need pity."

"I'm trying to be open and honest with you right now, Savannah, to tell you what I want and how I feel."

"And what about what I want?" My voice shakes with emotion.

"You asked me yesterday and here I am telling you and you're just shooting it down, invalidating anything that I feel for you, as if it's not real." I wipe furiously at the tears that have begun to fall one after the other.

I see his face soften and it's like he's telling me what he thinks he should tell me, but it's not what he wants.

"How are things with Barrett?"

"What does that have to do with anything?" I bite.

"He's a good match for you; you even said it. I just don't want you passing up something that's good for you, something that's maybe what is meant to be because you're hung up on me."

"*Hung up on?*" I shake my head and stand up from the chair in his office. I won't do this. I won't beg him to believe me. I won't beg for a second chance.

"Thank you for your time. I promise I won't bother you with my silly little problems again." I walk to the door without another word and leave.

This was a mistake.

Clearly, I was wrong about Warren Baxley.

19

WARREN

I'm in love with Savannah.

Head over heels, one hundred percent in love. Call me childish or pathetic or whatever, but I don't want *feelings*. I don't want to be her date when it's convenient. I don't want to fuck her when she's feeling in the mood.

I want all of her. Unconditionally. And I refuse to settle for anything less.

I'm not saying she can't develop a deeper sense of love or feelings for me, but right now, she's lost and confused whether she realizes it or not. It was only a few short months ago that she thought Easton might propose and she seemed willing to say yes.

For as much as I want to run after her right now and tell her all this, get her to realize that I'm the man she wants—needs—my mind is elsewhere.

Savannah's words echo in my head. *"I was coming over to your place to talk to you, but I got there right as you two were leaving."*

I reach down into my desk drawer and pull out the photos in the envelope. I look through them again till I get to the last two which were taken outside my building on Sunday. I look a little closer, but I don't see anything that would give away who took the photos.

I toss them back on my desk and run my hands over my face. My stomach churns as a cold chill runs through my body when I realize that whoever took these photos only got them because they were most likely following Savannah.

"Shit," I mutter as I grab my phone and call my lawyer.

"Hey, Warren. I was just emailing you actually. Got the footage from your lobby, but I don't think you're going to like it."

I wake up my computer and go straight to my inbox.

"The image doesn't give much away since he was wearing a hood over a baseball cap, gloves, and big sunglasses."

"Fuck!" I shout as I pull up the video. I squint, bringing my face to the screen, but it doesn't help.

"I'm sorry, Warren. But my investigator is working it. He says he has a guy that can access all the CCTV footage around your building for blocks so if this guy ever removes his glasses or hat while walking away from your building, we'll have him."

"How long will that take?"

"Not sure, could be a few days yet, maybe a week."

I sink back down in my chair and let my head fall back.

"Warren?"

"Yeah." I sit back up and try to imagine who would do this.

"You have any enemies? I know that's a loaded question when you're someone like you, but anyone you can think of who would want revenge?"

I run my hand slowly over the smooth wood grain of my desk. There's only one man I can think of who would stoop to something so low, so fucking vile.

"Yeah," I say slowly. "I can think of someone."

I hang up with Art and print out the video stills from the emails. I grab my keys, making my way down to the parking garage. I whip into traffic, cutting someone off in the process. I throw my hand up to apologize, but I'm met with a honking horn and the other driver flipping me the bird.

I navigate through the city traffic, heading out to the suburbs at a reckless speed. I'm white-knuckling the steering wheel. My blood pressure feels like it's about to blow through the roof. Finally, I'm pulling into the gated community in Hinsdale.

"Hey, Mr. Baxley." Jerry's face lights up, his bulbous cheeks squeezing his eyes almost shut as he smiles at me. "Haven't seen you out here in a while. How ya been?"

"Hey, Jerry. Been good, busy." I give him a quick smile. "Sorry, I'm in a bit of a rush tonight."

"Oh, no worries." He presses the button to raise the gate, allowing me to enter the subdivision.

I give him a curt nod as I navigate away from the booth, taking the first right and following it as it wraps all the way around the back of the community.

I put my car in park, leaning forward to look through the windshield. The lights are on. I walk to the front door and ring the doorbell, then pound mercilessly on the door.

"Open the fucking door, Eric. I know you're in there!" I shout, not caring if the neighbors hear me or not. I bang harder, my fist beginning to sting as the front door finally opens and I'm greeted by a disheveled and bearded Eric Oliver.

"The fuck is your problem, Warren?"

I push past him and enter the house. "Don't play coy with me, Eric. You know why I'm here."

I look down his body and notice the stained-up bathrobe that hangs limply from his frail-looking body. His usually clean-shaven face has a few weeks of growth, his white hair sticking up in every direction.

"To kick me while I'm down? Firing me for that cunt wasn't good enough?"

I step toward him but clench my fists instead, reminding myself that he isn't worth it.

"I know you had something to do with it, Eric, and I won't just roll over and let you get away with it. You've gone too fucking far this time." I spit the words right in his face as I tower over him, shoving my index finger into his chest.

"You wanna clue me in on whatever the hell you're accusing me of, tough guy?"

I didn't bring the photos. I won't give him the satisfaction of looking at them in front of me. Instead, I reach into my pocket and pull out the stills of the man who left the envelope in my building.

"That's Kane. You and I both know it. He took the photos and left them at my building."

"What photos?" He grabs the photo and stares at it before handing it back to me as he rolls his eyes. "Oh, please. That looks like any white man off the street. That all the evidence you got?"

I stare at him, considering lying and saying that's not all the evidence I have. That we have images of him walking away from my building with his disguise removed, but I decide to hold on to that till I have proof.

"You won't get away with this. Even if I never have enough proof to press charges, I'll fucking destroy not only you but your worthless son and your entire filthy bloodline."

Eric's lips curl into a nasty snarl before he erupts into laughter.

"Look at me. I'm in a fucking bathrobe and pajamas that I've been living in for weeks. After you fired me, Bailey left me. You think I give a fuck what you do to me?"

"You mean the twenty-two-year-old wife you met a month before you married her left? Shocking. And don't play that *woe is me* bullshit card; we both know you've got something brewing." I tap my temple. "Besides, I'm sure you'll be grooming wife number five here soon."

His shoulders tense and he narrows his gaze at me. "You better watch your tone with me, boy. You might be Warren Baxley to the rest of the world, but you'll always be an overgrown shit that's too big for his britches to me."

"Oh, what's the matter, Eric? Don't like it when someone calls you out on your pathetic behavior? Everyone in the industry knows you have to pay women to give you the time of day because not even your own son likes to be around you. Speaking of, where is the bastard? Jetting off to London to go scam some more investors?"

He steps toward me, puffing his chest out. "At least I have a son.

What do you have, Warren? Billions of dollars and an empire? Does that keep you warm at night? Who are you going to leave it to?"

I know he's only trying to get under my skin, but I'll admit, that one hurts. I don't let him see it though; I keep my expression calm and stoic.

"You're right, Eric. I might not be able to pin these photos and stalking charges on you and Kane... yet, but I do know about the investor fraud he has going with this app he's 'developing.' In fact, Riz Malik and I had a very interesting discussion about it."

I watch as his expression changes, his face going white and his mouth dry. I can't keep the smile from my lips as I watch panic seize his entire body.

"You know," I say as I turn and walk back toward his front door. "If I were you, my biggest fear right now wouldn't be Riz; it wouldn't even be the SEC." His eyes grow wide. "Oh, you didn't know they were aware of your little scheme? Well, they are."

A sense of giddy satisfaction courses through my veins as I give him a full, wide smile before narrowing my eyes at him, looking straight into his soul.

"My biggest fear if I were in your shoes—is me."

20

SAVANNAH

"Thanks again. I had a nice time."

I stand on the stoop of my building, Barrett leaning one arm against the wall above my head.

"Yeah? Nice enough time to invite me in?" He runs his nose against mine before pressing his lips to me. The kiss is soft but quickly turns into something more when he shoves his tongue into my mouth, dragging it against my teeth.

"Uh, easy." I laugh a little nervously as my hands press against his chest.

This is our third date. The date some would say is *thee* date. The sex date. But I'm nowhere near ready for that.

"Come on," he says in a whiny tone that isn't having the effect he wants.

"I'm not ready for *that*... yet." I add on the yet part against my better judgment. I hate that I feel I have to say something like that so I didn't risk pissing him off so bad I regret it.

His eyes turn soft. "I'm sorry," he says, stepping back. "I shouldn't push you." His eyes search mine as he reaches for my hands. "I did have an amazing time tonight. You are such an astounding woman; it

155

honestly makes me feel so honored that you'd even give me the time of day."

I smile and I feel a little bad for being so standoffish with him. He has been super nice, and yes, he comes on a little strong, but I've stated my boundaries and he's said he'll respect them. "Well," I say as I shrug one shoulder. "Maybe you could come in for one drink?"

His eyes light up and he pumps his fists in the air like Rocky Balboa. "Yes!" Which makes me laugh.

He follows me inside, looking around my apartment. "You have incredible taste."

"Thanks. How does a Malbec sound?" I ask him over my shoulder as I look through the bottles of wine I have on hand.

"Holy shit, a Wrensilva?" He whistles as he crouches down to run his hand over my record player.

"Yeah, it was a gift from my boss actually. He gave it to me on my one-year anniversary at the company," I say as I uncork the wine and pour us each a glass.

"May I?" he asks as he turns around with a record in his hands.

"Yeah, of course." I bring the glasses of wine over to the coffee table and quickly pull out my phone to send Callie a message while he puts the record on.

Me: *Hey, having Barrett over for a drink. First time. Wish me luck! And no, not doing it tonight.*

I slip the phone back into my pocket and smile as he holds out his hand toward me.

"Dance with me." He smiles and my stomach does a little flip. Not the excited kind of flip, the *the last time I danced with someone it was Warren* flip.

I place my hand in his and he pulls me up from the couch. I settle against his body as we begin to leisurely sway to the music.

I tell myself to relax and enjoy it. To stop trying to compare him to Warren or try so badly to feel a spark or sizzle between us with every little interaction. Sometimes love and passion aren't instant; sometimes they grow out of knowing someone.

"That's a pretty nice first-year anniversary gift from your boss."

"Yeah, he's a big giver like that," I say as I close my eyes and rest my face against his shoulder.

"Makes me wonder what you did to get it."

My eyes pop open and I lift my head to look at him. "What's that supposed to mean?"

He shrugs. "Just saying. Most people aren't gifted a ten-thousand-dollar record player for a year of work."

My spine stiffens and a feeling of unease replaces any amount of relaxation that was there a moment ago.

"Feels like you're saying something else." I stop dancing and break our connection.

"Stop. You're being dramatic." He grabs me and pulls me back toward him, but I put my hands up to push him away.

"I'm not being dramatic. You're insinuating—something."

"That you fucked your boss?" His harsh tone startles me, and I shake my head, like maybe I heard him incorrectly.

"Excuse me?"

"Well, did you?"

"That's wildly inappropriate," I say, reaching for my wine and taking a drink.

"It's only inappropriate if you did it. Did you fuck him?"

My mouth goes dry, and I feel panic start to well up in my chest. The almost maniacal smile that's on his lips is scaring me.

"That's none of your business and I'm not answering any questions like that. I think you need to leave."

"Oh, come on, Savannah." He grabs my hand, but I jerk it away. His eyes go from playful to angry in a flash.

"Ya know," he says loudly. "If you're unwilling to answer a simple question about fucking your boss, it tells me that you did." He starts to laugh maniacally. "Which is insane because you'll fuck an old man, but you won't even touch me, a solid ten who has fifteen years on the guy."

His face looks clown-like. Like something you'd see in a horror film before the killer starts chasing you around with an ax.

I slide my hand into my pocket, clutching my phone, my hand on the side button that will call the police if I hold it down.

"I said I think you need to leave." I repeat the words slowly and deliberately.

"Or what?" He takes a step forward, but I retreat just as quickly. He smiles again. He likes this. Toying with me, taunting me. Scaring me.

"Relax, Savannah. You're not worth it," he mutters as he reaches down and grabs his keys. He goes to walk past me but then grabs me around my neck before kissing me violently.

"A little something to remember me by." I try to pull back, but he squeezes harder. "You're gonna fucking regret this."

His threat hangs heavy in the air as he whips my door open, then slams it behind him. I scurry over to the door and lock the deadbolt, my heart about to thump through my chest as I sink down to the floor.

* * *

"HE SAID WHAT?" Callie's jaw is practically on the floor as she leans across the table. "Savannah, that's a threat; you need to go to the police."

"And tell them what? That my date got mad at me that I wouldn't sleep with him?" I shake my head as I push the salad around my bowl. "The cops won't do anything. They can't unless he *actually* does something to me. So messed up."

"Fine, tell Warren about it."

I look up from my salad at her to see if she's joking but the firmly planted arms folded over her chest tell me she's not.

"Tell Warren? It's been two weeks since our little episode in his office and he barely looks at me. He's not going to do shit."

She rolls her eyes. "Please, that man is in love with you, and he fired that dick that was like his mentor or whatever without a second thought. He'll handle this."

He probably would actually, but I'm not about to go running back to him to fight my battles. "Can you imagine? Hey, Warren, so that guy I was seeing that I told you checked the boxes, yeah, he threatened me, then kissed me against my will. I'm sure that would go over like a lead balloon. It's embarrassing."

"What's this guy's name again? Barrett Westmore? What did you find out about him when you searched him?"

"Searched him?" I take a drink of my lemonade.

"Yeah, like his social media?" I stare at her blankly. "Oh God. You did look him up before going out with him, right? Come on, Savannah, that's Dating 101 these days."

"I didn't know. I swear I just didn't even think about that."

She's buried in her phone already, tapping furiously with her thumbs.

"Hmm. Weird."

"What?" I strain my neck over the table trying to see what she's looking at.

"I can't find anything on this guy. No social media whatsoever. There's a few other Barrett Westmores in the Chicagoland area, but the youngest is fifty-four."

I shrug. "Who knows, maybe he's like me and doesn't have any social media. Who cares anyway, Cal; he's gone and I'm not seeing him again."

I stand up and toss my trash into a nearby wastebasket.

"I'm going to stop in the bakery around the corner. It was mine and Easton's little Sunday spot. I haven't been back since we broke up and I'd kill for one of their oatmeal raisin cookies."

She pats her belly. "I would, but I have to fit into that maid of honor dress for Tessa's wedding. Thanks for lunch, babe." She kisses me on the cheek and takes off down the street.

The bell above the bakery door rings when I step inside. The warm sugary scent hits me instantly, taking me back in time to lazy, easy Sundays.

"Miss Savannah!" Enrique, the owner, pops up from behind the counter with a huge smile on his face. "How are you?"

I smile. It's so good to see him. "Hey, Enrique. I had to cut back," I lie and he laughs. We spend a few moments catching up before he

159

steps aside to assist a long line of kids that come in holding each other's hands with a few adults dispersed between them.

I order my oatmeal cookie and tell Enrique bye as I make my way toward the door. I'm looking down at my feet when I open the door and bump into someone.

"Oh, sorry about tha—Easton?" I do a double take when I realize who I just ran into.

"Savannah!" His arms instinctively shoot out and wrap around me, pulling me in for the tightest hug.

"I'd ask what you're doing here, but duh." He laughs, motioning to the bakery.

"Yeah, got a craving," I say, holding up the giant cookie. "How are you?"

"Here," he says, motioning for us to step outside and away from the foot traffic coming in and out of the doorway. "You got a few minutes?"

"Yeah, I was just going to head back home. You want half of this? I feel like these things have gotten enormous."

"Sure, walk and talk?" he says as I break the cookie in half and hand it to him.

"So, how's life been?"

"Good." He nods as he chews. "Nothing too crazy or exciting. Working a lot and playing in this kickball league that Jason started."

I laugh. "You guys finally did it!" He and Jason had been talking about starting their own kickball league for months.

"Yeah, it's a blast. You should come watch us play. Might convince you to join." He nudges my shoulder. "So, what about you? How's work? You dating anyone?"

I let out a heavy sigh. "Work is good, been busy, but you know that. Dating, what can I say?"

"That bad for you too, huh?" I nod. "So, we're both single."

A comforting silence settles between us as we aimlessly wander through the streets of Chicago. It feels just like the old days.

"Hey." I turn my face toward him. "You ever think that maybe"—he stops walking—"maybe I made a mistake?"

That makes me stop too. "A mistake? Like ending things between us?" He nods. "Oh, I dunno. I did at first for sure, but then I guess I kind of chalked it up to the fact that we're better as friends. Why do you ask?"

He finishes his cookie and starts walking again. "I guess seeing everyone else around us get married."

"Maybe it's just that we haven't found the right people yet so we naturally want to look back on who we were with previously because they were safe, like a childhood blanket that we used for comfort."

He laughs and loops his arm around my neck. "I've missed you, Savannah. You're always so smart. I think you're probably right on this one, just like you always are."

"So can we be friends then?" I wrap an arm around his waist, and he kisses the top of my head.

"Of course. I think that's what has really made me sad lately, missing your friendship. You always made laugh. No matter what we were doing, you turned it into a good time."

I think about the Black Ties and White Lies masquerade ball this weekend and consider asking him, but then I remember the way Warren threw it back in my face when I asked him to an event as a friend.

"What's with the look? What's on your mind?"

"Oh, nothing," I brush it off, but he stops again and stares at me. "Okay, fine. I have this stupid event this weekend, a masquerade thing for work and I don't have a date."

"Say no more!" He smiles and then bows. "I'm happy to be your date, m'lady."

I laugh and playfully smack him. "It's a masquerade ball, you goof, not a period piece drama."

We both laugh and continue our walk, catching each other up on life and what movies we've seen lately. It feels like old times and gives me hope that even Warren and I will be able to work through things and be friends again someday.

21

WARREN

I scan through the crowd nervously, looking for Savannah.

Most everyone has on a mask so it's harder to recognize them. Maria loops her arm through mine as we make our way across the ballroom floor to the bar.

"White wine and an old-fashioned," I say to the bartender.

"Such a gentleman." Maria smiles at me. "Thanks again for being my date here. I know it was kind of pushed on you by Ester."

"Nonsense. I'm happy to. Especially if we're about to be in business together." We raise our drinks and toast. "Besides, it gives the goblins something to talk about."

We both look over to where a small group of people are doing a shit job of pretending not to look our way. Their heads shift back and forth like a flock of flamingos as they pretend to avert their gaze when they notice us staring at them.

Maria laughs. "No offense to you, Warren, but my days of dating are over. I'm about to be free of all responsibility when this merger goes through, and then I'm jetting off to the South of France."

I tip my glass to her. "Sounds like a dream."

I take a sip of the liquor, the burn slowly dissipating from my throat, through my chest as my eyes land on Savannah. Her back is to me. She's in a floor-length black gown with gold details that are woven throughout. Delicate straps hang off her shoulders. I'd recognize her anywhere.

My mouth suddenly feels dry when I see the man standing next to her snake his hand around her waist.

Who the fuck is that? Mr. Dreamboat?

"Ready to meet a few people?" I extend my arm toward Maria and she obliges.

"Maria, this is Diego, our new CFO. Diego, this is Maria Syler, Syler Systems."

"Maria, yes! I actually just read that fantastic interview with you in *Forbes*."

She smiles sweetly and shakes his hand.

"So Warren tells me you're selling?"

She nods. "I am. And I couldn't be happier."

Diego and Maria instantly immerse themselves in each other's company as my gaze goes in search of Savannah again.

I spot her in the far corner of the room, alone. I take a few steps toward her when I feel someone watching me. I turn to my right and see a tall figure that's fully masked, looking at me, then Savannah. I turn to walk toward the man, but he quickly ducks into a crowd and I brush it off.

I'm making way toward her when her date approaches her again. She's turned now, right toward me so I know there's no going back.

"Savannah, hope you're having a nice weekend," I say as I approach.

She slowly lowers her mask, her bright-blue eyes sparkling against the dark smoky makeup that surrounds them.

"Good evening, Warren." Her tone is flat. A hint of a smile almost appears, but then it's gone. "You remember Easton?"

Easton drops his mask, reaching for my hand enthusiastically as he smiles.

This fucking guy again?

"Easton, yes, I remember you. Pleasure to see you again." It's a lie. I don't want to see this guy ever again. The fact that the last time I did, the tables were turned doesn't go unnoticed. I feel frustrated that somehow, I'm now the man she doesn't want to engage with at an event.

Easton nervously looks between Savannah and me as an awkward moment passes between us.

"I'll go grab us some drinks." He touches Savannah's elbow and she smiles at him as he steps away.

She looks back to me before turning to walk a little farther away from the crowds of people and I follow her. She keeps her back to me and I can't help it; I reach my finger out and gingerly touch the gold strap that hangs off her shoulder.

Goosebumps break out on her skin and she looks over her shoulder at me, but she doesn't pull away or flinch.

"You look—beautiful." I say the words softly as I run my finger up her shoulder. "Are you and him back together?"

This time she shrugs her arm to remove my finger. "I don't think it's really any of your business," she says as she looks across the room toward Maria who is still talking with Diego. She tosses her head back and laughs heartily at something he's said.

"I told you, it's business."

"Right."

"Look at me, Savannah." My tone comes out harsher than I intended, but it gives the desired effect. Her eyes turn toward me. "I'm not dating her. Nothing has happened between me and her and she has zero expectations. We've been very clear with each other that it's purely business."

"I'm not sure why you're telling me this. The reality is we are boss and employee, and you don't owe me any explanation, Warren. You made it very clear in your office what you want things to be like between us."

My eyes fall to her exposed neck, and it takes everything I have not to lean forward and run my tongue against it. To bite down and feel her gasp beneath my touch.

"Don't look at me like that," she says just above a whisper.

"Why, Savannah? Why can't I?" I can't resist, and I reach out and touch her again. I see her eyes flutter and close for a second. "I never said I didn't still want you."

She sighs, her head falling slightly to the side as her eyes close. I lean in and press my lips against her skin; it's hot, begging for me to drag my lips across it, but she steps forward.

"Because I'm not yours, Warren. Don't toy with me; it's cruel." She walks away, not bothering to look back.

The next hour feels like pure torture. Every time I look up from my drink or away from whoever is speaking to me, I find Savannah. It's like I'm being drawn to her.

I hate that I was weak earlier. I want to be strong, but I feel like I'm slowly losing my grip on reality. All I can think about at work is her. All I see when I close my eyes at night is her.

I notice the man again. This time he doesn't seem to see me. He's completely focused on Savannah who is talking with a few people.

Why does he look so familiar?

I turn my attention back to the small group conversing in front of me, but I can't stay focused. Something tells me things are off.

Savannah laughs while she speaks and then excuses herself. I watch as she fidgets with her purse and makes her way across the room toward a long hallway where the restrooms are located. As soon as she rounds the corner and disappears down the corridor, the tall, blond man cuts through the crowd and follows her.

I place my glass down and navigate through the crowd, bumping into a few shoulders along the way.

"Sorry, excuse me."

"Warren, good to see you. Hey, have a qu—"

"Sorry, Richard, in the middle of something, but I'll come find you," I say with my back toward him as I reach the hallway.

It's dark, and my shoes echo as I walk hurriedly, trying to find where Savannah went. I push open the bathroom door.

"Savannah?" I don't hear a response. "Savannah, are you in here?" I repeat but again, no answer.

I hear the sound of heels on the marble floor behind me. That's when I see a large empty room, the door ajar. I open it further to see Savannah standing alone near a massive window with a balcony.

I step inside the room just as the blond-haired man comes into view; this time he's not wearing a mask. He appears practically out of nowhere from the shadows with his arm outstretched. He grabs her elbow, jerking her to face him just as the moon shines through the room and illuminates his face.

"Get your fucking hands off her!" I shout as I push the door open further and step into the room. His head jerks toward me as he pulls her even closer against him.

Panic and confusion mar her face as she looks at the man, but then it turns to recognition. She knows him too.

"Barrett? What? What the hell are you doing here?"

Then it hits me. That's how Kane was able to follow her; that's what his motivation was for blackmailing me... because I fired his father.

I walk slowly toward them, my eyes focused on Kane.

"I'm only going to tell you one more time, Kane. Take your motherfucking hands off her or I'll do it."

He laughs. It's loud and chaotic, bouncing around the walls of the marbled room.

"Who is Kane? How do you know him?"

Fear floods Savannah's voice, her eyes growing wide as they bounce between me and him.

"That's not Barrett, Savannah. That's Kane Oliver, Eric's son."

22

SAVANNAH

"Sorry, sweetheart." Kane winks at me as he tightens the grip on my arm, jerking me in front of his body like a shield.

"I don't understand. Why?" I begin to cry uncontrollably.

"Why? *Why!*" He screams the word in my ear and I flinch. "Because you two destroyed my father. My father who gave everything to you!" He points at Warren who doesn't see fazed. He stands there calmly, his hands in his pockets.

"You'll both pay for this. He has nothing now. His wife left him, his legacy is destroyed, all because you two wanted to fuck and he called you out on it."

Warren tosses his head back and laughs. "You think your dad has nothing? I was just in his multimillion-dollar home in the suburbs. I also noticed his four luxury cars in the driveway. Seems like he's living just fine. Oh," Warren says as he begins to walk closer to us, "and let's not forget I let him leave with a full pension, stock options, and equity. Not that any of that will matter when you're both in prison."

"Prison? You think I'm going to prison? You are! My father is suing you for not only wrongful termination but conspiracy to commit fraud. You seduced her away from Code Red to get intel and then turn around and buy the company."

"What?" I turn my head to look at Kane and jerk my arm away from him. "Nobody seduced me to work at Baxley Tech. I applied for that job and I got it based on my merit, you sexist prick!" I step away from him, my fear slowly turning to rage.

Kane glares at me and hauls his hand back, bringing it down to land square across my cheek. I stumble, stars bursting behind my eyelids as I right myself. Warren lunges at Kane in a blur, grabbing him by the lapels of his coat and lifting him off his feet up against the wall by the window.

"You think I'm scared of a pencil dick little daddy's boy like you?" Warren drags him from the wall and stands him upright before kicking him right in the chest. He tumbles right into the windows, flinging them open and falling back onto the balcony.

"Warren, stop!" I shout, but it's no use.

He reaches down, grabbing a handful of Kane's shirt, dragging him to the edge of the balcony. He grabs his coat again, jerking him up and pressing his back against the railing.

Kane panics, reaching for Warren's arms to grab on to as Warren bends him over the railing.

"Help!" Kane shouts, but it has no effect on Warren.

He grits his teeth, bringing his face inches away from Kane's again.

"You better run home to daddy and ask him about our conversation regarding the SEC and Riz Malik. You think you want to add extortion and blackmail to those charges? I'll make fucking sure you never see the light of day again, and then I'll piss on your fucking corpse when you finally die in federal prison, alone."

"Everyone will know!" Kane shouts as he struggles to pull a packet from his pocket. He tosses it to the ground.

"You *ever* fucking touch the woman I love again, I will kill you." His face is red as he spits the words out, his nose so close to Kane's. I've never seen him like this.

My eyes fall to the papers that have scattered around my feet and that's when I realize they're photos... of me... and Warren. I bend down, trying to get my eyes to focus on the images of us, naked, wrapped around each other, but my head begins to feel dizzy. The room spins and it sounds like rushing water in my ears.

"Savannah? Savannah, look at me." I can feel Warren's hands on my upper arms, but his muffled voice sounds a million miles away. "Sweetheart, stay with me."

I shake my head and begin to slowly inhale deeply through my nose and exhale through my mouth. I lean against Warren's warm body as he stabilizes me.

"The pictures," I say as tears prick my eyes. A flood of emotion feels like it's about to break through. I drop back down to my knees and scramble to pick them up.

"Let me," he says as he gathers them.

"Did you know?" I ask as I stand back up.

He nods slowly. "He left a copy of them with my doorman a few days ago."

"A few days ago?" My voice comes out louder than expected.

"Yes, and I'm sorry I didn't tell you. I honestly was trying to handle it and make it go away so you never had to know."

I don't know what to feel. I'm angry but I'm not sure it's directed at Warren, or if it should be.

"My lawyer is on it; we have a private investigator getting us proof it was Kane who left them, and obviously now with him admitting to it and his fingerprints all over these, it's pretty much an open-and-shut case, I'd assume."

I cover my face with my hands and begin to cry. Warren pulls me against him, his hand running up and down my back. "Are they on the internet?"

"Honestly, I can't say, sweetie."

"Wait, where is he?" I look around in panic.

"He ran off. It's okay."

I look up at Warren; his eyes look so heavy with sadness.

"It's my fault," he mutters as he steps away from me.

"How?"

"I didn't protect you. I should have noticed what Eric was doing to

169

you. I should have pressed charges against him for sexual harassment. This—" He doesn't finish the sentence, just shakes his head.

"It's not your fault." I step toward him, placing my hands on his back. "I'm the one who would press charges and I didn't want to. It's not worth the risk of everything that goes with trying to do that in our judicial system, and odds are nothing would even be done. I would have only made him angrier. Then who knows what Kane would have done? He might have—"

"Don't," Warren says, turning around to hold me in his arms again. "Don't even think that." He reaches up and wipes away a few remaining tears. "I'm so sorry, Savannah. I should have been there for you." He presses his forehead against mine.

We stand there for a moment, just holding each other. I have no idea what this means for us. I turn to my left and shockingly, nobody is standing there watching us. I fully expected with all the commotion that it would have drawn a crowd. I don't even know how long I've been away from Easton.

I turn back to Warren. "Now what do we do?"

"I've turned over everything to the SEC that I have, and I'll make sure law enforcement has all this stalking and blackmail evidence tonight." His cold facade is back in place. "Stay with Easton tonight and for the forseeable future till this prick is locked up."

He steps away, my arms falling from him as he reaches up to run his hands through his hair and adjust his bow tie before walking a few steps past me. Something makes him stop and reconsider. He turns back around and marches right toward me.

He grabs me behind the neck with one hand, the other coming to my waist as his lips slam against mine. His kiss is hungry, demanding. His lips caress mine hard but gentle at the same time, his tongue commanding mine with every lick and roll of it in my mouth.

Then just as quickly, he steps back without another word and exits the room, leaving me breathless and confused and all alone.

23

WARREN

I don't look back at her when I leave the room.

I know I'll never leave her alone again if I do and I need to get the fuck out of here. I need to go somewhere where I can clear my head, let myself think before I act irrationally and end up in prison for murder.

I walk through the main hall, finding Maria. "Apologies, Maria. I have an emergency and need to leave. Will you be okay?"

"Yes, absolutely. I'll get a ride home; don't worry about it. Everything okay?" She studies my face.

"Yes, it will be. Apologies again and thank you for understanding."

"Of course, I'll be in touch about the next steps."

I nod and quickly make an exit to find my driver and head home. On the way, I send a text to my pilot to ready the chopper to head out to the yacht on Lake Michigan and another to the crew on board.

I pack a bag as soon as I get home, grabbing random items and throwing them inside without thinking about it, then head to the harbor.

By the time I make it on board the yacht, I send an email to my assistant letting her know I'll be unreachable for the foreseeable future.

Then I shut my phone off and grab a bottle of whiskey to drown my sorrows and forget that I've not only hurt the one woman I've ever truly loved, but I failed to protect her.

* * *

"YOU DON'T LOOK GOOD, SON." My lawyer, Art, takes the glass of whiskey I hand him and sits in the deck chair to my left.

"Son? Haven't whipped that one on me since I was in my twenties."

He shrugs. "You haven't been this unhinged since your twenties."

I laugh. "I don't feel great either." I run my hands over the beard that has grown in the last several days. "Is that why you came out here? To lecture me?"

"I think we both know that would be about as successful as trying to bathe a cat."

I turn to look at him, my tumbler paused at my lips. "You trying to say I'm stubborn?"

"Wouldn't dream of it." He smiles. "I just know you're the kind of man that if backed in a corner, you'll always find a way out. Just like your father."

I nod slowly, remembering the first time I met Art at my dad's office. I was a sophomore at Harvard at the time, convinced I was ready to drop out and start my own company like Jobs or Gates. My dad was fit to be tied and brought me to Art to talk some sense into me. It worked.

"You remember how he used to call you up when he felt like he couldn't get through to me?" A smile slowly pulls at the corner of Art's mouth. "Why do you think he did that?"

"Oh, I assume it was the reason most parents do things like that. Sometimes you're too close to it all, need a third party who seems *neutral* to say the same thing your father wanted to say in different words." He winks.

"Is that what you did with Nathaniel?" I ask, referring to his son who has recently taken over his law firm.

He chuckles. "Nathaniel was a special case. The only person that could ever get through to him when he was in a mood was his mother, God rest her soul."

The sun will be setting soon. I look at Art, the corners of his eyes now permanently adorned with wrinkles that crinkle even deeper when he smiles. I'm the only client he still works for since his retirement, but I know it's only a matter of time before I lose that privilege.

"So what's the news?" He looks at me. "Well, I assume you didn't come all the way out on the lake just to reminisce about Dad."

He places his tumbler on the table between our chairs and reaches into his briefcase, pulling out a folder and handing it to me.

"My guy was able to get the security footage from two different buildings down the street from yours that show Kane without his disguise but there's a problem with it."

I crook an eyebrow at him as I leaf through the documents.

"It won't be admissible in court since it was obtained—outside the legal grounds of attainment. Also, it doesn't prove that he was in your building with the photos, just that he was in the neighborhood wearing the same vague outfit of jeans and a dark hoodie."

I look through the stills from the surveillance video. In one, he's practically looking straight at the camera; there's no denying it's Kane Oliver. I slam the photos onto the ground and stand up, gripping the banister of the deck.

"So what now? He just gets away with it?"

"Not quite. You know the SEC has enough on him to put him away for a decade on fraud charges."

"That's not enough." I look over the water, the panicked feeling like he's going to get away with the invasion of mine and Savannah's privacy making my chest tighten. "I want him to fucking burn, Art."

"Now, Warren, I'll advise that you let the law handle this. I know it's not what you want to hear, but he's going to go away, that's guaranteed."

"I know he's going to pay for the fraud charges, Art, but this"—I turn around to look at him—"this isn't okay. He took photos of the wo —of her naked, in my bed, in my home. And there's nothing I can do to rectify that? To make that right by her?"

"The woman you love? Is that what this is about, you on this boat avoiding everyone? Avoiding life?"

I hang my head and sit back down in my chair. "I don't know what to do. I feel like I failed her. I'm sick to my stomach that he was even able to do this, and now he's going to get away with it?"

"How could you have known? How could you have prevented it?"

"I should have seen the way Eric harassed her. I should have made her feel safe, like she could talk to me about it. I should have sent a loud and clear fucking message to that cockroach and destroyed him when I heard the things he said to her, but I didn't, Art." I shake my head and for the first time since my father died, I feel broken.

"What would that have done?"

"If I had stripped him of everything and pressed charges, maybe his void of a son wouldn't have felt it was okay to fuck with her like this, to cross me."

"It's not too late." I look over at him. "If you can convince Savannah to press sexual harassment charges against him and he's found guilty, then according to your company's bylaws, which I wrote, he would forfeit any pension, retirement, or equity in the company."

I sit back and let his words sink in. It might take some convincing with Savannah, but if there's one, there's most likely more at Baxley who he did this to.

"As for Kane, I'm not sure we could convince a judge to give us a warrant of his place based on hearsay. Nobody else was around to hear him confess to taking the photos at the event, correct?"

I shake my head no.

"Without the drone or camera and the original files, we have nothing to go on. Unless..." He pauses.

"Unless?" I press.

"Unless he's stupid enough to do something else."

Art stands up when Kevin appears to tell us the chopper is ready.

"We'll get it figured out. Don't do anything stupid in the meantime. Let me handle the law." He places a hand on either side of my biceps and gives me a sympathetic smile before following Kevin down the deck.

"Oh, one more thing," he says. "Your assistant told me to tell you to get your ass back in the office so she doesn't have to tell Savannah six times a day that you're still not back."

24

SAVANNAH

"He's still not in, Miss Monroe."

Sophie peers over her glasses at the computer screen in front of her, not even bothering to look up at me. I don't take it personally. I know she's stressed with the amount of people who keep asking about him and trying to reschedule this entire last week he's been out.

"Okay, can you—"

"I'll ping you if he shows up or I hear from him."

She finishes my sentence, already knowing since I've asked it every single day this week.

"Thanks."

I check my watch and head to the elevator to meet Easton for lunch.

* * *

"Still no word from him?"

I shake my head no as I swallow down the bite of my sushi.

"So weird. He just ghosted at the Black Ties thing and that was it? No reason?"

I lean back in my chair. "That's not exactly true. I didn't tell you everything."

That piques his interest. "Oh, yeah? Any particular reason why?"

"Warren and I..." I push a piece of ginger around my plate with my chopsticks.

"Were sleeping together? Yeah, I knew. It was pretty obvious when I saw you guys at the alumni fundraiser. The man couldn't keep his hands off you."

My mouth falls open. "You knew? I mean, we actually weren't sleeping together then. Happened shortly after that though."

He laughs. "Savannah, you and I might not have worked out as a couple, but I know you damn well. First of all, the way you talked about him when we were together, you were in awe of him, and honestly, I thought it was just a little crush you'd get over, but it seems like that isn't the case."

"God, yeah, that's pretty accurate," I groan.

"So how did that play into the thing last week? You guys have a big fight?" He shoves a roll into his mouth, his eyes focused on me with anticipation.

"First, let me just say that this is going to be confusing and crazy and just let me get it out."

"Okay, now I'm invested." He wipes his face with his napkin, then sits back in his chair like he's ready for me to spill all the hot gossip.

"Yes, I've had a crush on Warren, but I never expected to act on it. After we broke up, I thought giving casual dating a try would be fun so I made a dating profile."

"Casual dating? You?"

I wave him off. "I know, not my style, but anyway. I matched with a lot of guys, one in particular who seemed like a 'perfect' fit for me, but he was out of the country on business so we said we'd go out when he came back. My dumb ass thought since I couldn't stop thinking about Warren, I'd offer him this one night together and well, he took it. Oh, before this, his CFO, Eric Oliver, that creepy-ass dude I've told you about, he fired him for sexually harassing me at the office."

"You finally told him? 'Bout damn time, Savannah. I've been telling you that for years."

"Not exactly. He did it in front of Warren at his yacht party. He didn't know Warren was standing around the corner. I explained it all to Warren and he was shocked. He had no idea and I think he felt a lot of shame because he felt like he should have picked up on it, noticed it around the office. But yeah, he fired him on the spot that night."

"Damn, good for him. That dude Eric freak out, I bet?"

I grimace. "Yeah, big-time. So Warren and I hooked up a few times, and then it all just got complicated."

"Because it wasn't before?" He laughs.

"I know, I thought I had things under control, but I think I was a touch delusional. So that guy I thought I had potential with online, yeah, he came back and we went out like three or four times total and I never slept with him."

"Why not?"

"I couldn't—you know I'm not good at casual sex. With Warren, I trust him. I've known him for years; we're friends, and obviously I'm attracted to him, but with this guy, I didn't know him. He was very attractive, but when we kissed or he held my hand—sorry, is this weird to hear?"

He bobs his head as if he's unsure. "Meh, no. I want you to be happy."

"Thank you. But yeah, there was no spark or chemistry, it was weird. It felt like my brain knew something subconsciously or like sensed that this guy wasn't right. He pressured me to sleep with him one night and got a little too physical when I said no. He ended up leaving my place and threatened me."

"Holy shit!" He sits up straight. "Did he? I'll kill him."

"No, no, he didn't but it was crazy how his eyes and entire face changed right in front of me. I've always heard people say stuff on those murder mystery shows how they saw evil in someone's eyes and I never understood it till now."

"So where's this piece of shit now?"

"That's the thing, it gets worse. He apparently has been following me or Warren and took photos of us when we were—ya know, being intimate."

"Okay, this is getting out of hand. What the fuck, Savannah? Please tell me this guy is behind bars?"

I shake my head and explain to him the whole situation about who Barrett turned out to be, the photos, how I found out about them, and Warren threatening him at the party in the other room.

"And then he kissed me and stormed off and went on his yacht, I guess." I take a sip of water like all of this is just normal even though Easton's face tells me this is by far the craziest shit I've ever gotten myself into.

"So what's going to happen to him? He's just out there right now and might come for you?"

"I don't think he'd do anything like that, especially not after Warren threatened him. Oh, I almost forgot, Warren mentioned something about the SEC and fraud charges with Bar—er Kane and his dad. I think Warren has enough to put him away so he's probably laying low right now."

"Or maybe that's why Warren's on the lamb, he killed him." We both laugh. "Shit, Savannah, I feel so bad. I had no idea. I just wish—" He leans forward and takes my hands. "Are you okay?"

I let out a puff of air. "Honestly, I have no idea. I weirdly feel numb. When I first saw the blackmail photos or whatever you want to call them, I got dizzy and thought I was going to puke and pass out, but then I just became calm. I know Warren and I have no doubt he'll make sure that this guy pays. I mean, I am a little sick to my stomach thinking that someone has naked photos of me and could post them online."

"Yeah, you are strangely calm about all this. Not that you've ever been the type to fully freak out."

"I think part of it is just knowing there's nothing I can do about it right now. I'm choosing to believe that Warren will make sure it's taken care of. I know with his money and power he can make sure they don't end up online. Besides, I'm not even sure if that was Kane's goal. I think more than anything it was a power move. If he thought he could get them on the internet, it would damage Warren's reputation? I dunno."

"Well, shit." We both stare at each other, neither of us sure what to say. "I guess since we're both being honest, there's something I want to say to you too."

"Oh yeah? Do I need lunchtime saki for this?"

He chuckles. "Maybe, but I doubt it. I want to say something that you might think is bullshit, like I'm just trying to make you feel better after telling me all this, but that's not the case. I mean this."

"You're making me a little nervous."

He smiles and reaches for my hand again. "Savannah, you were my true love. You were the one woman whom I've dated that I felt I could truly be myself with. I felt, and still do, like you won't judge me and you made me feel safe and content in the relationship. I still see you as my best friend."

A lump forms in my throat and I grab a napkin to dab at the corners of my eyes with my free hand. "Okay, now you're making me cry."

He rubs my hand. "I didn't break up with you because I didn't love you; I still love you. I don't think either of us are in love with each other in a non-platonic way and I don't think we have been for some time. Neither of us seemed particularly satisfied or fulfilled in that kind of a relationship with each other."

"You're right. I wasn't ready to see it back then. I think I felt so safe with you that I wanted to be in love with you like we were a long time ago, but we couldn't force it."

"Exactly. I hate the whole *it's not you, it's me* cliché but that is the case. It's not that I didn't want to love you like that, it's just that—" He hangs his head.

"What?"

"I think I'm in love with someone else."

"Oh, that's not what I was expecting. Um, does it go both ways? Are they in love with you?"

"It's Jason."

"Tessa's fiancé's brother Jason? Your best friend?"

"Yup." He releases my hand and leans back in his chair, his eyes nervously searching mine.

"Oh my God." I smile. "Does he know? When did you realize?"

He just shrugs. "I think I've known for a long time but was scared to admit it to myself. I think Jason knows; he just does. There's been some tension, some flirty moments."

"Ohhh, have you guys kissed?"

"Maybe, once. We were both so drunk though and we never talked about it again." He waves it off like it's nothing.

"Don't act like it's nothing! That's huge. I'm so happy for you, Easton. That's all I want for you too, to be happy and loved. This is such exciting and good news; you've made my day honestly."

He stands up and pulls me toward him for a hug. We both stand there, smiling like idiots.

"Are you in love with him?" I pull back to look at Easton. "Warren, I mean?"

"Yeah, I am and it sucks." I laugh. "He said he's in love with me too, or he called me *the woman I love* when he was threatening Kane."

"So what are you going to do about it now? You both can't use the stupid excuse of miscommunication because while you've had months of that, you both know you love each other."

"I know. I just worry about it all working out. I think he feels a lot of guilt when he sees me."

We pay and walk slowly back toward my office.

"So does this mean I'm going to see you as Jason's plus one at the wedding?"

"Tell you what. I'll be brave enough to put it out there to him if you're brave enough to do the same with Warren. No holding back."

I look up at him. "Deal."

I spend the rest of the afternoon and early evening up to my eyeballs in reports and analytics for Syler Systems. My eyes have grown dry and red from staring at my screen for too long.

I shut down my computer and head to the elevator, punching the button for the garage. I close my eyes and lean back against the wall till the elevator dings and the doors slide open.

I reach into my purse, digging around for my keys as the echo of my heels clicking across the cement bounces off the garage walls. I finally find them and look up to point them at my car to unlock it when I see Warren leaning casually against my car.

"Hey." The word comes out breathier than I mean it to, but he takes my breath away.

He's in a crisp white shirt underneath a charcoal suit. His hair is styled perfectly. As silly as it sounds, I think that over the last week, I forgot just how good-looking this man is, the way he instantly sends my heart into overdrive and my thoughts into the gutter.

He pushes off the car and walks right up to me. I tip my chin upward to meet his gaze as he towers over me, the scent of sandalwood hitting my nostrils and making my head swim.

"Hello, beautiful. We need to talk."

25

WARREN

I watch shock turn into recognition and then a warm smile slowly spreads across her face as she comes to a halt in front of me.

Her brows slowly stitch together, a *V* forming between them, and she pulls her hand back and smacks my chest.

"Where the hell have you been?"

"On my yacht."

"Sulking?"

I chuckle, and she plants her hands on her hips.

"More like thinking and strategizing."

"About?"

I don't answer. I just let my gaze take her in. My eyes roam her face and it's like I'm noticing certain things about her for the first time. Every time I look at her, my heart stops and it feels like the air is sucked from my lungs. Like I'm seeing her for the first time and it's everything I could ever hope for, all at once.

"You're angry with me?" I know she has every right to be, and we certainly didn't leave things on good terms before the whole incident at the Black Ties and White Lies masquerade party.

Her shoulders drop and she releases her hands from the balled-up fists on her hips.

"I'm not. I'm not sure if it's because I'm still processing everything or because there's no point anymore. Being mad at you for not wanting what I want isn't going to solve anything. I'm just happy you're safe and back. You're back, right?"

"I am. There's a lot I want to fill you in on about the photographs and other illegal activities Kane and Eric have been involved in."

"Like?" she asks and I glance over my shoulder when I hear a car start in the distance.

"I went to see Eric. This was right after I received the photos. He denied knowing anything about them and also denied that it was Kane. I didn't have the proof that it was him and what proof I have now won't be admissible in court."

She sighs and rolls her head to the side, readjusting her purse strap.

"Obviously we don't have a warrant to search his place and while the feds will with the SEC, they can't get a warrant specifically for items like a drone or camera in his house. Now, hopefully he's stupid enough to keep the images on his computer which will be seized by the feds since he's going to be brought up on fraud charges."

"Okay, so he'll be going away for fraud, right? I mean there's no way he'll be able to talk his way out of that?"

I nod. "Yes, but I want him charged for what he did to you."

"Warren, as long—"

"No, Savannah. That piece of shit went too far and I won't let him get away with it. I actually just came here from Eric's house for the second time. I told him that if he can convince Kane to hand over the original images on a thumb drive, I'm willing to not pursue legal action."

"But you just said—"

"I know. I lied to him. If Kane hands over that thumb drive, I'm going to make sure the police are there to witness him handing it to me."

"Oh." Realization sinks in. "That's actually an amazing idea."

"It was either that or you would need to press charges against his father." Fear flashes across her face. "Don't worry. I put some feelers out in the company and found out that you're not the only woman he's harassed. Two have come forward so far and are willing to file charges and testify."

Her hand shoots up to cover her mouth. "Oh my God."

"Sick fuck," I mutter as she throws her arms around me unexpectedly, knocking me back a step. "Whoa, you okay?"

I hear her sniff and she nods her head against my chest as her face stays pressed against me.

"Hey, sweetheart, it's okay." I rub her back softly as the sound of a car draws closer. "Hey, look at me."

She pulls back and I use the pad of my thumb to press softly against her cheek, wiping away the tears. Her eyes dart back and forth. I push her hair behind her ear and lean my head down a little further.

I'm so close.

Her pillowy soft lips call to me.

I can't resist. I close the distance and our lips touch just as the sound of a revving engine and squealing tires explode behind us.

I whip around, blinded my someone's headlights right in my line of vision, but it doesn't stop me from realizing what's happening. The car is barreling right toward us.

I grab Savannah around the waist and push her back against her car, shielding her body with my own as the car whips past us and drives out of the garage.

"Give me your keys," I demand.

She's shaking, stumbling with them as she hands them over to me. I unlock the car and push her inside the passenger side as I jog around the back and climb behind the wheel.

"You're coming home with me tonight and staying there till we get this motherfucker put away."

"Who? Was that Kane?"

"I couldn't tell, but who else would it be?"

I throw the car in reverse and pull my phone out as we drive to my building.

"Hey, Kevin. Sorry, but I need you to pull the surveillance footage from the office garage from tonight and send it to me immediately. Thanks."

I hang up and reach for Savannah's trembling hand.

We arrive at my building a short while later.

"Mind if I take a shower? I'm feeling overwhelmed and just want to decompress in that fancy steam shower of yours." She smiles weakly at me.

"Absolutely, take your time. I'll lay out some pajamas for you on my bed and work on dinner." I kiss the top of her head, her hand lingering in mine as she walks away. I'm tempted to tug it so she's pulled back to me, but I can't keep doing this.

I open the fridge and pull out the salmon, asparagus, and potatoes my housekeeper prepared for me earlier. I preheat the oven and toss everything inside before going in search of a pairable wine.

I grab a red, reading over the label when my phone buzzes in my pocket. Kevin's name flashes across the screen.

"Hey, what'd you find?"

"Hey, boss. Pulled the footage like you asked and just emailed it over. It's Kane clear as day; the idiot didn't even bother trying to disguise himself this time."

I walk to my office and sign on to my computer to open the email with the video. I watch as Kane pulls into the garage two hours before he attempted to run us over. His car circles around the garage, then slows and stops behind Savannah's car. He gets out of the car, looking around before walking right up to the driver's side door. He looks through the windows, then circles the car slowly. I lean in closer to the screen to watch his movements, making sure he didn't plant anything on the car, but he never actually touches it. He pulls out his phone, snaps a picture of her license plate, then gets back in his car and drives up to the top level to lie in wait.

"Does he just sit in the car for the next two hours?" I ask Kevin.

"Mostly. He does get back out and stretch. Walks around for a few minutes, then gets back in until about the last fifteen minutes or so when your driver dropped you off."

I fast forward to that part and sure enough, Kane gets out a few times to go check and see that Savannah's car is still in the garage. Kane is turning around to walk back up to his car when my driver pulls in, causing Kane to stop and crouch down. He watches as I exit the vehicle and walk over to Savannah's car to wait for her. He then sprints back to his car.

"My guess is you showing up threw him off. If you hadn't been there, who knows what he might have done. Maybe kidnapped her?"

Anger courses through my body, my stomach becoming nauseated almost instantly.

"Thanks, Kev. I'm going to need you to take this to the police right now. Make sure it gets into Detective Montclair's hands, okay? I'm emailing him now along with Art."

We hang up and I draft an email to the police detective I know on the force. I don't ever use my name and power to sway politicians or government officials, but I do have a few connections, one of which is Detective Montclair, a man I've already been in contact with about the sexual harassment charges pending against Eric Oliver. I make sure I CC my lawyer, Art, and hit send.

By the time I get off the phone with Kevin and dinner is done reheating, Savannah has emerged from my room showered, her hair hanging in wet strands down her back.

"Thanks for the pajamas, again."

"They look good on you." I pull out her chair and she takes a seat.

"This smells amazing."

"Wish I could take the credit."

I pour us each a glass of wine and take a seat as we dig in to the meal.

"I just spoke with Kevin. I watched the garage footage."

"And?" Her fork pauses halfway to her mouth.

"It was Kane, clear as day." She drops her fork and her bottom lip begins to tremble. "Hey, hey." I reach for her hand. "This is actually a good thing."

"How? I feel like I'm never going to be able to sleep again." The pain in her eyes tugs at my heart.

"He fucked up. I emailed the detective I know on the police force

187

and Kevin is taking the footage there now. You can't deny it's him in the video; it's crystal clear, and he tried to run us over, attempted murder at the least. They'll probably go arrest him tonight."

Her eyes soften. "Really?"

"Yes," I say, not knowing for sure if they will tonight, but I need her to know she's safe now. That no matter what happens with all these possible fraud charges, she can rest assured that with this new evidence, Kane Oliver won't be tormenting her any longer.

She pushes back from the table and stands, walking around to my chair and crawling into my lap.

"Thank you," she whispers against my neck, her warm breath coming out in a soft puff against my skin.

I close my eyes, savoring the feeling of her warmth against me.

"We need to talk."

She leans back, her hands resting on my shoulders as she looks at me.

"Okay, let's talk."

"Not like this." My hands rest on her waist. "I can't think straight when you're sitting on my lap."

We stare at one another, my mouth close to hers. I almost lean in and kiss her, but instead I lift her off my lap and help her stand. We both grab our wine and walk to the living room. The sun has completely set, the city still ablaze with lights down below. I hit a switch and turn on a soft light from the settings as she takes a seat on the couch, tucking her feet beneath her.

I stare at her for a moment. She looks so small in my oversized pajamas. She's rolled the waistband of the pants a few times so the hem doesn't drag beneath her feet. My eyes settle on her breasts that sway ever so subtly as she adjusts herself against the back of the couch. She's clearly not wearing a bra, evidenced by her nipples poking against the fabric.

"Why are you looking at me like that?"

I don't respond at first. I pull my lip into my mouth, running my tongue against it as images of my tongue swirling around her rosebud nipples flood my brain. I feel my cock twitch and I close my eyes, willing myself to regain control.

"I can't do this anymore, Savannah."

"Do what?"

"This back and forth. The flirting, the way you—the way you fucking look at me."

Her eyes don't sway from mine.

"How do I look at you?" she asks softly.

I will myself to stay standing right where I'm at.

"Like you know exactly what you're doing. Like you can see every filthy fucking thought I'm having and you want it just as bad."

"What do *you* want, Warren?"

"You, all to myself," I answer without hesitating. I'm done hiding my feelings and pretending I'm okay with a casual fuck here and there. I take a step toward her.

"You told Kane I was the woman you love. Did you mean that?"

"Yes. I'm in love with you, Savannah. I have been—just too afraid to admit it to you or myself."

She's still perched on the couch, her hands folded in her lap as she listens to me. My hands are shoved deep in my pockets to keep from grabbing her.

"That's why I reacted so poorly in Vegas. It's a shitty excuse, especially as an adult who should be able to handle his emotions, but I felt like I was losing you."

Her brows furrow. "Losing me?"

I nod. "I wanted to go, want to go I should say, to your friend's wedding, but I wanted you to want me to go as your date, as your lover. I felt like you were using me, but not in the sense that it was without feelings, just that you wanted me there for different reasons." I shake my head. "I feel like I'm not making any sense."

"You are," she says, sliding her legs out from under her as she stands and walks toward me. "Keep talking." She's standing right in front of me.

"I want it all with you. I want you to be mine, but I know there's a lot we need to work on. I think we both struggled to express what we truly wanted in this relationship and we both had our reasons for doing that. I've been terrified of losing you, of not being enough for you or of abusing the trust you've put into me as your boss and mentor. I know I also betrayed your trust and I need to work on getting that back and being your friend first."

She steps closer, finally placing her hands against my chest and tipping her head up to look at me. Her blue eyes look so vibrant in the dim light of the room, her cheeks flushed with pink.

"You're my best friend; that's never changed. You didn't betray my trust, Warren. Something happened completely out of your control, and since then, you've done everything within your power to rectify it. Please, stop blaming yourself."

I can feel the tension growing thick between us, making it impossible to ignore no matter how hard I try.

"Do you want to know what I want?" I nod my head yes. She stands on her tippy-toes, pressing against me as her lips graze my ear. "I want to be yours, completely yours." And then she says the words I've been dying to hear for three damn years. "I love you."

I hear myself make a low growl-like sound that vibrates through my chest as I clench my hands into fists inside my pockets.

"Why won't you touch me?"

"I'm trying to be good, sweetheart."

"Why?" Her voice is pleading and it shoots straight to my cock.

"Mmm, fuck me. I promised we'd work on being friends first."

She slowly begins to unbutton my shirt, trailing hot kisses down my chest.

"Please don't be good," she whispers as her hands slowly drag down my body, to my waistband where she attempts to undo my belt, but I shoot my hands out of my pockets to grab hers, stilling them.

"Look at me, Savannah." She obeys; her eyes heavy-lidded with desire meet mine. "Are you begging?"

She nods slowly, her teeth biting down on her bottom lip.

"More."

"Please," she says again, and it makes my cock pulse with desire. "Please do all the filthy things you want to me."

SAVANNAH

is eyes darken the moment I say the words.

"Listen to me." He holds my hands in one hand as he tilts my head backward with the other. "We're going to have a serious discussion about things between us when I'm not about to use you as my little fuck toy, understand?"

I nod.

"Say it."

"I understand."

He releases my hands, his own sliding into my hair to tilt my head as his lips overtake mine. He kisses me like he's starving, like he needs the air from my lungs to survive. It's wanton and needy and so delicious it already has my thighs quivering with anticipation as his tongue demands entrance.

I drag my hands back down his stomach, reaching for his belt and finishing what I started. I unzip his pants, sliding my hand beneath the waistband of his underwear and straight to his hard cock.

I'm not shy about my need for him. My hands grip him, stroke him as I kiss him. He moans into my mouth as my thumb grazes the underside of the tip. I feel it jump in my hand and he breaks the kiss.

Without a word he pushes my hands away as he lowers his pants enough to pull his cock free; at the same time he grabs a fistful of my hair and guides me to my knees. I don't need instruction. I lean forward, lips parted, and take him in my mouth. I tilt my head enough that I can watch him. His head is back, eyes closed as he stands there with my head in place. Then he slowly lowers his chin, his eyes finding mine.

"Watch your teeth," he says as he tightens the hold on my hair, then slowly moves his hips forward till his cock hits the back of my throat.

"Keep still just like that." His words are strained. Veins bulge on either side of his neck as he watches himself slide in and out of my mouth. "I'm going to fuck your pretty little mouth for a minute."

I hold still as he continues to thrust his hips, each stroke nearly gagging me, but I remind myself to breathe through my nose and relax my jaw. I can feel his control slipping as his cock grows even harder, but then he releases me, lifting me back to my feet and stuffing himself back in his pants.

"Was that okay? Did I do something wrong?"

"It was too good, baby. I don't want to come yet." He grabs my hand and leads me across the room and down the hall to his bedroom.

He spins me around to face him, his shirt half undone as well as his pants. He reaches down and lifts my shirt over my head, then tosses it on the floor. He tugs the pants down my legs and tosses them with the shirt. Then he stands back up and steps away, looking at me fully naked.

"What are you doing?" I feel my arms start to creep up my body to cover myself.

"Don't," he commands. "Let me look at you." He reaches his hands out and cups both of my breasts, swiping his thumbs over my nipples, eliciting a gasp.

"You are so fucking beautiful." He fondles my breasts, squeezing them together. "I've fantasized about sliding my cock between your tits so many times. Something about seeing my cum marking your smooth skin drives me wild."

He leans down and sucks a nipple into his mouth as he plumps the other breast with his hands, then repeats the process on the other one.

"Lie back on the bed," he commands as he undoes the last few buttons of his shirt and slides it down his arms. I love watching the way his muscles ripple with the movement.

I lie back on the bed and he steps closer. He looks so tempting standing there with his pants undone, slung low on his narrow hips. I let my gaze wander over his sculpted body, the black smattering of hair across his chest that winds its way down his six-pack till it disappears beneath his waistband.

Every little thing about this man drives me insane. The attention to detail he has as he removes his watch. The way his fingers move quickly to undo buttons. He's always in control. Always.

He lifts the material of his pants as he slowly squats down in front of me. I raise myself up on my elbows as I look down my body. He looks back up at me as his hands softly slide up my calves to my knees, pressing my thighs apart.

"I've also fantasized countless times about your taste. I'd watch you cross your tempting legs in your seat as you sat across from me and I would wonder what color your panties were, if they were wet." He runs one finger up my slit and my body tenses. "Fuck, the way your sweet little cunt pulses under my touch. You're practically dripping, baby."

I let my head fall back, hanging between my shoulders as his tongue slides slowly up my folds.

"You taste like heaven. So sweet," he says as he does it again. "I could spend hours buried between your thighs. I'd die a happy man if I only ever tasted you for the rest of my life." This time he buries his face between my thighs and devours me till I come undone against his tongue.

He stands and removes his pants, kicking them aside as he crawls up my body.

"I'm going to try to go slow, sweetheart, to make love to you, but I can't promise I'll be able to honor that." He kisses me, his fingers replacing his tongue as he slides two in and out of me at a leisurely pace. "I'm going to play with you for a bit, okay? I'm going to make you feel so good, baby. Just relax and let me tease you. I want you begging, clawing at me to fuck you."

It already feels like every nerve ending in my body is on high alert, two seconds from firing off as he does exactly what he just said.

His fingers explore every inch of me.

He rubs them against the arch of my foot, then follows the movement with his tongue, dragging it slowly up my arch till my toes curl. I've never been into foot stuff, but holy shit, the way this feels. He lowers the foot and does the same with the other, my body already needing release.

"Please," I pant as he drags the tip of his cock slowly between my folds.

"Please what, Savannah?"

"Please fuck me," I beg as I play with my own nipples, trying to find any sort of relief.

"Okay, sweetheart." He presses into me. "You need to relax for me, baby. Let my cock in."

"Oh God," I moan, already my walls clenching around him so tightly.

"Look at you trying to come on my cock already. You're a greedy little thing, aren't you?" His words are starting to become strained too as he presses in even further. "Just like that, fuuuuck yes!" He fills me completely. He pulls back and slides in again. This time I feel his balls against the underside of my ass as he presses all the way in.

"I'm the only man who gets to fuck you, Savannah. Understand?" He leans over me, propped up on one hand as he begins to quicken his pace. "You're mine." He wraps his hand around my throat, pressing against it as his eyes darken. His hair falls forward over his forehead, and his eyes start to roll back in his head as his hips piston back and forth, his cock slamming into me over and over. He uses the grip around my throat to pull me back down onto his cock with every thrust.

"I'm gonna co—" I don't even get the words out as my orgasm

finds me. "Don't stop," I beg as my nails dig into his biceps and my lungs burn, screaming for more oxygen. He releases my throat and the pleasure builds into something I've never experienced before.

He doesn't stop till I've ridden out every last wave of pleasure, then he pulls out suddenly, climbing over me to press my tits around his cock. His head falls back, and he moans loudly as he pumps his hips fast and erratic, fucking my tits before he spills himself on them.

He's breathing hard, his chest rising and falling in rapid succession as he looks down at my body where he marked me. A naughty smile spreads slowly across his lips.

"Knew you'd look good with my cum on your tits." He reaches down and puts his fingers back inside me. "I'm going to make your pussy feel so good, baby."

"You already have," I murmur as he slides them in and out.

"Oh, that was just the appetizer, baby. I'm going to spend all night with my cock buried deep inside you. Fucking you till you can't move. Reminding you who you belong to."

* * *

I LAY naked across Warren's warm body, both of us still sleepy from what little sleep we actually got last night. He did not exaggerate when he said he was going to spend the night buried inside me.

"Ow," I wince as I move my legs and attempt to sit up.

"Where do you think you're going?" Warren tosses a heavy arm over my torso, pinning me against him.

"I need coffee and a shower."

He nuzzles his nose against my neck. "You need to stay right here."

I shove his arm off me, wriggling free and sliding off the bed to grab the shirt from the night before.

"I have brunch with my friends today in an hour. I'm going down to make coffee. I'll be right back."

"Fine," he mutters, tossing a pillow at me playfully. "I'll go start the shower." He stands up in his fully nude glory. "Unless you want to get in a quickie?" He grabs his half-rigid dick and glides his hand over the shaft.

I'm tempted, so tempted, but even the thought has my body reminding me of the pain I'm already in from last night.

I look him up and down and shrug. "I think coffee would do the trick better."

He lunges forward, but I turn to run just as his hand lands a loud smack against my bare ass.

I fix our coffees and bring them back upstairs where I join Warren for a much-needed relaxing shower. He massages my shoulders with the shower gel, the steam engulfing us both as tension leaves my body. I still have so many questions for Warren, not only about the Kane situation, but about us. I know he said I was his, that he wants me only to himself, but I need to know that wasn't just a fantasy or some in the moment, lustful bullshit.

I dry my hair after the shower, but I don't have any clothes here so Warren has agreed to drive me home so I can do my makeup and hair there before meeting my friends.

"What should I wear?"

I look over at him as I slide my shoes on. "To drive me home? I don't think it really matters, does it?"

"Is this brunch appropriate?" He walks out from behind the closet wall, his arms outstretched. He looks delicious. Dark denim jeans with a casual baby-blue polo and camel-colored boat shoes.

"You look like one of those naughty frat boys from an Ivy League school that's spending a summer on the coast, looking for trouble." I step toward him, running my hands over his biceps. I can't resist; I step up on my tippy-toes and kiss him.

"Mmm, does that mean you're the innocent young woman who's determined to lose her virginity this summer by a positively rakish asshole?"

I giggle. "We should definitely role play that later when I get back. Are you coming over later?"

He smirks. "I'm going with you to brunch. Why do you think I asked if this outfit was appropriate? So yes, I am coming over later since I'll be with you."

I step back. "It's not that I don't want you to come, but is this how things are going to be now? You bossing me around?"

"I am your boss." He smirks and I roll my eyes and step away.

"At work, yes, but this isn't going to fly. I'm not your property, and you're not just going to tell me where I can go or who I can hang out with."

He reaches his arm out and places it firmly behind my head. "You are mine." He points his finger in my chest, then drags it up till it's beneath my chin. "And until Kane is behind bars, I'm tagging along. I'm not telling you who you can hang out with or where you can go. Don't go looking for a fight where there isn't one."

I know it probably goes against every girl power movement and ideal, but when this man tells me I'm his and tells me that he's going with me, it makes me want to fall to my knees and say, *yes, daddy.*

"Okay. Let's get going so I have time to fix all this," I say, motioning to myself.

While he drives us over to my place, I pull out my phone and send a text to the girls.

Me: *Soooo Warren is coming. I'm sorry! I know it's our last brunch before your wedding Tessa, but I'll explain it all later. I promise.*

* * *

I'm NOT sure if Tessa and Callie even realize I'm here. They're both fawning over Warren to the point that it's embarrassing.

"You have a yacht? Like an actual yacht?" Tessa asks in disbelief.

"Yes."

"Do you know Beyoncé and Jay-Z?" Callie asks which makes Warren chuckle.

"Seriously, guys? You could have asked me all these questions about him over the years and save yourselves some embarrassment."

"Hey, I've never met a billionaire before," Tessa says. "Oh, by the way, sorry if this is awkward, Warren, but whatever happened with

Easton? You said you guys were friends again but never told us how that happened."

"Yeah." I look over at Warren. "I actually never told any of you that. Callie, I ran into him that day you and I had lunch and I said I was going into the bakery for a cookie. He came in and we just walked around the city for like hours and talked."

"*Talked?*" Warren gives me a curious look. I feel him slide his hand over my thigh beneath the table.

"Yes. We were both just painfully honest with each other and it was so refreshing. We both talked about how we realized that while we cared for each other, loved each other even, we weren't in love. We weren't fulfilling each other's needs in that capacity."

"Damn, that is some serious growth. I mean it. Cheers to you both because if you can salvage a friendship from a breakup, that is maturity."

"That's why he was with me at the masquerade party." I look over at Warren. "Neither of us want to get back together; there is *zero*," I say, emphasizing the word for everyone at the table, "desire there like that for us. Besides, he told me he had feelings for someone else and I think he's pursuing that, which makes me so happy for him." It's not my place to share any details about Easton's private life beyond that so I'll let him be the one to tell when he's ready.

"Wait, does this mean you're coming to the wedding then as Savannah's plus one?" Tessa asks Warren. "I still have a place setting marked for a date for you."

"Uh, we haven't discussed that actually," I answer nervously, glancing at Warren as I take a sip of my mimosa.

"Yes, I will be coming, as her boyfriend." I feel his hand tighten against my thigh.

I cough which causes the mimosa to almost come out my nose. I grab a napkin and manage to swallow it.

"I didn't realize we agreed to that. What happened to not bossing me around?" I give him a sassy side-eye and he doesn't skip a beat.

"No? I thought you liked when I told you what to do. You certainly did last night."

My mouth falls open, and Tessa and Callie burst into laughter.

"Don't encourage him!" I scold them as his hand moves dangerously higher on my thigh. I try to squeeze them together tighter so he can't get beneath my dress that's trapped between them, but it's a losing battle. He pinches me and I fumble, giving him a chance to get his fingers right up against my panties. He rubs his finger in circles over my clit briefly as he leans in to whisper in my ear.

"The more you deny me, the harder I'm going to fuck you."

Then he removes his hand and downs the rest of his mimosa.

"I'll grab another pitcher from the bar." He stands up and looks down where I'm sitting, dazed. "Sweetheart?" He holds out his hand for me to go with him.

We walk inside, me following behind him like I'm a child in trouble. The bar is busy. He pulls me in front of him and stands behind me, resting his hands on my hips.

"You're a little tease, you know that?" he murmurs in my ear.

"I'm the tease?" I look over my shoulder at him. "You just had your hand against my panties."

"I did, didn't I. Are you wet?" The bartender approaches before I can answer. "Pitcher of mimosas, please." Warren puts in our order, and I take the opportunity to return the favor. I arch my back, pressing my ass right into his crotch and giving it a little wiggle.

He grips my hips harder, trying to still my movements.

"Stop, Savannah."

"You're not the only one who can tease," I say, biting down on my bottom lip as I look back at him. I reach up and brush my hair off my shoulder, pushing the strap off my dress in the process. "Oops."

I don't have time to turn back around before Warren is turning me away from the bar toward the back of the restaurant. He stays practically pressed up against me as he marches us toward the restrooms. He reaches his arm around me, pushing the door open and thrusting me inside before shutting and locking it behind us.

"What have I said about toying with me, Savannah?" He spins me around, placing his hands beneath my ass and hoisting me onto the counter.

"I thought you liked when I was a little slutty for you." I reach out to touch him, but he catches my wrist in his hand, jerking me forward.

"I love when you're a slut for me, baby, but only when I can punish you for it how I like."

He grabs both straps of my dress and pulls them down, my bare breasts bouncing free with the movement.

"No bra, I see?" He shakes his head. "Tsk, tsk. You are a naughty little slut, aren't you?" He bends his head down, biting me, hard. My hand shoots into his hair and I tug on it, but he doesn't relent. When he does pull back, there's a perfect red bite mark on my breast.

"You're mine; don't ever fucking forget that."

He pulls me off the counter, spinning me around and pressing against my lower back to bend me forward. His movements are erratic at best as he fumbles with his belt. When he frees himself, he doesn't even bother with foreplay. He grabs the back of my neck and turns me back around.

"Spit on it," he says with his cock in his hand. I look at him, then back to his dick. "You wanna play a little slut, baby, then spit on my cock so I can fuck you hard."

I've never done this before but it's exciting. I do as he says, then I'm back to being bent over, my panties pushed aside, and he's pressing into me as I plant my hands on the counter to brace myself.

It's hard and fast, rough and painful but in an oh so delicious way. He's grunting, holding me by one shoulder, his other bunching my dress up away from my ass so he can watch. I reach my hands forward, pressing them against the mirror for more leverage as he thrusts into me even harder.

I'm so close. I attempt to say his name but I'm not sure what actually comes out of my mouth. I can feel myself about to lose control when suddenly he stills, a loud grunt echoing through the restroom as he leans over me.

"Did you?" I ask, looking behind me as he pulls out and readjusts himself.

He grabs a paper towel and wipes between my thighs, turning on the water to wash me with a wet towel before readjusting my panties and dress.

"You bastard." I shake my head, and he steps forward, grabbing my chin and kissing me.

"I told you I'm not the type to be toyed with. Maybe next time you'll think twice about teasing me in public."

27

WARREN

I love watching her squirm.

She refuses to look at me, her cheeks flushed pink as we take our seats back at the table.

"Everything okay? They have to actually hand-pick the oranges and squeeze them at the bar?" Callie eyes us both suspiciously.

I slide my hand back under the table to Savannah's thigh and she jumps. "You know Savannah, likes to make sure things are done properly and thoroughly." She smiles tensely at her friends as she tries to pry my hand from her thigh. I squeeze it tighter. "Isn't that right, sweetheart?"

She reaches for her glass and refills it from the fresh pitcher of mimosas. She brings it slowly to her lips, savoring the sweet tanginess before placing the glass back down.

"I dunno, sometimes even the best still can't get the job done right so you have to just do it yourself later."

I can't help but smile as confusion settles over Tessa's face. "Why do I feel like we aren't talking about making mimosas now?"

"Because we aren't," Savannah snaps, leaning forward to take a last bite of her pineapple upside-down pancakes.

I reach my thumb to the corner of her lips where a small dollop of whipped cream sits. I wipe it away, then place my thumb to her lips for her to lick it off. She does, a little too thoroughly. She snakes her tongue out, wrapping it around the tip of my thumb, then closing her lips around it. She sucks and it sends a jolt to my cock. I bite my lip to stifle a moan, but at the last second she bites down, hard. I pull back my thumb; there's a look of warning in her eyes.

Damn, this woman.

"Bottom line is, you can't trust a man to do a job that you can do yourself with a one hundred percent success rate."

She flashes a cocky smile to her friends as she crosses her arms and sits back in her chair.

So that's how we're gonna play it?

"Oh, I don't think that's an accurate statement." I snake my arm around her neck and press the pad of my thumb into the base of it, dragging it slowly back and forth. I see her eyes flutter and she squirms in her seat... again. "In our years together, I don't think I've ever failed to deliver one hundred percent satisfaction in any task. You just haven't learned the value of delayed gratification yet, baby."

I can see the effect my words and the movement of my fingers against her skin are having on her. She's fighting it, trying to pretend that if I spread her right now, I wouldn't find her soaking wet.

"As fun as this weird mindfuckery is that's going on here," Callie says, standing up, "Tessa and I promised Brendan and Patrick that we'd meet them at the golf course."

They both reach for their wallets and pull out cash, but I wave it away. "My treat, ladies."

"Are you sure?" Tessa asks and I insist.

"Thank you so much, Warren, and it really was great to finally meet you." I smile and she realizes she fucked up. She looks at Savannah who's looking at her with an annoyed expression.

"*Finally*?" I say, raising an eyebrow.

"Uh, just that we've all heard about you as her boss and it's finally nice to officially meet you because I know Callie has in the past and in Vegas, well, we didn't actually meet you—"

"Okay, Tess, we get it. You guys have fun and give the boys my love," Savannah says, popping up and hugging both her friends. Callie whispers something in her ear which makes Savannah laugh and playfully smack her.

We walk back to where the car is parked and get inside to head back to Savannah's place. "So what was that about?" I look over at her as I start the car.

"What was what about?"

"Your friends saying it was good to *finally* meet me?" I don't put the car in gear yet. "Do they know about us?"

She gives me a look. "Seriously? You showed up to Vegas and dragged me up to your suite after telling my friends we needed to 'talk' and then kept me all night."

I grin, remembering that night together, but it's quickly soured when I remember how it all fell apart so quickly.

"Do they know about the rest of things between us?"

"Meaning?" She gives me a bit of an exasperated sigh.

"Savannah." I slide my hand on her thigh again.

"Can we please talk about this later? I just want to get back to my place." She turns her body to look out the window.

I don't press the issue for now. I ease the car into traffic and make the drive across town to her building. I put the car in park and turn to ask her once more.

"What's wrong?" I give her thigh a squeeze, but she pushes my hand away. "Hey." I reach across and grab her chin softly so she turns to look at me.

"Oh my God, you are so frustrating!" She throws her hands in the air as she reaches for the door handle, pulling it open and marching around the car toward her building.

"What the hell?" I mutter to myself as I exit the car and lock it, making my way slowly into the building to avoid her tearing my head off. She must have taken the stairs because she's nowhere in the lobby and the elevator is empty as I ride to her floor. When I reach her apartment, I turn the handle and it's unlocked.

"Savannah, sweetheart, what's going on?" I walk down the hall just as she exits the bathroom and crosses the hall into her bedroom, but she ignores me. I take a seat on the end of her bed. She pulls open the drawer on her nightstand and rummages through it, muttering something before slamming it and walking into the closet.

"So I guess we're fighting then?"

Ten seconds later she emerges from her closet with the pink vibrator in hand. She points it at me as she marches past toward the bathroom.

"Like I said, why rely on a man to do a job you can do yourself."

I shoot up and lunge for the toy, but she dodges me, running down the hall and slamming the door behind her just as I reach it.

"Savannah! Open this damn door right now!" I pound against it. "You really think a toy can make you come like I can?" I jiggle the handle. I had fully planned to give her every orgasm she wanted when we got done with brunch; I just wanted to teach her a little lesson in the meantime.

"Guess we'll find out," she shouts through the door. I hear a buzzing sound begin and a slow moan. "Ohhhh."

"Goddammit, Savannah!" I pound on the door harder, not giving a shit if the neighbors can hear. I'm like a man possessed, completely out of control. I pound against the door harder as she moans louder.

"Yes! Yes! Yes!"

I can't take it any longer. I step back and kick the door right below the handle. The wood splinters, sounding like breaking spaghetti as the door flies open.

Savannah jumps, a startled look on her face. She's sitting on the toilet, one leg casually crossed over the other as she holds the vibrator out in one hand. A smile slowly spreads across her face.

"Gotcha."

"You fucking tease." I grab the toy and toss it into the hallway. My cock throbs in my jeans, demanding to break free. I grab her, pulling her to her feet and spinning her around to face the mirror.

I reach down for the hem of her dress and pull it up and over her body in one move, tossing it aside. I grab her thong, twisting it till the fabric tears and falls from her body.

"Put your hands on the counter and don't fucking move."

Sweat beads on my forehead. I unbuckle my belt and slide my zipper down, reaching inside to fist my cock and pull it free. A bead of precum is already on the tip. I swirl it over my head as I crouch down behind Savannah. I spread her ass cheeks, running my tongue between her folds and right up her ass crack.

"Ohhh." She pushes back from the counter, pressing into my tongue.

"Are you going to obey me?" I ask as I drag my tongue slowly up her spine.

"Yes," she says, the word practically a hiss.

"Good girl." I grip a handful of her hair as I position myself at her entrance and press hard. She groans, "But you still need to learn your lesson." I smack her ass hard as I push myself inside her.

I'm filling her, my balls pressed against her. I grip her hair tighter as I grab her shoulder with my other hand, closing my eyes and taking in a deep breath so I don't blow my load already. I rear back, then slide into her again.

"Are you sorry?" I ask, repeating the process, only this time slamming into her a little harder.

"No." She lifts her head to meet my eyes in the mirror. Her eyes are ablaze with desire.

I cock my hand back and bring it down again with a sharp slap. I repeat the process over and over. I pull out, slamming into her, then spanking her.

Our groans and shouts echo through the bathroom as I lose control. My hands fall to her waist as I pull her back onto my cock over and over again, fucking her with everything I have in me. Her hands slip and slide over the counter as she loses grip. Finally, she stretches her arms overhead, pressing them against the wall behind the counter as an orgasm finally brings her relief.

Mine is a minute behind. I shout, digging my fingers into her flesh as I still myself buried deep inside her. My balls jump as I flood her with my release.

We're both silent except for our heavy breathing and the subtle buzzing coming from the floor. I look around for the vibrator and pick it up, bringing it around the front of Savannah to her clit as I slide myself back into her.

"Oh God!" She jumps, then giggles. "I'm so sensitive."

"You want me to stop?"

"N—no." Her giggles turn into moans as I feel her walls clench my cock. She grips the edge of the counter, her mouth hanging open as I press the vibrator to her clit.

I give her two more orgasms in the bathroom before picking her up and carrying her to her bedroom where we spend the next several hours using her toy in all the filthy ways I'd imagined.

"So you ready to answer me?"

She lifts her head lazily, propping it up on an elbow as she flings her leg over me.

"I told my friends about us, yes."

"Just about the sex?"

"No, about everything. They've, uh… they've known I've had a crush on you for a while." She blushes.

"Is that right? Do tell."

"I've always been attracted to you. I think most of Chicago is, but I never thought about it because well, you're my boss obviously, and then as we became friends, I realized that it could ruin everything."

I know that feeling all too well. I reach for her free hand and intertwine our fingers. "So what made you throw caution to the wind and go for it then?"

She shrugs. "Honestly, I'm not sure because I did have a lot of fear about us ruining what we have, but at the same time, I couldn't stop thinking about it. I guess I hoped that if all we did have was one night together, our friendship could handle it, and if it turned into something more between us, then I guess I figured it was worth it to try."

"Were your friends supportive?"

"They were, they are. They're the ones who helped me realize that maybe I wasn't the only one having feelings in our relationship. I think in my stupid mind I'd convinced myself that to you it would be just sex, that as a man you could easily compartmentalize it and it wouldn't affect things."

I laugh. "I wish it was that simple. Maybe if I wasn't crazy about you, I could have done that, but I think the depth of our friendship was proof that my feelings for you were more than just something casual or even professional."

"Yeah, I kind of missed that. I was scared to admit my own feelings to myself. I knew I was in love with you. I knew that what we had, our friendship, was more intimate and special to me than any actual relationship I've had with any other man."

I smile. "Really?"

"Yeah. The other dates I went on, all I could think about was you and not just in a sexual way. I just love spending time with you and I didn't feel that way with others. When Kane kissed me—"

"Whoa, he kissed you?" I sit up.

"Yes," she says slowly, "Nothing more. We just kissed. But I didn't feel anything. No spark, no excitement, absolutely nothing."

I swallow down the jealousy. I have no right to be upset with her for trying to move on; after all, I pushed her to go be with him, before I knew it was Kane, obviously.

"I'm not angry. I was the one who told you he was who you should be with. Was he ever pushy or anything with you?"

She tilts her head down, averting her gaze and my stomach drops. "Savannah?"

"Just once." She explains when he came to her house and tried to seduce her, how he reacted and the threat he casually shouted at her when he left. I can feel anger course through my veins.

I stand up and slide on my pants and grab my shirt.

"Where are you going?"

"I need to go see Detective Montclair and make sure this piece of shit is arrested and locked up tonight."

* * *

"Mr. Baxley, we did arrest him."

"When?"

"This afternoon. He's currently waiting in holding, waiting to be processed, but I have to warn you, with his money and connections, I'm not sure this case will get very far."

That makes me laugh.

"*His* money and *his* connections? First of all, Jim, that's not his money; it's the investors he's defrauded, and the connections? Those are his dad's connections which are people I know. If anyone in this dynamic has money and connections, it's me, but somehow that doesn't seem to matter to you people."

He narrows his gaze and points at me. "Easy, Warren. I'm not saying we aren't going to punish this man within nine tenths of the law, but I'm just saying, be aware of your expectations."

"What about the garage footage Kevin dropped off?"

He looks at me funny. "Garage footage?"

"Yes. I emailed it to you and Kevin dropped it off. It shows Kane clear as day attempting to run Savannah and me over in my own fucking office garage!"

"I didn't get any footage."

"You gotta be fucking kidding me," I mutter as I pull up my sent emails and see it clear as day.

Jim taps around on his computer. "It went to spam. Looking at it now." He clicks the video, his face close to the computer screen. "Okay, yeah, this is pretty damning. This is exactly what we needed."

"No kidding!" I shout in exasperation. "Kevin said you were out when he dropped the footage off so he left it with the officers at the front desk."

"They lose shit all the time; I'll get on them about it."

I shake my head and stand up. "Keep that motherfucker locked up, Jim. I'm heading over to the regional SEC office to check on things. Keep me posted."

I head over to Jackson Street to meet with my contact over at the SEC.

"Terry, got a minute?" I knock on his office door and poke my head inside.

"For you, Warren, absolutely. Come on in." He gestures to a chair across from his desk. "Want some coffee?"

"I'm okay. Just tell me what you've got so far."

"Actually…" He reaches down into a drawer and pulls out a massive folder, then another, and another. "I was just about to call you. We are moving forward with charges now and plan to file a motion this week."

I stand up. "This is your evidence?" I pick up one of the folders and start to flip through the documents.

"This is just what we've gathered from two investors, Warren. There are about fifteen others."

"Fifteen plus investors he defrauded?" I'm in actual shock. I knew Kane and Eric were both arrogant, but this level of fraud is beyond anything I'd imagined. "I'm not sure if I should be impressed or laugh at how ballsy these greedy bastards were. How did nobody catch on earlier?"

Terry shakes his head. "They were smart, Warren. Covered their tracks and sadly, they used your name a lot."

"My name?" I lean forward.

"Everyone knows Eric Oliver was your finance wizard for the last fifteen years. Your reputation has always been well aboveboard so when he backed his son and they both mentioned that you'd offered Kane a position at Baxley and were considering investing yourself, that opened so many doors for them."

I feel sick to my stomach. Not only for the fact that these assholes are risking my reputation, but that they defrauded so many people while they hid behind my name.

"What do I need to do, Terry?"

"Right now? Sit tight. I'll have a few agents to your office this week for some questions, but in the meantime, I need you to do absolutely nothing. Don't try to cowboy this investigation; trust me and the SEC that we will make sure they both end up locked away for a long time."

I stand up. "You better, Terry, or I'll handle this my way."

"Warren, I mean it," he says sternly, pointing a finger at me. "There is one thing you can do that will be a huge asset to the trial."

"What's that?"

"Would you be willing to testify?"

"Absolutely."

28

SAVANNAH

TWO WEEKS LATER...

"I now pronounce you husband and wife. You may kiss the bride."

The small crowd bursts into cheers as Patrick dips Tessa back and kisses her dramatically. When he stands her back up, they grab hands and hold them in the air in triumph.

The wedding was small and intimate, each of them only choosing one person for their wedding party. Callie looks stunning in her lavender bridesmaid dress and Patrick's brother Jason looks handsome in his gray suit.

"Such a beautiful way to end the summer," I say to Tessa as I pull her in for a hug. "You looked stunning and you both look so happy."

"Don't make me cry." She fans her face, her eyes blinking rapidly so she doesn't ruin her wedding makeup. She turns to Warren. "Warren, good to see you here." She gives us both a quick hand squeeze as we move through the line.

The ceremony was held in a beautiful garden in back of the mansion where Tessa's favorite tapas restaurant is housed. It's the location of her and Patrick's first date. A few weeks after they started dating, he admitted to her that he brought her there because he knew she loved sangria and he was hoping that if he ordered a pitcher of it, it would make her enjoy the date even more and agree to a second one.

There's a tented building with glass walls on the grounds where the reception is taking place. Twinkle lights hang from the ceiling in strings that all gather in the center of the ceiling. Outside, the trees are also decorated in lights, and decorative lanterns line the sidewalk that lead to the reception area from the garden.

"To Patrick and Tessa!" Jason, Patrick's brother and best man, lifts his glass and we all follow.

"Seems like things are working out." I nudge Easton who's staring at Jason with a flirty smile on his face.

"Yeah, seems like it. Who would have guessed we'd be seeing each other at our friend's wedding, each with different dates."

I glance back at Warren who flashes me a wink. "Crazy, right. So you two? Are you a couple now?" Easton kicks nervously at nothing with his shoe. "Don't be shy. It is really cute how flirty you two are."

"I came here as his date and we are seeing one another."

"Exclusively?"

He shrugs but I can see he's trying to hide a smile. "Maybe."

"So you guys are boyfriends?" The smile finally bursts through and I clap my hands in excitement. "Oh my God, I'm so happy for you!" I throw my arms around him.

"Stop, you're going to jinx it and your boyfriend is glaring at me." He tries to pull my arms from his neck, but I just hug him tighter.

"Am I going to have to keep an eye on you two?" I spin around as Jason approaches us.

"I'm just so happy for you guys is all." I smile and Jason wraps his arm around Easton, kissing his temple.

"So are we."

The three of us walk over to the table and take a seat. Callie's mouth is on the floor.

"I cannot believe what is happening right now. We're all sitting here in relationships, happy, celebrating love." She starts to fan her face dramatically. "I promised myself I wouldn't cry." It doesn't work; two seconds later she's full-on crying as Brendan rubs her back.

"Sorry. This baby is just ruining my emotions," she says through broken tears. Yup, two days after we went to brunch a couple weeks ago, Callie called Tessa and I over in a panic because she missed her period and was too scared to take a pregnancy test alone.

So, Tessa and I both showed up with a few boxes of tests and sat with Callie as she took all eight of them... which all came back with a big fat positive.

"I still can't believe you're pregnant, and ten weeks pregnant at that without even realizing it."

"I know. We have our twelve-week scan on Monday and I'm so excited but also terrified to see an actual baby on the monitor. Like—how?"

Brendan laughs. "I've got a pretty good idea."

"I was on birth control though. Not that we aren't ecstatic, we have been talking about trying anyway."

"Babe, you took your birth control pills about as regularly as most people floss."

Callie smacks his shoulder and he flinches.

"You take yours regularly, right?" Warren leans in and whispers in my ear.

I smile nervously and reach for my water. "Yeah," I say but a little voice in my head reminds me of at least two times I was very late, like two days late taking my pill during all this stressful shit with Kane and Eric.

"Hmm."

"What?" I say, turning to look at him.

"Just think it might be cute to see a little Savannah running around." He places his hand softly against my lower belly.

"You want a baby?"

His eyes search mine, and then we both stare down at where his hand rests against me. A million thoughts burst through my brain. Thoughts of seeing Warren holding our child, images of me pregnant, my belly swollen. Suddenly my heart feels like it's aching, like it's realizing for the first time how much I want a family with Warren.

"We can talk about it later." He kisses my ear softly. "But right now, let's dance."

He pulls me up from my seat and leads me toward the dance floor, but then instead of stopping, he walks to the back of the room and through a door that takes us back outside to the grounds.

It's still warm out, even though the sun has set. The gentle sounds of crickets echo around us as the door closes and the sounds of the party inside are muffled.

"Here," he says, leading me underneath a massive tree that is glowing with twinkle lights. He pulls out his phone, opening a music app and hitting play. Smooth jazz hums from his phone as he slides it back into his pocket and takes me in his arms.

"It's kind of our little tradition to have a private dance alone."

We sway to the music, Warren's hand still burning a delicious path over my too-warm skin.

"You still make me nervous," I say softly.

"I make you nervous?"

"Mm-hmm, in a good way. I still get goosebumps when you touch me and butterflies."

He smiles and dips his head to kiss me. We stop our movements, Warren's hands coming up to cup my cheeks as he deepens the kiss.

"I'm more in love with you every day," he whispers, his forehead pressing against mine. "You're my entire world, Savannah."

We spend several minutes in each other's arms, neither of saying anything. He spins me around to face the building where the reception is being held. We watch as everyone dances and laughs.

"What kind of wedding do you want?"

I lean my head back against Warren as his arms wrap around me.

"I always thought I'd do the big wedding thing like this but now, I don't think I would."

"No? Why not?"

I shrug. "I don't have any family, you know that, and honestly I just think I want to share the moment with my husband. I think coming back and having a party could be fun to celebrate with friends but the actual wedding part, I just want to be a completely intimate affair."

"Good to know; I'll keep that in mind." He nuzzles my neck.

"Oh, yeah? You think you'll be my husband?"

"I think the real question is, would you be my wife?"

I still in his arms.

"Are you asking?"

"What would you say if I were?"

I spin around and plant my hands on his chest; I can feel his heart thudding just as fast as mine.

"Don't tease me like this."

"I wouldn't dream of teasing you about this, Savannah." My eyes search his for any signs that he's joking, but they're not there.

"What would you say if I asked you?"

"Yes." The word is out of my mouth before I even think about it because the truth is, I don't need to think about it.

He spins me back around to face the building again, one arm wrapping around my body. "So when should we tell them you're going to be my wife?"

Warren's other hand reaches for my left hand as he slowly slides a massive diamond solitaire on my ring finger.

I stare at the ring, my eyes seeing it but my brain still trying to play catch-up.

"Is it too much? When I saw it, I thought of you. It's so delicate yet bold." He holds my hand in his, extending it out in front of us so it catches the light.

"It's—" I'm speechless. I want to cry and run inside and tell everyone but at the same time, I want to savor this moment between us. I feel tears fall over the brim of my eyes.

"Are you okay, sweetheart? Happy tears?" Warren's face is twisted in concern. He spins me around to face him, holding me back to study me.

"Happy tears," I finally say as I smile and jump into his arms. "I can't believe—are you really asking me to marry you?"

He laughs. "Yes, I am."

"How long have you loved me?" My arms are linked around the back of his neck, his hands on my back as we sway beneath the tree.

"For a while now." He's being coy.

"How long?" I pinch his side and he jumps.

"Okay, okay, fine. Honestly, when I think about it, it feels like I've always loved you. I know that's vague but it's the truth. But specifically, I remember that day you fell off your counter, attempting to change a lightbulb." He starts to laugh which makes me laugh.

"Oh God, that day." I shake my head. "I was mortified! Wait, that was when you knew you loved me?"

"No, I knew before then, but that day specifically comes to mind. I know I was already fighting with myself every night for weeks before that."

"Fighting with yourself?"

"Yes, I knew I *shouldn't* want you, that was for sure, but having feelings for you? I knew I was venturing into incredibly dangerous territory. If it had been just lust, I knew I could get over it eventually, but love?" He shakes his head. "I never got over it."

"I'm glad you didn't. Do you think you ever would have pursued something with me had I not propositioned you?"

"I'd like to think I could have remained strong but the reality is, sweetheart, I've been hanging by a thread for so long that it was only a matter of time before it snapped. That day you sat on my desk and poked me with your foot..." He crooks an eyebrow.

"I knew it." I playfully poke his chest. "I could sense some serious tension between us before Eric ruined it."

"Glad it wasn't just me then."

"Would you have made a move if he hadn't walked in?"

"I think so, yes. The moment I swiped my thumb across your foot I was fucked. All I could think about was doing it with my tongue and then dragging it all the way up these lovely legs of yours." He leans in and nuzzles my neck.

"So it seems like we're both madly in love with each other, can't keep our hands off each other, and should have just admitted all this to each other a long time ago."

"I agree. So when are we getting married?"

WARREN

"Where are we going?"

"Don't worry about it; just pack your bags."

I kick back on Savannah's bed as she leans against her closet door.

"Well, that's kind of the point in why I'm asking. I need to know what to pack. You tell me we're going on a three-month long vacation with zero hints." I shrug and she rolls her eyes. "You're infuriating, you know that?"

"Sweetheart, it doesn't matter what you pack. You'll be naked most of the time anyway." I slide off the bed and walk over to her. "It will be warm and sunny with maybe a few cooler evenings." I kiss her on the forehead as she snuggles against me.

"See, was that so hard?" Her hands come to rest softly against my chest, and I notice that they're bare.

"Where's your ring?"

"Oh." She wriggles her fingers. "I don't wear it at work so I took it off this morning and then just forgot to put it back on."

"Are you hiding me, Miss Monroe?"

"No, we just haven't discussed how it's going to be at work. Besides, I haven't told my friends yet."

I spin her around and press her back against the door of her closet. I grab her wrist and pin them above her head. "And why's that?"

"I just haven't had the time. Since the wedding, Tessa's been on her honeymoon and Callie is busy being pregnant, and I've been busy with work."

I press my groin against her, my cock growing more rigid by the second. It aches for relief. I lean into her. "Sounds like excuses to me." I run my tongue up her neck, biting her softly beneath her ear.

"Ahh," she gasps, her body betraying her.

"Maybe you need a little reminder about *who* you belong to?" I slide my hand up her thigh slowly till I reach her sweet, warm center. "Did you do it on purpose, Savannah?"

"No," she whimpers.

"Are you sure you didn't forget your ring just so I'd notice? Just so I'd teach you another lesson?" I glide a single finger over her panties, back and forth slowly.

"Please." The word is a single please, her eyes closed as she strains against my hands, begging for relief.

"So responsive." I slide her panties aside and repeat the same motion with my finger now over her bare pussy. She moans and attempts to thrust her hips forward so my finger slides inside of her.

"I can feel you pulsing, baby," I tease her, swirling my finger over her bud as she begs for release.

"Now," I say, pulling my finger from her. "Get undressed and put your ring on." I slowly lick my finger that is glistening with her juice. "I want to fuck you with it on."

* * *

WE MAKE it to the airport with only minutes to spare.

"Evening, Mr. Baxley."

"Evening, Tom," I say to the pilot, and turning to the copilot, "Pete."

I scheduled for Savannah and me to take an overnight flight on my private jet since we'll be in the air for several hours. We land in Paris in just over nine hours before reaching our final destination in Athens where we'll board my yacht and take a tour of the Mediterranean.

"Apologies we were cutting it close. I had some end-of-the-day business to attend to."

"No worries, sir. We'll be wheels up shortly."

"Some business to attend to?" Savannah gives me a look. "Is that what I am, business?"

We sit opposite each other as we prepare for takeoff.

"Would you rather I tell them I needed to fuck some sense into my wife? That I needed to remind her that she's mine because she conveniently hasn't told her friends and is hiding me at work?"

I try to hide the annoyance in my voice, but I'd be lying if I said it doesn't bother me. I get her fear about how it will look at work, but she's engaged to me, the damn owner of the company.

"That really bothers you, doesn't you?"

I look out the window, avoiding her gaze.

"Baby." She unbuckles her seat belt and slides to her knees, resting her hands on my thighs as she looks up at me. "I'm not hiding you from anyone. I just want some time for just *us*. To enjoy our bubble a little longer before everyone knows and it turns into a big thing. I'm proud to be yours and I want to be your wife more than anything."

I look down at her big doe eyes staring up at me. I reach my hand out and run my thumb over the edge of her jaw.

"Do you trust me to handle it at work?"

"What do you mean? Like telling everyone?"

I nod. "Yes, and just managing responses."

"Yes, but that doesn't mean I'm not still worried about what people will think or say."

"Don't worry about that, sweetheart. Besides, you already worked for me for years and once you say I do, that's your name on that building, not just mine."

She flashes that coy smile. "Oh, I'm taking your last name?"

"Was that a serious question?"

She shrugs. "I haven't given it much thought. A lot of women are hyphenating their last names now."

I feel my brows furrow. "Is that what you want? I'll take your last name if you want. I don't give a shit. I'll change the name of the company if I have to. I just want you to be mine."

"I am yours, Warren. Just because we haven't signed a marriage certificate doesn't change that and neither will a last name. I will gladly take your last name though."

Relief washes over me. "Good, now get your pretty ass up in that seat so we can take off and I can spend the rest of this flight reminding you how good I can make you feel."

She blushes as she looks up at the passing flight attendant. "Discretion," she mouths to me as she fastens her seat belt.

"You think this entire crew doesn't know what I plan to do to you in that bedroom once we're at altitude? Get ready to join the mile high club, baby—several times." My response does little to quell the growing pink that creeps over her skin.

The captain makes the final announcements as we prepare for takeoff.

"Flight time to Paris is eight hours and forty-seven minutes."

Savannah's eyes light up. "Paris? We're going to Paris?"

"That's just the first stop, baby."

Between the hours we spend exploring each other and sleep, the flight time passes quickly. Upon arrival, we deplane and our driver takes us directly to The Four Seasons Hotel George V.

"Holy cow." Savannah's mouth falls open when we enter the grand lobby of the hotel. She looks around, her eyes taking in the detailed paintings and crystal chandelier that hangs in the center of the room. "This is—unreal."

We check in and make our way to the Eiffel Tower Suite. I normally opt for the penthouse, mainly because it affords me privacy, but I want Savannah to experience Paris and I know she'll love this room.

"Here is your room," the bellhop says as he opens the door. "Someone will be up with your bags shortly."

I watch as Savannah takes in the room. She silently walks through the rooms, her eyes dancing from place to place like she's trying to memorize it. She drags her fingertips lazily along the bed linens, then steps into the bathroom where a full soaker tub stands in the middle of the room. The large windows bring in natural light that bounces off the white marble of the room.

"Come here," I say, holding out my hand toward her. She places hers in mine and follows me as I lead her to a large bay window in the corner of the suite. It's adorned with a window seat and a large bouquet of fresh pink peonies on a table next to a chair. "This is why I booked this room."

I pull her to stand in front of me. She gasps when she sees the unobstructed view of the Eiffel Tower in the distance. She's silent.

Ever since I asked her about the little statue she's kept on her desk for years, I've dreamed of being with her when she finally saw it.

"Did you buy that at the base of the Eiffel Tower, one of those tourist shops?" I point to the relic next to her computer. She leans around the screen and looks at it before picking it up and smiling.

"It was a Christmas present from my foster sister, the only Christmas present anyone had ever given me when I was a kid. She and I had watched Funny Face *together one night when we couldn't sleep and I had told her that my dream was to see the Eiffel Tower in person."*

"What do you think?"

"I just can't believe that I'm standing here in the Four Seasons, with a view of the Eiffel Tower. If someone had told me, an orphan with no future, when I was eleven that I'd be experiencing this, I would have laughed." She spins around to face me. "Thank you."

"You deserve it, sweetheart. You deserve the world and I'm going to give it to you."

Paris is everything I'd hoped it would be and more. We spend afternoons walking through the city, enjoying lazy mornings and snacking on macarons and pain au chocolat. We indulge in French wine and picnics by the Seine where we join a group of locals who have gathered for dancing by Pont des Invalides.

"You ready for part two of our adventure? Sunning yourself in the Mediterranean?"

Savannah yawns and stretches her arms overhead.

"I am, but I'm not sure I'm ready to be in a swimsuit after the amount of pastries and baguettes I've consumed these last two weeks." She rubs her belly.

"Who said you'll be wearing anything?" I nip her ear and she giggles.

"I'm not sure my clothes will fit by the time we get back home."

"So we buy you new ones." I continue trailing kisses over her ear and down her jaw till I reach her lips, then her breast, then—bliss. I spend an hour exploring her body with my tongue before I finally bury myself inside her and gain relief.

The flight from Paris to St. Tropez where my yacht is docked is quick, barely ninety minutes. Savannah spends the time napping, much needed after I wore her out this morning, and I spend the time catching up on things at home.

I respond to a few work emails, but I'm mostly focused on the updates from my lawyer about the case against Kane and Eric. I read through the email and see that between the investigation by Chicago PD and the SEC, there are enough charges being brought against both of them from conspiracy, multiple fraud charges, attempted homicide, and sexual harassment that these two will both be going away for a long time. I close my laptop and breathe a sigh of relief that even though both men are currently out on bail, they're confined to their residences with an ankle monitor and both institutions are taking these charges seriously.

* * *

"Oh yes, right there, don't stop."

I grip Savannah's hips as she rides me. Her back is arched, her head falling backward as her hips move in time with my thrusts. The sun glistens off her tanned skin, her tits bouncing with each thrust, driving me closer to the edge.

Sweat pools beneath my ass on the outdoor bed on the deck but I don't care. She's begging me not to stop and I'm not going to.

"I'm so close." Her hands slide up her own body, toying with her tits.

"Fuck, me too." I close my eyes and let my head fall back as I pump into her two more times. I grit my teeth, willing myself not to come yet, but it's no use. Her walls quiver and clench around my cock, my name tumbling from her lips in ecstasy as we both orgasm together. Her body slumps forward onto mine as we both catch our breath.

It's been four days of absolute bliss in the Mediterranean. The weather is perfect; the seas are smooth sailing, and Savannah can't get enough of my cock. It's to a point where I'm pretty sure my balls are bone, but I'm not complaining.

We spend our days stopping at different islands, Corsica and Sardinia and heading to Sicily next, and our evenings are spent exploring each other.

"Should we shower and take a little nap before dinner?"

"Nap, then shower," she says, nuzzling against me before quickly falling asleep in my arms.

* * *

"Sweetheart, dinner is in less than an hour." I gently rub my hand up Savannah's arm and she stirs awake. "You've been asleep for almost three hours, baby."

"I have?" She sits up, looking around the deck and then down at her naked body. "Oh, I forgot I was naked out here."

"Don't worry. I told the crew to avoid this deck all afternoon." I stand and hold out my hand to her. "I have the shower running already. Let's go get ready for dinner."

After our shower we step back into the bedroom where I've laid out a simple white satin dress I picked out for Savannah back in Paris.

"What's this?" she asks, running her hand over the silky material. "It's beautiful."

"Something special for tonight."

"What's tonight?"

"Get dressed, and then meet me out on the main deck." I kiss her forehead and exit the room to go check on things.

I look around the deck. It's lined with dozens of pillar candles and rose petals, the soft sound of jazz coming from the speakers.

"Evening, sir." My captain approaches. "Everything is ready to go."

"Thank you." I clap him on the shoulder.

He exits, leaving me standing there nervously waiting for Savannah to emerge. I know I'm taking a risk here with hoping that she says yes tonight, but I don't want to go another second without her as my wife.

I see her exit the hallway and walk across the large room that leads to the deck. She sees me and smiles, and then her eyes glance from side to side as she takes in the candles and rose petals.

"This is so romantic," she gushes as she walks into my arms.

"You look stunning." She smiles. "Marry me."

"I already said yes." She holds up the ring.

"No, I mean tonight, right now. Let's just do it. Let's get married."

"But how? We don't have a minister or judge and we haven't even talked about a prenup or anything."

"Prenup? Savannah, I don't care about any of that. I'm not asking you to sign a prenup. What's mine is yours." She's stunned and I'm actually shocked she thinks I'd make her sign one.

"But, Warren, this is your empire, your life's work. I won't be offended or think you love me less if you want to protect that."

"Sweetheart, I've waited my lifetime for you. I'm not worried about protecting anything from you because if I lose you, I've already lost everything that matters to me."

Her lip quivers. "Don't cry, baby."

"What about—"

"Captain Howard can marry us." I look over her shoulder as he walks up the stairs in his full uniform.

She spins around. "Are you serious?" She's smiling from ear to ear. "Are we going to get married right now? Here?"

"That's what I'm saying, baby. Just say yes." I hold her hands in mine and bring them to my lips to kiss them.

"Yes," she says. "Yes!"

Captain Howard performs the ceremony. It's quick and even though she had no idea this was going to happen, somehow she has the most perfect vows ready off the top of her head.

"I now pronounce you husband and wife. You may kiss your bride."

I pull her to me, kissing my wife.

We enjoy the three-course dinner the chef has prepared for us, and I take Savannah's hand and lead her back to our private quarters.

"One second." I walk over to my record collection and pull the Miles Davis record that Savannah always chooses for us to dance to at my annual yacht party. I place the needle down and the music fills the room as I walk back over to where she's standing.

"Dance with me," I say as I take her hand in mine and pull her against me. "Every time I held you when we danced to this song, on this boat, I dreamed that someday I'd get to do this with you as my wife."

30

SAVANNAH

"You okay?"

"Yeah, just feel a little off." I shrug. "Think that lobster bisque from last night is just sitting weird."

"You want to head back to the yacht and lie down?"

"No, I'll be fine." I smile.

We stroll hand in hand through the cobblestone streets of Santorini, the midmorning sun bouncing off the stark white walls of the buildings.

"Hey, mind if I stop in this little mart really quick and use the restroom?"

"Of course." He ushers me toward the building.

"You can just stay out here. I'll be right back." I reach up onto my tiptoes and kiss his cheek before ducking into the store. I make my way through the aisles quickly, searching for what I need. In the last aisle, tucked away in the back, I find it—a pregnancy test. I grab it and pay, quickly shoving it in my purse before heading back outside to meet Warren.

We spend the day sunning ourselves on a local beach, popping into different shops, and settling on a gorgeous restaurant for dinner that overlooks the ocean as the sun sets.

By the time we make it back to the boat, the pregnancy test is burning a hole in my purse. I know it's best to take it first thing in the morning, but there's no way I'll be able to sleep tonight if I don't take at least one of the two tests in the box. Besides, if it's negative, I can always take the second one in the morning.

"Night cap on the deck?" Warren asks, his arm looped lazily over mine as we make our way back onto the yacht.

"Of course. I'm just going to freshen up really quick."

"Don't be too long." He grabs a handful of my ass as he dips his head to kiss me. Per usual, the kiss doesn't stay quick or chaste. Passion takes over as his tongue sweeps into my mouth. He picks me up and my legs instinctually wrap around his waist as he presses me against the wall.

"Wait, wait," I pant between kisses as I unwrap my legs and slide down the front of his body.

"Dammit, woman, you really know how to test a man's patience." His cock is at full attention, threatening to tear through his linen pants.

"I just need two minutes. Go out to the deck. I'll be right out."

He groans and hangs his head as he begrudgingly walks out to the deck.

I dart to the bathroom and pull the box from my purse, opening it and taking out one of the tests. I pee on the stick portion and put the cap back on the test and place it on the counter.

While I wait, I search through my items for the sexy sheer bra and panty set I picked up in Paris and put it on. I look at myself in the mirror. My breasts definitely seem fuller; even my nipples seem a touch darker to me. My normal C cups are almost spilling over the bra that fit when I tried it on when I bought it several weeks back.

I turn sideways and hold out my hands. My once-flat stomach protrudes a touch over my panties and while I have been indulging in more pastries and rich foods than normal, I've also been walking and... having marathon sex sessions that have to burn a ton of calories.

I grab one of the fluffy robes hanging in the closet and pull it on, shoving the pregnancy test in the pocket without looking at it. I make my way back up to the deck to join Warren who is sitting halfway reclined in a chair, his legs propped up on the railing in front of him.

I take this moment to stare at him. His hair is wind tossed and a little longer than usual. The black hair on his arms and chest seems a touch darker compared to his bronzed skin.

"Hey," I say as I walk toward him.

"Hey yourself, beautiful. You got cozy," he says, his eyes dropping down the robe that's wrapped tightly around my body. "Come here."

I walk toward him and he guides me onto his lap. "Hard to believe our trip comes to an end next week. Not sure I'm ready to go back and share you with the world."

He gently moves my hair out of my face as a warm breeze brushes past us. I feel nervous but more than anything I feel excited about the possibility that we might be starting a family.

"I need to tell you something." I reach my hand into my pocket nervously and wrap my fingers around the test.

"Everything okay?" He looks at me quizzically.

"I think I'm pregnant."

His eyes grow wide. "You think you are? What—why?"

I stand up and slowly undo the belt on the robe and it falls open.

"Holy fuck." His eyes go to my almost-naked body. "You trying to distract me now?"

"Look at my breasts," I say, cupping them.

"Oh, I'm looking, baby." He scoots to the edge of his chair as I stand between his thighs.

"Feel them though, don't they seem so much fuller?" I grab his hands and place them on my breasts. "And my nipples, they seem darker, no?"

He plumps my breasts in his hands, rubbing his thumbs over my nipples as he eyes them. I can't stop the effect it's having on my body.

"And my sex drive is out of control. I mean, I've always had a healthy appetite, but haven't you noticed that I'm insatiable?"

He gets a devilish grin on his face. "Oh, I've noticed, baby, but I'm not complaining."

"Yeah, but it feels like more than just horny. It's like the second I orgasm, all I'm thinking about is my next one."

"Does it hurt when I squeeze?"

I wince. "A little but like right now, all I want is for you to be inside me, like now." I close my eyes and enjoy the sensation that's settling between my thighs as he pulls the cups of my bra down. He stares at my breasts as he holds them in his hands.

"They do seem bigger."

I stand back up and drop the robe from my body, removing the bra completely as I turn sideways. "I have a little belly now too and my ass seems wider."

"Wait, you're on birth control though."

"Yeah." I drop my eyes. "I wasn't so diligent about taking my pills as I led you to believe. I know, I know, I've never been this irresponsible before. I think with everything going on with Kane and Eric and —us, I got overwhelmed and stressed and I missed at least two."

"Honestly, sweetie, I think it's probably in your head. We've been out of our normal routine and maybe you put on a few pounds from the food, but if you're worried about being pregnant, why don't we grab a test tomorrow?"

I pick up the robe and slide it back on, reaching into the pocket. "Actually, I did already." I pull it out.

"Holy shit. Well, what's it say?"

"I dunno. I was too scared to look at it alone."

"When did you—whatever, that's not important. Okay," he says, grabbing my hand with the test. "Let's look at it together but before we do, just know that no matter what it says, it's fine."

"Do you—" I hesitate. "Want it to be a certain outcome?"

He looks at me and I hold my breath, hoping he wants the same thing as me.

"Yes, I want it to be positive."

"Me too," I whisper, a tear falling down my cheek.

"Don't cry, baby." We both exhale as I turn the test over.

There it is, two pink lines.

"It's positive." My hand shoots to my mouth. "It's positive," I repeat as I fall forward into Warren's chest.

* * *

THE COOL BITE of Chicago autumn has settled into the air and I'm not happy about coming home to it. After three months basking in the sun on a yacht, hopping from island to island, I'm seriously dreading when the frigid temperatures arrive.

I pull my coat tighter around my body as I step into the Baxley building and make my way to my office. I told Warren when I left his penthouse this morning that I was just running over to my place to grab a few things, which is true, but I also wanted to stop by my office to grab my laptop which I knew he'd fight me on if I told him. It was hard enough getting out of his place alone. Now that we know I'm pregnant, he's watching me like a hawk and questioning if every single thing I do is safe. Not to mention, the fact that I still have my apartment is a bit of a sore subject.

My phone buzzes in my pocket and I pull it out to see a text from Callie.

Callie: *Hey, now that you're back, when are we hanging out? We want to hear all about the vacation!*

Me: *Yes! Can't wait to see you guys and tell you all about it. How about Thursday? Dinner at Postino?*

She responds with an affirmative yes and lets me know she'll extend the invite to Tessa and Patrick.

I'm about to slide my phone back into my pocket when it rings. It's Warren.

"Hey, I'm ju—"

"Where are you? We need to leave for the doctor's appointment in less than thirty minutes."

"Warren, calm down. I was just about to say I'm walking into your building."

"*Our* building. *Ours*," he repeats again.

231

"I'll see you in thirty seconds." I hang up the phone and step into the elevator. I walk through the entryway, fully expecting a pouting Warren, but I don't see him.

"Babe?" I walk further into the penthouse, poking my head into the living room and then making my way toward his office which is also empty. I take the stairs and instead of taking a right toward the bedroom, I look to the left and see him standing in a doorway.

"There you are. What are you doing in this room?" I look past him into the spare bedroom.

"This should be the nursery. It's closest to our bedroom and it has the en suite for when the baby is older."

I smile and wrap my arms around him from behind and rest my cheek against his back. "It's perfect for a nursery."

"Why don't you call it our home?"

"I'm sorry. I didn't mean anything by it. It's still all so new to me. This has always been your building, your home, your life. It doesn't mean that I don't think of this as my home. Anywhere I'm with you is home."

He grabs my hands and pulls them tighter around his body. "You're my home too, Savannah."

"I'm not holding on to my apartment for any reason other than I haven't got around to hiring movers and talking to the landlord about my lease. I wasn't expecting to get married on our trip and we hadn't yet talked about living together." I walk around to face him. "Okay?"

"I'll call the landlord and movers and handle everything."

I roll my eyes. "No, I can handle it."

"Fine." He plants a kiss on the tip of my nose. "How about after the doctor appointment we stop by your landlord's office?"

"No, we are going to go to the appointment, then we're going to come back home and bask in the confirmation that we're going to be parents in less than a year. I'll call my landlord later this week, and then I'll schedule the movers."

"Damn, I marry you and you turn bossy." He pinches my ass.

"Just wait till I'm nine months pregnant, raging with hormones with swollen ankles and my back about to give out."

"Mmm, can't wait, baby." We both laugh as he kisses me. "Seriously, I'm going to soak up every single minute of this. Whatever you need, no matter what time of day or night or how asinine you might think it is, ask me. I want to make things as easy and as comfortable for you and baby as I can."

"How'd I get so lucky?"

"Let's go find out when I knocked you up."

The doctor's appointment goes smoothly, but it doesn't come without shock.

"Twelve weeks? I don't understand," I lie against Warren's chest on our couch, a warm fire crackling in the fireplace, both of us staring at the sonogram photo in my hands.

"Must have happened the first night in Paris," Warren says. "Or maybe even the flight there."

"I just feel so guilty that I drank on our vacation."

"The doctor said the baby is healthy and you didn't know, sweetheart. Besides, I think you drank maybe three drinks at most before you stopped."

He places his hand on my lower belly, rubbing it softly.

"Think it'll be okay to tell everyone at dinner on Thursday?"

"I think so, as long as you're comfortable with it."

"I won't be able to hide it much longer and the girls will wonder why I'm ordering Sprite when we go to Mitzy's."

I lift myself up and turn around to crawl into Warren's lap to straddle him. "I read online that women tend to get *very* amorous during their second trimester. Think you can handle more?"

He lets out a loud, hearty laugh. "Are you seriously asking if I can handle *more* sex with the most delicious"—he leans down to kiss my neck—"sexy"—he kisses me lower, unbuttoning my shirt—"mouthwatering"—another kiss—"woman I've ever met?"

This time he doesn't stop kissing me. He finishes unbuttoning my shirt and pushes it from my shoulders, his fingers making quick work of my bra and tossing it to the side barely fast enough before his lips are latching on to my nipple.

I can't help but moan. My breasts are so sensitive right now it's like it sends a bolt of lightning directly to my clit.

"Give me one second," Warren says as he moves me off his lap and walks out of the room. He's back in a flash, something behind his back as he sits back down on the couch. "I bought this to replace the pink one."

I take the toy from his hand as he stands me up and finishes undressing me. I place a knee on either side of his hips again as he fishes his cock free from his pants. He helps me position myself above him.

"Wait, are you ready?" He runs his fingers over my folds. "Oh, fuck yes, you're ready. Damn, baby." The words come out strained as I slowly slide down his cock. He takes the toy from my hands and turns it on, a low buzzing coming from it as he slowly presses it against my clit.

"I want you to use me, baby. Fuck yourself with my cock while I help you with this, okay?"

I nod as I lift my body up, then back down as he presses it against me. It's incredibly intense, like sparks are igniting all over my body. I'm coming within seconds of having the toy pressed to my clit, but I don't stop riding him. I come over and over like this till my body is wrecked and Warren is hanging on by a thread. My body is limp as he lifts me up and down his shaft, finally able to let his own release go.

"Mmm." I sigh as my eyes begin to flutter closed, sleep within my grasp. "Thank you."

"No need to thank me, sweetheart, but don't think you're going to sleep." He slides his hand up my back and into my hair, pulling my head back so my neck is exposed to his mouth.

"I'm just getting started with you, Mrs. Baxley."

* * *

"You're so tan!" Tessa and Callie hug me at the same time.

"I'm so jealous. You guys are both all cute and refreshed and glowing from your honeymoon, Tessa, and your Mediterranean vacation, Savannah, Warren," Callie pouts, her round belly really starting to show. "I just feel sweaty and gassy."

"Stop, you're glowing! You look adorable." I pull her coat apart so we can get a better look at her bump.

We all catch up on how life has been the last three months. Tessa and Patrick tell us about their amazing honeymoon in Aruba, and Callie and Brendan tell us about how their home renovation project and the pregnancy are going.

"So what about you guys? Anything crazy happen on vacation like Tessa and her near-death jellyfish episode?"

I laugh nervously and reach for Warren's hand under the table. I don't know why I'm so scared to tell my friends all our happy news, but I am.

"Well, yes, one thing did happen," I say as I slowly drag my hand out from under the table and dramatically reach for my glass of water.

"Holy shit, what is that?" Callie practically lunges across the table for my hand as she and Tessa lean in to look at my rings. "Oh my God, you're engaged?" She immediately starts to get weepy.

"Not exactly." I smile.

"Wait, there are two rings there," Tessa says in shock and I nod.

"You got married!" Callie is practically yelling. "Without me there?" Here come the tears again. "I'm sorry," she says, grabbing a napkin and dabbing her eyes.

"We did and yes, I know you guys weren't there. It was honestly spur of the moment on my part, but it's what we both wanted, something small with just us." I look at them with pleading eyes and they both smile.

"Oh, Savannah, I don't care that I wasn't there. Honestly, I shouldn't have said that. I'm just so happy for you both." Callie holds my hand and looks back down at the ring. "Seriously, this thing looks like it could sink the *Titanic*."

"I didn't want to take away from your big day since it just happened, Tessa."

"Don't be crazy and trust me, you did it the smart way. So expensive and draining and all the thank-you cards." She shakes her head and Patrick agrees.

"Yeah, cheers to that," Patrick says.

"I tried warning you." Brendan laughs.

"So you guys are married. Congrats. I can't believe it but at the same time, it's about damn time," Callie says, raising her glass. "Here's to the next steps. Moving in together, I assume?"

"Yeah, eventually. We haven't really discussed it though." I look at Warren and laugh.

"She loves to try my patience." He winks at me and leans in to kiss me. "But yes, she's moving in asap. She kind of has to, actually."

"Has to?" Callie and Tessa look at me in confusion.

"Yeah." I sigh and reach into my purse. "There's something I need to tell you guys. I—we went to the doctor today and we got some news." My expression is serious. "I thought I had more time, but it turns out"—Callie gasps and clutches her chest—"I'm already three months," I say as I place the sonogram photo on the table, no longer able to hide my smile.

"Wait, what?" Tessa grabs the photo, but Callie snatches it from it her.

"You bitch!" she shouts before jumping out to run over and hug me. "I hate you so much; I thought you were dying." She sobs, her words coming out broke and almost unintelligible. "I can't believe we're pregnant together. Tessa, come on, get it together. You're next." She looks over at her.

"Abso-freaking-lutely-not," she says emphatically as she picks up her glass of wine. "Just had my IUD put in right before the wedding. No chance in hell we're having kids right now. I'll just be the cool auntie to your little bundles of joy."

"To Mr. and Mrs. Baxley and their bundle of joy," Callie says, raising her glass once again.

I smile at Warren. "I think that's the first time I've heard someone call me Mrs. Baxley." I take a sip of my water as Warren leans, whispering in my ear.

"Tsk, tsk," he scolds, "the first time you heard someone call you Mrs. Baxley was when you were impaled on my cock."

I turn my head, our lips centimeters apart. "I guess I forgot."

He slides his hand up my thigh beneath the table, cupping me. "I think you just might need another lesson on who you belong to."

Moments later we're in the car on the way home, his cock buried deep inside me as he reminds me exactly who I belong to.

EPILOGUE

WARREN-NINE MONTHS LATER...

I lay on my back in bed, my three-month-old son fast asleep on my chest and my wife curled against me.

This right here is the ultimate fantasy.

"How do you still look so good after spending half the night awake with him?"

Savannah lifts her head to look up at me, propping herself up on an elbow as her hand rests gently against Simon's back.

"I'm not sure I do, sweetheart. You're just delirious from lack of sleep too." I wink at her.

"Still gives me butterflies when you do that." She leans in and softly plants a kiss on my lips. "I told Callie I'd go to a postpartum spin class with her this morning but ugh, I just want to stay in bed with you two."

Since our son Simon's birth, life has been more than perfect. Even through the never-ending dirty diapers, the lack of sleep, and the general anxieties of being a parent, I'd do it a million times over for this little man.

"Go to your spin class this morning, baby. Me and little man will be just fine."

"Are you sure? I feel guilty leaving you both." She pouts, jutting out her bottom lip, and I reach my hand out and run my finger over it. She darts her tongue out for a second, then bites down on my finger.

"You better or I'm going to work you out a lot harder and you'll have to explain to Callie why you missed class."

She giggles and stretches her arms overhead before tossing the covers aside and climbing out of bed. My t-shirt she's wearing sits just below her ass so when she bends over to grab her panties from the floor, leftovers from last night's fun, I get a delicious glimpse of her naked backside.

"Goddamn, baby, you trying to drive me crazy this morning?" Simon stirs on my chest and I run my hand over his back to calm him.

She stands back up and looks over her shoulder. "You like the view?" She hikes the shirt up a little higher, teasing me.

"Go to class now," I tell her slowly, my tone changing. "When you get home, we'll take a nice long shower together, and then I'm going to bend you over like that and eat you out from behind, taking my slow, sweet time. How does that sound?"

"Yes, sir." She smiles before disappearing into the closet.

I've come to realize that Savannah is easily motivated when it comes to rewarding her body with my tongue and I'm not mad about it. Tasting and savoring her is one of my all-time favorite activities.

"Okay, I'm off!" She emerges moments later in some skintight black leggings and a matching sports bra. She walks to the side of the bed and leans down to kiss our son, then me.

"Don't push yourself too hard." I run my hand up the back of her thigh to grab a handful of her plump ass. I've tried convincing her to keep a few extra pounds of the baby weight, but so far I've been unsuccessful. "Can't wait to peel these off you later."

Simon begins to fuss so I get up with him and walk around the penthouse with him in my arms. It's a surefire way to get him back to sleep. I make myself some coffee and while it's brewing, I gently place him back in his crib.

I step into my office to catch up on some work when my phone rings.

"Riz, how are you?"

"Good, Warren. Sorry for calling so early on a weekend morning, but I figured you've heard the good news from your lawyer?"

I sign on to my computer and go to my email, searching for something from Art.

"I didn't but I'm looking at my email now. What's the good news?"

"The judge gave them each fifteen years and they've been ordered to pay restitution in the amount of $350 million."

"Think you'll ever see that money?"

He laughs. "Not a chance but I'm not worried about it too much. Just glad that they were finally brought to justice."

I let out a sigh of relief when my phone alerts me to another incoming call. I look at the screen.

"Hey, Riz. Art's calling me now. Thanks for letting me know. I'll see you in LA next month."

I hang up with him and answer Art.

"Hey, Art. I just spoke with Riz."

"Morning, son. So you heard. Well, that was the federal case. They're going to be tried in district court now for the blackmail, photos, violent threats, and attempted homicide. I spoke to the DA this morning and have it on good authority that they'll both plead guilty and take a deal to avoid a very public and humiliating trial. With the amount of evidence the DA has, they both know it'll be a slam-dunk case if they did go to trial."

"I hope so, Art. I just want this all behind us, and if Savannah and Eric's other victims don't have to testify at trial, that would be ideal. I don't want to put her through that, especially after Simon's birth. She's got enough on her plate."

"How's she doing? How's your son doing?"

"Good, they're both doing great. Her delivery was uncomplicated and she's already back to work part-time from home. Nothing can stop that woman."

"Sounds like you. I'll keep you updated on things with the case, Warren. See you at the shareholders' party."

I hang up with Art and lean back in my office chair. I check the baby monitor. Simon is still fast asleep in his crib so I take my coffee and slip quietly into his nursery.

These are some of my favorite moments. I sit in the rocking chair in his nursery while he sleeps and I talk to him. I tell him stories about how I met his mom, what my father was like, what kind of life I hope he has. I know he doesn't understand what I'm saying, but it feels like a father, son bonding moment.

"More than anything, little man, I want you to be happy. I don't care what path you choose in life. If you don't want to take on the company, I'll never resent you or be disappointed. All I care about is that you're happy and feel loved and supported by your mom and dad." I whisper the words over his crib, leaning down to kiss his fuzzy little head before heading back to the kitchen to make a smoothie for Savannah when she returns.

I get a text from Art not thirty minutes after we hang up.

Art: *Spoke to the DA again. They took a deal. Fifteen years for Kane, six for Eric. It's done, Warren.*

I slide the phone into my pocket and let out a huge sigh of relief. Finally.

* * *

"How do I look?" Savannah asks nervously as she smooths her hands down the front of her floor-length black velvet dress. It hugs her newfound curves like a glove. The thin straps dip into a delicate *V* in the front, accentuating her full breasts.

"Mmm." I run my hands up her sides and settle them against her waist. "What's the back?" I spin her around and see the back plunging low, all the way to the top of her ass. "Fuck me, that's delicious." I run my hand over her exposed skin, dipping it beneath the material when I reach her lower back. I grab a handful of her ass.

"Hey, easy, big guy. Everyone will be here shortly."

"Seriously? You walk out here in that, and I'm not allowed to have a little fun?"

241

"Is it too much?" She looks at herself in the floor-length mirror, ignoring my question.

"Absolutely not. It's too much for me to keep my hands off you all night, though, so I'm pretty sure your *rule* might get tossed overboard."

She turns around and cocks her hip. "Warren, we have a *no fooling around at work events* rule for a reason, remember?"

"First of all, I never technically agreed to that rule and second, you're very much to blame too."

She rolls her eyes and checks the time. "Callie and Tessa are probably on their way up." The women and their husbands are coming over to watch Simon tonight while Savannah and I attend the annual shareholders' event on the yacht. Savannah was a mess at the thought of leaving Simon for the first time, but after Tessa and Callie both agreed to watch him, and since Callie is also a new mother, she finally agreed.

"For the record, it's my company and my goddamn office. If I want to bury my tongue in my wife's pussy on my desk, I can, and it's nobody's business. You needed relief; you were insatiable, and it's not my fault Sophie heard you screaming and thought something had happened and burst through the office doors. They were closed for a reason!"

Savannah walks over to me and places her hands on my chest. "Baby." She slowly slides them up around my neck. "I know and I agree, but we can't be traumatizing any more employees. How about"—she leans in and kisses the corner of my mouth—"on the drive to the marina"—she kisses the other side of my mouth as she drags one hand agonizingly slow down my body till she gets to my cock, palming it—"I give you a little special attention?"

I groan into her mouth as she slides her hand up and down my shaft a few times.

"Now, let's go make sure Callie and Tessa have what they need and say good night to our son."

I grab her wrist as she turns to walk away and pull her back to me, kissing her like she's the air I need to breathe.

It takes us another forty-five minutes to get out of the penthouse and into the car. I'm about to fucking explode by the time we're on our way to the marina and Savannah's slowly lowering her head down and wrapping her lips around my cock.

I try to maintain composure but I'm losing it. I let my head fall back for a second but quickly lift it back up to watch her. My hand rests on the back of her neck as she bobs her head up and down my length.

I'm so close. I can feel my balls tense.

"Baby, I'm close." I grit my teeth as she quickens her pace. "I'm, I'm —" I don't get to finish the statement before I explode. Savannah's lips remain locked on my cock as she swallows down every last drop I release.

"Oh fuck, that was good." I'm panting. One of her straps has fallen off her shoulder and I reach into her dress and palm her breast. I swipe my thumb over her nipple. "Did you pump?"

"Yes."

"They're so full. Fuck, I need more." I attempt to pull her to straddle me, but she stops me.

"We're almost there."

"Sweetie, please," I'm the one begging this time, but she pulls the strap of her dress up and pulls out a makeup compact to fix her lipstick and check the rest of her makeup.

"Later, I promise." She gives me a peck on the lips and reaches for my pants to fix my zipper.

"Don't touch." I laugh. "Or I can guarantee you we won't make it out of this car." I look up at her as we prepare to exit and head out to the yacht. "Thank you, baby."

The party is agonizing. The only good thing is I get to talk about my son and show pictures of him which everyone is eating up.

I have a few people ask about the Kane and Eric situation, but I shut it down quickly, making it clear that chapter is closed and I have no interest in any more conversation about it.

Otherwise, everyone is drunk and happy since the Code Red deal and the Syler Systems deal are both done and they're a whole fucking lot richer thanks to it.

I watch Savannah work the room, her infectious smile and laugh pulling at my heart. I still can't believe she's mine. I grab a bottle of champagne and two glasses from the bar and head up to the private quarters where I know she'll find me soon enough.

A little while later I hear delicate high-heeled footsteps moving up the steps and down the deck.

"I feel like you're hiding away earlier and earlier each year." She walks toward me where I sit in a chair in the far corner of the room near the record player.

"Hi," she says when she reaches me. She stands between my outstretched legs. I reach up and place my hands on her ass.

"Hi, sweetheart. You feeling okay?"

She nods. "I am." She reaches around to grab my hands and tugs on them so I stand up. "Dance with me."

I find our record and put it on, pulling her body against mine as we sway to the music. It's a tender moment, both of us holding each other, but it doesn't last long. She looks up at me with need in her eyes.

"What do you need, sweetheart?" I brush her hair away from her face and kiss her lips softly, teasing her. I nip on her lower lip, then suck on it, my tongue touching hers for a brief second.

"Don't tease me," she pleads.

I spin her around so her back is to me, my tongue and lips exploring her exposed neck. I press on her lower belly so her ass grinds against my firming cock and she moans.

"We can't," she says, but it's not convincing.

"Sure, we can, baby; it's our boat."

I let my hand slide up her body till I reach her breast, cupping her while my other hand starts to gather her dress. I slide my hand beneath the fabric, running it softly over her ass.

"Are you sure we can't?" I say as I slide my finger beneath the material of her thong and pull it to the side. "Are you sure you don't want me to give you some relief?" I slide a finger down her ass crack, right to her slick center, toying with her.

"The rule," she says without conviction.

"Yes, the rule. It would be a shame to be naughty and break the rules." I bite down on her earlobe as I slide my finger inside her. "Just think, baby," I say as I slide my finger in and out of her at a slow pace. "All those people down there have no idea that sweet, professional Savannah is up here, being a naughty little slut for her husband."

She starts to pant, her mouth falling open as her release builds. Her head falls back against my shoulder and I bend to kiss her.

"They'll never know when you go back down there that you've just been fucked by your boss. That you not only have my cum in your belly, but in this delicious little pussy."

She's close, I can feel her quivering against me.

"So if you want to keep that rule, I understand, but maybe," I say as I slide two fingers inside her and she moans my name, "just this once, we can break the rules."

Her eyes open, hungry for me, she pulls me to her mouth to kiss me and I can see her giving in. Her eyes fall closed again as she presses back against my fingers inside her, arching her back so I get deeper.

"Just this once."

If you love naughty billionaires, make sure you check out the other complete stand alone books in this series!

KEEP READING FOR A SNEAK PEEK OF BEG FOR IT

You know that feeling when you tell yourself over and over again that you shouldn't do something, but you know you're going to anyway?

That feeling when your resolve slowly starts to slip and you realize that this man isn't just your dad's best friend who's twenty years older than you, he's your new boss…but it's too late, there's no turning back now.

Get ready for another scorching hot off limits age gap romance in *Beg For It.*

CHAPTER 1

BRONTË

"Congratulations to my daughter Brontë on her graduation from grad school. Your stepmother and I are incredibly proud of you."

My father Jonas Ramsay lifts his champagne flute toward the sky as he toasts to me. The room fills with cheers and echos of congratulations as I smile shyly and nod my thanks.

I'm still not used to this kind of wealth. The kind of wealth where spending probably fifty thousand on a graduation party at one of the most exclusive restaurants in Chicago is merely a gesture.

"Come here sweetie," my dad approaches and wraps his arm around my shoulders. "Have you thought anymore about my offer to join Ramsay Consulting?"

I look down at my glass of champagne and shrug.

My dad is one of the most, if not the most powerful billionaires in Chicago but he's only been a part of my life for the last year. He and my mother met when they were young and had me at only twenty-five, something I later learned was unplanned and a source of contention between them. As expected, they divorced when I was seven after dad was unfaithful and mom moved us to the suburbs where we lived a quiet, normal middle class life away from the glitz and glam of the world's elite.

"I've thought about it a little but I'm still just—unsure."

"Well that's why I think it's a great idea. You can come in at an entry level position, feel it out, see if finance and business are what you want. I can tell you for sure though that they're in your blood." He squeezes my shoulder and I look over at him. He's referring to my mother.

Nadia Spencer my mom was an accountant for as long as I can remember and she loved it. That's how she met my father, in college they were both finance majors and they hit it off. After I was born mom stopped working to raise me but once she and dad divorced, she went back to work to support us. Dad wasn't yet the billionaire tycoon he is now but I do know she received child support and alimony payments every month but she always said she refused to be beholden to a man and wanted to show me that a single mom could do it on her own.

She was fierce and incredibly brave. It's been almost three years now since she's been gone and not a day goes by that I don't miss her. It's because of her actually that I'm working on my relationship with my father...or that I even have a relationship with him. On her deathbed she made me promise that I'd forgive him and try to get to know him and my half-siblings. I put if off for about two years but now here I am, having this elaborate graduation party thrown by him in my honor.

"That's part of the problem though, I know everyone will just assume I'm working there because you're my father which will prob-ably lend to some resentment amount my peers because they'll assume I can get away with anything or they'll just wonder why I'm working in the first place like I'm trying too hard to prove myself to everyone."

I gulp down the half a glass of champagne I've been nursing and grab a fresh one off of a waiters tray that's passing by. Even talking about my future instantly stresses me out. I feel like an asshole, like I'm complaining about my gold shoes being too tight with the amount of opportunity that's sitting in my lap but I want to be fulfilled with my career, like my mom was.

I want to now that I'm making a difference in the world.

"I think you nipped that fear in the bud when you took your mother's last name." He doesn't have to tell me that it disappoints him that I'm not proudly a Ramsay.

"Oh trust me, with social media nowadays, everyone will know who I am the second I get hired on at your company." He nods once, giving a half hearted smile before looking down at his shoes. I feel guilty. "I'm not ashamed of you dad, that's not it." I reach my hand out to his arm, "I'm just feeling a little lost is all. You know how it is to be twenty-four."

I give him a smile and his eyes brighten, his own lips curling into a smile. The truth is I am ashamed of the Ramsay name. For years my dad didn't have a great reputation. I know he's changed, or that's what his new wife Chantelle says, along with a few others but it's hard to trust that when the only version you've known of him was an angry, cheating liar who walked out on you when you were seven and barely showed back up, only to drop off a check or make a half-hearted attempt to celebrate a birthday or milestone too late.

"Okay this is my last resort. My good friend Beckham Archer, own Archer Financial just across the street from my building, he's looking for an admin immediately. His last one left unexpectedly. I could send him your resume and set up a meeting?"

"Now you're pawning me off onto your friends who need assistants?" I crook an eyebrow at him, "Dad, I appreciate the offer but I'm just not sure."

"Okay, just promise me you'll think about it."

"I promise."

"Come on," he motions with a quick nod of his head.

"Where?"

"To your gift." He smiles and grabs my hand, leading me toward the center of the room.

"Dad," I groan, feeling like I'm that young girl all over again who just wants to spend time with her dad, instead of be showered with elaborate gifts. "I told you I didn't need or want any gifts besides donations being made to the Chicago Boys and Girls Club."

"Oh psh," he waves away my suggestion in classic Jonas Ramsay fashion. Sure he gives to charity, what billionaire doesn't donate more money in a year than most of us will see in a lifetime to various causes but do they care about them?

My dad doesn't. Which is why I haven't told him that for the last several years I've volunteered at a few different non-profits in the city for underprivileged children, something has become such a passion of mine I can't help but keep coming back to the idea that maybe I should start my own non-profit.

"Ladies and gentleman it's gift time!" He grabs a spoon off a table and clinks it against his glass, the guests turning to listen to his announcement.

"I cannot wait to see what he got you for a gift." My best friend Sylvia stands next to me along with our mutual friend Taylor who are both giggling.

"Stop it," I give them both a glare but it only eggs them on.

They've been by my side for this entire journey with my father and they've been in the room with me while he's on the phone trying to talk me into letting him buy me a new house in the suburbs, a penthouse downtown or even a flat in London or Paris.

"I wanted to do something special for my baby girl because she not only deserves it but, she's always wanted one." My dad smiles at me and motions for us to head outside.

I'm so confused as to what might be on the other side of these walls. I walk next to him as the host walks ahead of us and dramatically opens both doors of the restaurant in a sweeping gesture.

I gasp when I see it.

Parked on the street in front of the restaurant with a giant bow on top is a brand new, cherry red Porsche 911 Carrera Cabriole.

"Dad, this is too much."

"Nonsense," he walks me over to the car and slides the key in my hand. "Remember when you were just a little girl and you'd beg me to take you driving in mine with the top down? You couldn't get enough of that car."

He smiles so proudly as he looks at it and for a second I think I almost see a tear in his eye. I'm not sure if it's a tear about my childhood or if it's because he loved that car so damn much. He conveniently doesn't mention when I accidentally crashed my bike into the rear fender and he screamed at me like I did it on purpose. I remember sobbing in my room for hours, my mom coming to rub my back and comfort me but my dad pulling her out of my room because I needed to think about what I did.

"It's a hundred thousand dollar car dad, I don't have anywhere to put it."

"We can sell your old car."

"I like my car," I say nervously, "And it's only three years old."

I feel guilty for not being super excited about a gift I not only didn't want but one I don't need. I like the fact that I saved up and worked hard, busting my ass doing double shifts at the restaurant I worked at to buy my Kia. I was so proud when I did buy it since it was not only knew but had cooled and heated seats plus a moonroof.

"Chantelle enjoys having a few different cars. She says it's nice to have one as a daily driver and one when the weather isn't so great."

"Yes well you two have a ten thousand square foot garage, I have a single parking spot."

I can see his smile fade again as he leans in to plant a kiss on my cheek.

"Tell you what," he says taking the key from my hand, "you can keep it parked at my house. When you come over to our neighborhood we can drop the top and take her out for a spin, how about that?"

"Sounds good dad."

I stand there staring at the car along with two valet guys who are admiring her from every angle.

"That's what he enjoys doing you know?" I turn to my right where Chantelle, my stepmother has sidled up beside me. "Giving gifts is one of his love languages."

"Or maybe that's an excuse that rich people give instead of actually taking the time to think out something thoughtful or meaningful or just respect the person's wishes when they said no gifts?" Her lips form into a thin smile and I shake my head, "Sorry, that was rude. You're just being kind."

Chantelle is clearly a lot younger than my father but she's also probably one of the best things that has ever happened to him. I still struggle with the notion that people can really, fully change who they are at their core but I also feel like a hypocrite when I see the way my father has changed because of her. When I heard that he was forty, marrying a woman that was my now age, I laughed. I didn't think for a second that it would last, it was merely a cliche life crises move. But here they are, ten years and two kids later and he couldn't be happier.

"He's working on it Brontë. I know it's practically a slap in the face to ask for your patience and understanding with him but I promise you," she says softly, reaching her perfectly manicured hand out to rest on my arm, "he wants a genuine relationship with you. He talks about it all the time."

"I know, sometimes it's just hard to forgive and forget."

"I have no doubt. You're justified in those feelings Brontë. The boys were upset they couldn't come tonight by the way, Silas in particular. He and Jenson made this for you." She reaches into her clutch and pulls out a hand drawn card that brings a huge smile to my face.

Silas and Jenson are the two little gems that came out of my family's toxic breakup. From the first day I got to meet them it's like I've always been their big sister. And one thing that Chantelle always makes sure they know is that we are brother and sister, no half this or half that.

"Awe, those boys. I need to come see them this weekend."

"They would love that and your father would love it to, so he can take you out in your new car." She winks at me. "I better go find him but I want to throw a fun little family cookout in the next few weeks, kick off summer right and celebrate your birthday. The boys will want to show you all their new flips and trick they learned in swim lessons over the winter."

"That sounds lovely Chantelle," I pull her in for a tight hug, "Tell the boys I missed them and I'll see them soon."

I head back inside to find my friends, "Hey, you guys want to go grab a drink somewhere else? I'm feeling a little celebrated out."

"Oh yes please!" Taylor says grabbing her clutch and hopping down from her stool.

"Just a second," I say looking around for my dad. I spot him and head over to him and let him know we're leaving.

"Thanks again dad," I give him a hug and he squeezes me so tight, like he's trying to make up for years lost.

"I'm so proud of you Brontë, your mother would be too."

This time I can clearly see the tears and for some reason, maybe because I don't want to disappoint him or maybe because I'm tired of feeling guilty I agree to the meeting with his friend.

"I'll do it. I'll meet with Beckham Archer for an interview."

A few moments late Sylvia, Taylor and I are making our way into a dimly lit speakeasy type bar in The Loop. This isn't our usual neighborhood and the bars here are filled with finance bros in overpriced suits and clearly veneered teeth, all trying to shout over each other about their "big win."

"You sure you want to stay here?" Sylvia asks looking around and I shrug, grabbing a high top table. "Doesn't seem like our vibe."

"Yeah it's close by, I don't feel like Ubering anywhere. I just need something stronger than the glasses of champagne I downed."

"Did your dad manage to talk you into working at his company?" Taylor asks.

"No but I did something stupid." I roll my eyes. "I agreed to take an interview at his fellow billionaire friend's company Archer Financial. I guess he needs an admin or something. Ugh, I'm so disappointed in myself I didn't just tell him I want to work in non-profit and maybe start my own someday."

"Honestly Brontë I think it's a smart idea." Sylvia shrugs and I look at her sideways. "Remember when you met me in undergrad? I was the teacher's assistant and I told you that if I was unsure about getting my masters in education? Well, I didn't listen to that gut feeling and now I'm a teacher and honestly, I kind of hate it."

"You hate it?" Taylor's ears perk up.

"I don't *hate* it all the time but it just doesn't feel like it was my passion, what I'm meant to do, it's something I'm good at so I convinced myself it was my dream. Sometimes I don't think I've even figured out what my dream is yet but I know it's not in the education world."

"So you think taking this job, if I get it, would be a way for me to try out the financial world before I either fully commit or walk away?"

"Exactly!" She slaps the table dramatically, "and if you think there's an interest there I'm sure you could move into a financial position within the company. With your forensic accounting masters, you'll be able to find work at any financial firm. Fraud is always going on. You know what they say, scammers are the new serial killers."

"True," I say laughing at her comment. I'm feeling better already about my decision.

"But first," Taylor says looking around the bar, "we need to get you laid because it's been over two years now and you've graduated so no more excuses."

I duck my head in embarrassment, "Okay, maybe yell it a little louder next time so the bartender can hear you?"

I slide off my stool, flipping her the bird as they both fall into a fit of giggles.

"I'm getting a round of old fashions."

I walk to the bar and wait for the bartender to notice me when a shadowy figure to my right catches my eye. This guy is not your average twenty something frat boy. His suit looks expensive, bespoke like it was made for him. It hugs his arms and shoulders, accentuating a very toned physique. A lock of his dirty blonde hair has fallen over one eye as he reads something on his phone.

I take the advantage of going unnoticed by him to really look him over. His jaw is rough with stubble but it's cut and angular. His lips full. He reaches for his cocktail, bringing it to his mouth to take a sip before placing it back on the bar top without looking away from his phone.

"What's with you finance guys?" A burst of confidence surges through me as I make small talk with the stranger. "Always working." I shake my head and place my order as the man turns to look at me.

He glances over his shoulder to make sure I'm speaking to him before sliding his phone in his pocket and turning on his stool to look at me. He does't hide his gaze as it slowly travels down my body then back up again before he replies.

"Guilty." He smirks.

The dim light catches his icy blue eyes and makes my stomach do a little flip. Maybe that champagne hit me harder than I realized because this man is so sexy I feel my mouth grow dry.

"Married to the job?" I say coyly, dragging my teeth over my bottom lip seductively like I'm in a cheesy rom-com. I brush my hair back in a flirty manner, leaning a bit forward on the bar top so it presses my breasts together.

Who the hell am I right now?

"Afraid so. She's my wife, mistress and lover." He tosses back the rest of the amber liquid in his tumbler and places it on the bar top.

"Shame," I smile as the bartender places my drinks down in front of me and I go to hand him my credit card.

"Allow me, please?" He says nodding toward my card.

"Thank you." I pull my card back and place it in my wallet. I gather the three tumblers between my fingers and then I set them back down on the bar, not yet ready to break up this little flirt fest.

"So what brings a beautiful, young woman like you to a place like this?" The way he looks at me has my stomach doing all sort of little flip flops.

"You mean to a bar in the Loop filled with young finance gurus foaming at the mouth to be the next Wolf of Wall Street?" He chuckles and I shrug, "Just something in the way they all brag about how they can really see Jordan Belfort in themselves gets me going. Like it's going to make a woman's panties drop that they can resonate with a selfish, narcissistic scam artist like they really are Leonardo DiCaprio in the movie."

"You're fiery, funny as hell too." His eyes do that lazy perusal of my body again and it sends my stomach into summersaults. "Please tell me a woman as gorgeous as you hasn't been lured into the soul crushing world of finance?"

"You mean because I'm pretty it would be a shame?"

He nods, "Not a shame, we need more women like you that call it like it is but you're young, seems like there's probably more fun and exciting things to fill your time than long hours and hanging out at bars with men like me."

"Men like you huh?" I cock my head, bringing back my flirty demeanor. "And what kind of man are you?"

"The kind your dad wouldn't want you talking to." His voice is deep and a little ragged as he leans back in his seat, running his hand through his hair as his eyes drop down to my lips. I stare at him, debating on my next move when I notice the sexy lines at the corner of his eyes. It was obvious he wasn't a fresh graduate when I first saw him but it's only now that I can see he definitely has a few years on me.

Damn, an older man—my kryptonite.

"Look, I don't normally do this," he laughs at my statement, "Right, cliche I know, especially after your little ominous warning but," I rummage through my wallet for an old receipt and grab a pen from the bar, scribbling down my first name, last initial and my phone number and hand it to him.

"Is that an initial?" he looks at the paper then to me.

"Yes, I figure a man that looks like you, must have at least twenty different *I don't normally do this* women's numbers in his phone. So, with a last initial maybe I'll stand out."

"Only twenty?" He hooks an eyebrow at me, making me laugh. "Why only the initial? Scared to give me your last name?"

I grab the paper and write out the rest of my last name before handing it back to him.

"There."

He looks at it then his smile falters a little, "Brontë Spencer?"

"Yes, that's me. I guess you probably don't have a lot of Brontë's in your phone so the last name is a little redundant now that I think about it."

"Yeah," he says almost nervously as he runs his hand over his jaw. "That's for certain."

"I'll be right back. The ladies are frothing at the mouth over there for these." I say as I look over at my friends who are giving me ridiculous hand signals and eye gestures thinking they're being subtle.

I walk the drinks over to the table and place them down.

"Holy shit you guys I just met the finest man I have ever seen in my life. I think I almost blacked out and peed myself talking to him." I whisper as if he could hear me over the loud ruckus the frat boys are causing in the center of the bar.

"And of course he's older," Taylor bounces her eyebrows, "daddy issues coming in stroooong." They both laugh, something they've always teased me about is my affinity for older men.

Is it daddy issues? I'm ninety-nine percent sure it is. We can thank Jonas for that.

"I gave him my number!" I shriek just as both of their faces fall. "What?"

"Uh, I think he just left?"

"What?" I spin around and sure enough, he's nowhere to be found. I walk back up to the bar and look around, "Where did that guy go?" I ask the bartender who shrugs and turns to help someone else.

And then that's when I see it, the crumpled up piece of paper left on the bar top with my name and number.

***

I groan and stretch my arms overhead, trudging to the kitchen to make a much needed espresso before getting ready for my interview at Archer Financial...a decision I'm now regretting giving in to.

Instead of taking time to learn about the company, I've spent far too long thinking about the rejection from a total stranger this weekend.

I make myself a latte and open my iPad to do a little research but my mind keeps drifting to that sexy smirk from Mr. Daddy Issues at the bar.

"Ugh," I shut my iPad and march to the bathroom for a shower, hoping if I get my day going it will take my mind off of Taylor's all too true comment that I haven't been laid in over two years and if I'm not careful, my virginity will grow back at any second.

I finish applying my makeup and pull my long hair up into a high, professional ponytail. I slide my feet into a sensible pair of black pumps and do a quick spin in my floor length mirror to double check my pencil skirt isn't tucked into my panties or there isn't a hole in my white blouse.

After this weekend's rejection, I really don't need a double dose of embarrassment for my self esteem. I look polished and professional.

"I'd hire me." I smile at my reflection before grabbing my portfolio and heading to Archer Financial.

I stop outside the reflective building and stare up at the towering sky scraper. My dad was right, it's literally across the street from his building. I feel my chest tighten as I watch several people walking in to the building, their heads turned down as they stare at their phone, completely oblivious to the world around them.

Is this really the life I want?

I square my shoulders and march into the building, reminding myself that this is a good opportunity and like my dad and my friend's mentioned, a way to feel out if a life in finance is really want I want.

"Hi, I have an interview with Mr. Beckham Archer at 9:30."

I smile at the man sitting behind the front desk but he doesn't reciprocate.

"Name." He doesn't even look up from his computer screen.

"Brontë Spencer."

"It's the fortieth floor, take the elevator bank behind me to your left. Here's your visitors badge. Make sure it's visible on your person."

"Thank you."

I walk timidly around the massive desk, my heels echoing against the marble floor as several others rush past me to enter the elevator. When I arrive on the floor there's a second reception desk with two women smiling at me. I repeat the process of introducing myself.

"Mr. Archer is ready for you." One of the ladies smiles as she stands and walks around the desk. "I'll show you the way."

She brings me to two massive wooden doors that she opens and ushers me inside before turning to walk back down the hallway.

I step inside the office, nervously looking around when I spot him. His back is to me as he faces the floor to ceiling windows, he's clearly typing furiously on his phone but finishes and slides it into his pocket to turn around and face me, a casual smirk on his face as he speaks.

"Thanks for meeting me Miss Spencer."

Holy fucking shit you have to be kidding me. This cannot be real.

I almost want to pinch myself, convinced I'm having a nightmare right now. Before I can stop myself, the words fall from my lips in a somewhat whisper.

"Mr. Daddy Issues?"

CHAPTER 2

BECKHAM

Her face says it all and it's fucking priceless."Pardon?"

I watch her delicate throat constrict as she attempts to swallow down the realization that the man she tried to pick up last night, is not only her dad's best friend but I very well could be her new boss.

"Uh, nice to meet you." She says clutching the folder to her chest, her cheeks flaming.

"Brontë Spencer then I presume?" I take her hand in mine.

"Ye—yes, that's me." She smiles nervously, shifting her folder and purse to shake my hand. "Pleasure to meet you sir. And thank you."

"Pleasures all mine." Her hand is thin and soft and I'm tempted to hold onto her fingers longer than professional or necessary. I gesture for her to take a seat in the chair across from my desk and she does. Crossing one slim ankle over the other as she smooths out her black pencil skirt.

"I've heard a lot about you from your father, all good things of course." I offer her a genuine smile to ease her tension but it doesn't work, in fact it seems to have the opposite effect. Her shoulders lift as she hugs the folder in her arms a little tighter.

"So why don't you tell me about yourself Brontë, what your background looks like, what interests you, what line of work you think you want to end up in?"

I lean back in my chair and fold my hands in my lap.

"Well, honestly I'm a little unsure what I want to do with my life which is why I'm here. My father suggested I come work for you till I figure out what I actually want to do." I chuckle and she nervously tries to backpedal. "Not that I don't think that this is a real job or anything, I'm extremely grateful for the opportunity and for you even taking the time to speak with me."

"No explanation needed," I hold up my hand. "I've been in your shoes before and I think it's a smart plan. Too often we're pushed into specific careers based on what we decided to study when we were eighteen years old. A lot can happen between now and then."

"I studied finance and accounting in undergrad and just graduated from grad school with my masters in Forensic Accounting. My mom was an accountant and she loved her job so I followed in her footsteps."

"But now you're unsure about that path for yourself?"

"Yeah, I guess so."

I lean forward in my chair and intertwine my fingers, "What is it that excites you? When you picture yourself twenty years from now, what career do you see yourself in?"

Her shoulders finally drop as she chews on the corner of her lip.

"Helping people. I like volunteering and I think non-profit is something I could see myself in long-term."

"Well that's good news, we have some great relationships with a few here in Chicago. In fact, we have a foundation, The Archer Foundation that focuses on single mothers or women in need of prenatal care...basically families in need. We do fundraisers and group volunteering throughout the company. We also offer five paid days off per month for volunteering."

Her eyes grow wide as I explain about our efforts here at Archer Financial to give back to our community and help those in need.

"That sounds wonderful. My mom was big into volunteering and took me even before I can remember. Anyway, I do like finance as well, I enjoy solving problems and finding errors. I just—it's a big commitment to choose a career and jump in when you're not one hundred percent certain."

Gone is the bold, flirty woman from last night who shamelessly approached me at the bar—replaced with an almost timid and nervous little creature. Her eyes dart from mine to the floor and back again as she speaks. They sparkle when the sun hits them through the blinds behind me. Her lips are full, almost too large for her delicate features yet they fit her perfectly. Everything about her seems ethereal, like she could be a Disney princess locked away in a tower by an evil witch…a far cry from her commanding and at times tyrannical father.

"Tell you what Brontë, if you were to accept the position here at Archer, you would be hired on as my assistant. I am in desperate need of someone who can help me manage my calendar and gate keep my time, also someone who can attend meetings with me, book travel, manage my emails and messages. Basically, my right arm. I'm not looking for someone to work twelve hour days or pick up my dry cleaning. I'm pretty easy going and approachable. I do—"

"I'm really sorry about last night." She interrupts me, blurting out her apology nervously. "I had no idea who you were and I *never*" she gestures with her arms like she's an umpire calling a runner safe, "do that. I had some champagne at my graduation party, that's why we were there, we were celebrating. I don't know what came over me but I wanted to be bold and felt confident and I just…I'm so sorry."

She shakes her head and I can see the shame on her face but it doesn't stop me from chuckling.

"Absolutely no need to apologize about it Brontë. We are two adults and asking someone out is part of life. I uh, I feel like I owe you an apology actually. When you said your name I recognized it immediately and because of who your father is…and because he's one of my closest friends I removed myself from the situation."

"My ego appreciates the explanation," she looks down as she says it, a sly smile on her face and it feels like her nervousness is melting.

"I should have offered you an explanation but I panicked. I think I was just in shock at the coincidence considering you were on my calendar this morning. Guess I should have just explained that right then but felt it might have been embarrassing...then again, showing up to find me behind this desk today probably wasn't any better." She shrugs and we both laugh again. "So, water under the bridge on both our parts?"

"Deal," she smiles.

"Great. So back to the job, how does all of that sound? And for the record, I am fully aware that if you took this job, you could realize in a month that you hate it and want to leave, that is completely fine and won't be an issue. I just wanted to extend the offer to you if it was in any way something you feel you would be interested in."

"I appreciate it. I think it sounds perfectly manageable on my part. When do I need to give an answer?"

"How about the end of the week? Give you enough time to think things over?"

"Yes."

"Perfect. Here," I grab my business card and scribble down my personal cell number on it, "this has my email and work phone but this is my personal cell. If you have any questions or need more time to make the decision, just shoot me a text."

My fingers graze hers as she takes it from my hand. The touch is quick and subtle but it instantly sets my nerves ablaze. Her fire red nail polish isn't helping the matter because all I see when I look down at them is having them wrapped around my cock.

"Looks like I got your number after all," she giggles, that blush spreading up her neck and over her cheeks again. "Sorry, that wasn't professional. I don't know why I said that."

It makes me laugh again, "Don't apologize, we're not that uptight here." She looks up at me from where she's still sitting in her chair that I'm towering over and for some stupid reason, I take it a step further. I reach out and tip her chin upward so she's looking up at me, "I promise I don't bite Brontë, you can relax."

The tension in this second is palpable but just as quickly, it vanishes when she clears her throat and stuffs the card into her purse as she gathers her things to stand up.

"Thanks again for your time Mr. Archer, I will be in touch with you shortly."

"Beckahm." I correct her.

"Beckham," she nods and heads toward my office door. She stops just before she reaches it and slowly turns back around to face me. "Just one other thing."

"Hmm?"

"Could we keep last night between us? As in, don't tell my father."

I want to say I wouldn't dream of it because if your father knew that I even contemplated for one second taking his daughter home, he'd cut my balls off and feed them to his dogs.

"Of course, it'll be our little secret." And just to make things even more tense, I throw in a wink for good measure.

***

I'm not proud of it but I've spent the last three days thinking of very little but Brontë.

Something about her, beyond her obvious beauty is so compelling to me. The way she seems to hold herself back, the way she presents so innocently yet lurking beneath that surface I sense a curious woman begging for a man to coax out her naughty side.

I grip my golf club tighter as I imagine being that man. It excites me to imagine helping her find that confidence again she displayed the other night in the bar. To see her ask for what she wants, to demand it from me.

"Something on your mind? Awfully quiet today." Her father Jonas asks me, snapping me back to reality.

Is it fucked up beyond measure that I'm standing fifteen feet away from Brontë's father, imagining doing all sorts of debase things to her? Yeah, I'd say that's about as fucked as you can get but maybe that's part of the allure.

The forbidden fruit.

"Heard anything from Brontë about the job?" I ask as I take my position at the tee.

"No, haven't spoken to her since the graduation party. I can give her a call if you want?" He holds his cell phone up but I shake my head no.

"That's okay. Don't want her feeling pressured. I told her let me know by Friday, I'm sure she will."

"She's a very bright woman, just like her mother. I just worry she'll end up wasting her aptitude for finance and problem solving on some silly do-good endeavor in non-profit. Now I know," he says lifting his gloved hands, "others need help and don't have the opportunity like I had but still, she's got something and it would be a shame to toss that aside. Even her professors have said as much, she's gifted."

I smile, not surprised at all that she's whip smart. I could tell just from our short interaction she's the kind of woman that has it all.

I'm trying to play it cool but I'm hoping she takes the job. I don't know why because I know that no matter how much I want to, no matter how much she wants me to...I can't touch her.

I *won't* touch her.

I tee off, the ball sailing down the fairway.

"Not a bad shot but still won't be enough to beat me. Get that checkbook ready." He laughs as we climb inside the golf cart.

We've had a long standing bet between us when we play golf. Loser has to donate winner's chosen amount to winner's chosen charity.

"We'll see about that."

"So any more thoughts about Pierce Investments? With almost twenty nationwide locations, it's only upside for Archer if you guys acquire them from Ramsay Consulting."

"I think you're right. I'm actually going to be meeting with them in the next few weeks. They want to come to Chicago and see how we do things here. If they end up not wanting to go through with the acquisition will you keep them?"

Jonas shakes his head as he reaches for his beer. "They've been on the chopping block for awhile with us. I think there's a lot of potential with them, could easily triple their locations nationwide but in the last few years I've backed away from investment firms. I think it would be right up your alley though to acquire them and rebrand them as Archer. Already have the overhead and infrastructure in place."

He's right. I've been looking to do a major expansion with Archer Financial and acquiring an already established company is the best way to do it.

"Bottom line," he says, "They want to expand their portfolio and footprint but they need the capital from somewhere and they know they're not going to get it from me."

We finish our game and I head back home to try and relax and push the ever present thoughts of my best friend's daughter from my mine.

I'm just stepping out of the shower when my phone chirps at me from the counter. I look down to see a text from a number that's not in my phone. It just reads: *I'll take the job.*

I smile and add Brontë's name to my contacts.

Brontë: *Sorry, I said I would email didn't I? Will send an email now so it's official.*

Me: *No need for the email Brontë, thank you for letting me know and for taking the job.*

And because I clearly can't seem to not fan the flames I say:

Me: *I was actually just talking about you.*

Brontë: *Oh?*

Me: *With your father.*

Brontë: *Oh.*

I want to read into her response. Was it disappointment that I didn't say I was telling a friend about a sexy little thing I met at the bar this weekend that has my brain doing all sorts of fucked up backflips trying to justify wanting to fuck my best friend's daughter?

Me: *He'll be happy to hear you took the job. Have a good night Brontë. See you Monday.*

Brontë: *Thanks again, see you Monday Mr. Archer.*

She doesn't correct it to Beckham and I don't want her to because standing here butt ass naked out of the shower, my cock growing harder by the second, all I want is to see her on her knees in front of me calling me that.

I look back over my shoulder at the shower, my cock throbbing, begging for release at the images in my head right now.

I know I shouldn't. It's fucked up. It's so wrong on so many levels that I'm pretty sure even Freud would have a field day with me.

"Fuck it," I reach back into the shower and turn on the water as I step and begin to slowly stroke myself.

WANT MORE CHICAGO BILLIONAIRES?

Dirty Little Secret
Those Three Words

Each book is a complete stand-alone with no cross-over characters or continuing stories.

ALSO BY ALEXIS WINTER

Slade Brothers Series

Billionaire's Unexpected Bride

Off Limits Daddy

Baby Secret

Loves Me NOT

Best Friend's Sister

Slade Brothers Second Generation Series

That Feeling

That Look

Men of Rocky Mountain Series

Claiming Her Forever

A Second Chance at Forever

Always Be My Forever

Only for Forever

Waiting for Forever

Four Forces Security

The Protector

The Savior

Love You Forever Series

The Wrong Brother

Marrying My Best Friend's BFF

Rocking His Fake World

Breaking Up with My Boss

Hate That I Love You

Business & Pleasure

Baby Mistake

Fake It

ALL BOOKS CAN BE READ AS STAND-ALONE READS WITHIN THESE SERIES

ABOUT THE AUTHOR

Alexis Winter is a contemporary romance author who loves to share her steamy stories with the world. She specializes in billionaires, alpha males and the women they love.

If you love to curl up with a good romance book you will certainly enjoy her work. Whether it's a story about an innocent young woman learning about the world or a sassy and fierce heroine who knows what she wants you,'re sure to enjoy the happily ever afters she provides.

When Alexis isn't writing away furiously, you can find her exploring the Rocky Mountains, traveling, enjoying a glass of wine or petting a cat.

You can find her books on Amazon or here: https://www. alexiswinterauthor.com/

Made in the USA
Monee, IL
17 August 2022

11824802R00157